From the Land of the Shamrock

From

The Land of the
Shamrock

BY
Jane Barlow

Author of *"Irish Idylls"* *"Bogland Studies"* *"A Creel of Irish Stories"* etc.

New York
Dodd, Mead and Company
1900

Copyright, 1900
by
DODD, MEAD & COMPANY

Contents

v

Contents

IN THE WINDING WALK

IN THE WINDING WALK

I

WHEN people go away from Clonmalroan, they go away, as a rule, very thoroughly. Their absence is an absence more complete than that of other persons from other places less out of the world and behind the times. Once any traveller's departing form has been beheld pass round the turn in the deep-banked boreen, or watched dwindle into a speck on the straight road streaking the wide bog-land, the chances are that little news of him will reach his former neighbours, till some day that same speck is espied growing into human shape again along that same road, and acquaintances remark to each other in the course of conversation: "And so Big Pat Byrne"—to put case—"is after comin' home wid himself."

For Clonmalroan is but meagrely provided with the means of communication, and its inhabitants are mostly ill-able to make use even of those which it possesses. It is as yet untouched by the wonderful thread of wire, which has put a running-string through the web of human lives—

3

puckered up in a moment from Hongkong to
Cambridge—and the shining metals with their
rush and roar, still halting many miles short of
it, are lamely prolonged by the wheel-tracks of
the jiggeting side-car with a slenderly filled mail-
bag on the well. The letters it brings are commonly brief and obscure, the difficult product of
certainly no excessive ease in composition. They
convey little more than an intimation of continued existence led among surroundings only
mistily imagined by readers whose own journeying has lain within the radius of a day's tramp.
Beyond that limit everything is vague and dim,
a mysterious region from whence the absentee
seems not so very much more likely to reappear
than do those who have been seen off with a
wake and a keen. Not that such returns even
as these are by any means unheard of at Clonmalroan. Would the friends of Michael Larissy,
who duly waked and buried him three years ago,
aver that they have never set eyes on him since?
Or ask anybody, almost, in the parish, why he
wouldn't take half-a-crown to be crossing after
nightfall that bridge over the Rosbride River
near Sallinbeg, where a poor tinker-woman was
swept away and drowned in a flood some few
autumns back. Then, everybody knows that several of the Denny family have "walked." Therefore the assertion: "It was himself or his ghost,"

is not regarded as containing a very unequally
balanced hypothesis, especially if "himself" has
been supposed away sojourning in those unknown
and imperfectly reported lands.

But there came one autumn when far and far
away from Clonmalroan began to happen events
which had such a heartburning interest for many
of its people that some news of them did pene-
trate the densest barriers of ignorant resource-
lessness. Mere sparks, perhaps, as it were blown
from some huge conflagration, whose distant
flames make only a sullen glare behind a smoth-
ering smoke-fog. Yet a spark may blacken a
body's home over her head, or sear the sight out
of her eyes. A great war was thundering and
lightening across wide seas, under alien skies; a
war which in no way behoved Clonmalroan, and
which might have stormed itself out little needed
there, had it not been for the circumstance that
Pat and Micky, and their brethren are "terrible
lads for goin' an' listin'," and that the regiment
they had for the most part joined was understood
to be "up at the fore-front of everythin'."

After awhile, moreover, it was not those wild,
irresponsible boys alone that this lurid cloud
engulfed in threatening glooms. The reserves
were called out, people said, at first without any
clear notion of what the phrase might signify,
but soon perceiving too plainly how it meant

that men whose soldiering days were long past
and nearly forgotten, except just the little pen-
sion, must now break the ties they had peaceably
formed, and once more set forth campaigning.
Murtagh O'Connor of Banacor, had to leave a
wife and five children on his bit of a holding "in
a quare distraction," his friends reported, "For
when he was killed, what could happen them but
the union?" And many another household on
that countryside had to consider the same woeful
question.

So all round and about Clonmalroan there
came to be an intense craving for the latest war
intelligence. Never had newspapers been in such
request. At Donnelly's bar the *Freeman* and the
Independent were as badly tattered as strips of
ill-preserved papyri by the end of an evening's
reading. The widdy Gallaher "would be walkin'
wild about the country the len'th of the day,"
folk said, "for the sight of a one. Be raison,"
they added, "of her two sons." And another
illiterate and sceptical old Mrs. Linders for simi-
lar reasons "was tormintin' everybody to read
her out every word there would be on the paper,
even if they tould her 'twas only the market
prices." The elders, indeed, were often at a dis-
advantage in this way, owing to the inferior edu-
cational arrangements under which their genera-
tion had risen. Big Brian O'Flaherty, who had

an independent and ambitious spirit, demeaned
himself to set about learning the alphabet from
that little spalpeen Larry M'Crilly, in hopes of
subsequently reading his news "and no thanks
to anybody." But Larry was impatient and sarcastic, and Big Brian slow-witted and irascible,
so the course of lessons one day ended abruptly
with "a clout on the head" to the taunting
teacher. With more modest aspirations old John
Connellan got the schoolmaster to print for him,
"the way it would be on the paper," the name
of Private Patrick Connellan; and he might be
seen on many a cold day sitting out on the rimy
grass-bank before his dark door, for the sake of
the light, and comparing with this scrap the un-
intelligible lines of the *Independent*. It was very
slow, puzzling work, since the columns were many
and lengthy, and his eyes none of the best. Old
John seldom could retain the loan of the wide
sheets long enough to assure himself completely
that his grandson's name was happily absent
from them. For no news was certainly the best
that could be looked for from the papers. What,
indeed, was likely to happen a lad save one of
those casualties which were so briefly recorded.
"Och, woman dear, they're sayin' at Donnelly's
that there's a terrible sight of officers kilt on the
Freeman to-day, so there'll presently be a cruel
big list of the rank and file. God be good to us

all, woman dear—and poor Micky and the rest. I'm wonderin' will they be apt to print it to-morra."

Thus the winter, always at Clonmalroan a season when cares and losses are ripe, was beyond its wont harassed and haunted by fear and sorrow. The calling away on active service of the Captain from the Big House was one of its incidents that tended to deepen the general depression. His stalwart form, and sturdy stride, and off-hand greeting were missed going to and fro, and much commiseration was directed to "poor Lady Winifred, and she not so long married, the crathur, left all alone by herself up at the Big House."

II

It was only comparatively speaking a big house at all, though it made some architectural pretensions with its pillared front and porch, and balustraded roof. Its lower windows looked out of a spacious hall, and a few ill-proportioned sitting-rooms; upstairs rambling passages and wide-floored lobbies cramped the uncomfortable bedchambers. Disrepair prevailed within and without, ranging from the rough work of wind and weather to the minuter operations of mouse and moth. Even at its best, all had been ugly and inconvenient enough. Nevertheless to be-

come mistress thereof, Lady Winifred had not
merely left a far statelier and more luxurious establishment, but had quitted it under a cloud of
disapproval, with an assurance that she was taking a long step down in the world. For her
Captain was a person so impecunious and impossible, with such an unsuccessful past career, and
such unsatisfactory future prospects, that nobody
could imagine what she saw in him, and everybody thought the worse of her for seeing it,
whatever it might be. The marriage was just
not discountenanced and forbidden outright, but
most austere visages were turned upon it, and
the wedding, Lady Astermount's maid declared,
"couldn't have been quieter if an affliction had
occurred in the family only the previous week."

Notwithstanding that inauspicious send-off,
however, Captain and Lady Winifred O'Reilly
passed a surprisingly pleasant year at this shabby
old house of his among the bog-lands. Lonesome and monotonous are the bog-lands, and
creep up very close to the Big House; but it
stands set in a miniature glen of its own, with a
wreath of shrubberies around it, and during the
months after they arrived, the O'Reillys busied
themselves much about additional trees and evergreens, wherewith to screen their domain more
effectually from the dreary outlook and roughly
sweeping winds in the years that were to come.

Many improvements, too, had to be made in neglected plots of garden-ground, where the Captain looked at geraniums and pansies and carna-
tions through another person's eyes, until at last
he saw something in them himself, and learned
with extreme pride to call them by their proper
names. This lore gave him more pleasure on the
whole than he had ever derived from his familiarity with the colours worn by jockeys or
stamped on playing cards, studies which had
hitherto engrossed a larger share of his attention.
His wife and he diversified their gardening with
long rides together on steeds not expensively
high-bred. Clonmalroan opinion waxed somewhat critical when the pair came trotting by.
Her ladyship, they said, didn't look the size of
wren perched up on that big, rawny baste of a
chestnut, with an ugly, coarse gob of a head on
him too, and the brown mare was something
slight for his Honour, who must ride well up to
fourteen stone. But the riders themselves were
satisfied with their mounts.

Their contentment had showed no signs of
waning in that mild November weather, with its
pearl-white mists and wafted odour of burning
weeds, when the likelihood of his going out
loomed up suddenly on their horizon. The
certain news came one morning while they were
working away near the back gate, where their

small bog-stream flows under steep banks, on
which they had designed a plantation of rhodo-
dendrons. In the black peat-soil these thrive
amain, and by next June would have lit a many-
hued glow in the shadowy little glen. Lady
Winifred tried hard not to see that this interrup-
tion of their labours was to the Captain scarcely
such an unmitigated calamity as to herself. Her
recognition of the fact made her feel doubly desolate; not that there was more difference in their
sentiments than had to be in the nature of things,
or than left him otherwise than miserable at their
parting. She tried further to go on with the
plantation, as he would no doubt return in time
to see it in blossom; but she was relieved when
a spell of bad weather presently set in, and let
her stay indoors. Yet indoors it seemed as if the
whole solitude of the great bog had pressed into
the empty house. All day it said, wherever she
went, upstairs or downstairs, one word to vex
her: *gone*. But at night she had various fortunes
in dreams good and evil.

And every morning at breakfast in the low,
broad-windowed book-room, she sat opposite to
the Captain's place, just as usual, except that the
place was empty. She chose that seat because
from it she could watch for old Christy Denny
coming by from Sallinbeg post office with the
mail-bag. That window looked out on a small

lawn, bounded by a shrubbery through which a
path ran leading round a corner of the house to
the front door.   The laurel-bushes straggled into
frequent gaps, so that between them the approach
of a passer-by could be fitfully descried.   And
any morning might bring the letter for her, the
foreign letter.   To think of how it was perhaps
in those very moments journeying towards her
in the battered old brown bag made her so hungry
and thirsty that she sometimes forgot to pour out
her tea, or cut the over-large loaf.   Nor was she
always disappointed.   Every now and then a
letter did come, and in its re-reading she would
find a refuge through the terrors of the day, as
in a flattering dream by night.   All the while,
indeed, she knew that she was in a fool's para-
dise: that, being so many weeks old, it could
give her no assurance of its writer's safety.   The
hands that had folded its sheets might ere now
have grown cold beside some far off stream,
where geysers of deadly hail broke out rattling
on the hills, and the wide air was as full of
murderous stings as a swamp of sweltering
venom.   She might more rationally rely upon
the newspapers with their flashed tidings.   But
these she never dared open herself, and she could
not forbear to hang her hopes upon that delusive
correspondence.

One midwinter morning she came down to

breakfast with her heart set more than ever
eagerly upon the arrival of old Christy. Partly
because she had not had a letter for longer than
usual, and partly because it was Saturday, and
on Sunday no mail comes into Sallinbeg. This
last was of course no reason at all for expecting
a letter; but it did 'seem to her almost improbable that fate could intend such harshness as
to make her wait two whole days and nights before she could begin hoping again. So she looked
out of the window with shining eyes, and set
about crumbling the bread on her plate before
she had tasted a bit, and thought Christy was
late before he had well started on his two-mile
trudge. It was hard weather, and on the corner
of lawn she looked into lay a sprinkling of frozen
snow; only a sprinkling; she had seen it whiter
last June with daisies spread to the sun. But the
frost was keen, as she would have felt by the airs
blowing through the open window, if she had
been at leisure to consider anything except the
possibility of their bringing the sound of foot-
steps on the hardened path.

Old Christy was late really, and she listened
in vain. When at length he did come, she saw
him first, a shadow moving along within the still
shadow of the laurels. Just opposite to the window a gap in them made a ragged arch, and Lady
Winifred knew that if Christy had anything

special for her, he would come through the opening, and straight across the grass to her, instead
of following the path round the house to the hall-
door. For a minute, a half-happy minute of
doubt, she watched him nearing the fateful place,
fearful, hopeful, blindly impatient, and then—
stunned. Old Christy had gone past the gap,
hurrying a little it seemed, as if he wished to get
out of sight. This in fact he did. "Sure now,
the mistress's face is all eyes these times," he
said to Mrs. Keogh in the kitchen, "and lookin'
at me they do be like as if she thought bad of me
not bringin' her aught. But bedad if she could
see to the bottom of me heart, she'd know it's
sorry I am I haven't got somethin' for her at the
bottom of th' ould bag. Troth would she so."
And Mrs. Keogh replied: "an' sure it's frettin' she
is, goodness may pity the crathur, she's frettin'.
And doesn't ait what would fatten a sparrow.
It's my belief she'll do no good."

The mistress did not appear to be fretting as
she sat without motion, and still gazed out over
the lawn. Though its aspect was quite un-
changed, it had become a grave wherein her hope,
newly slain, must lie buried until the sun had set
and risen, and again set and risen. Even by the
uncertain measure of years, the mistress was very
young yet, and otherwise younger still, so that
the edges of the experiences which make up life

had not been worn smooth for her, to expedite
their slipping past. A whole day looked nearly
as interminable to her as to a small child, who
gets out of bed with no clear prospect of ever getting into it again. And now her own bedtime lay
beyond more than twelve leaden-footed hours, so
early was this desolate sunny morning. It
seemed late, however, to some of her neighbours,
who were keeping round eyes on her movements,
and considered her as tardy as she had been
thinking Christy. Perhaps a chirp or a rustle
may have reached and prompted her unawares,
or perhaps she merely acted from habit, but by
and by she got up, and scattered her plateful of
crumbs upon the rimy window-ledge, where they
lay like a little drift of discoloured snow. As she
strewed them she said to herself bitterly towards
fate, and ruthfully towards fellow-victims: "why
should the birds go hungry, because I have no
letter?" and she was careful to shut down the
window-sash, lest the sleek black cat should, according to custom, lurk ambushed within to
pounce upon a preoccupied prey. Then she stood
aside, half hidden by the faded crimson curtain,
and looked out at nothing with a cold ache in her
heart.

The small birds arrived in headlong haste.
Some of them were pecking almost before the
window closed. For the frost's tyranny had

made of not a few among them desperate
characters, fluttering with reckless enterprise.
Even a scutty wren ventured out of cover, and
advanced along the ledge in a dotted line of tiny
hops, scarcely less smooth than a mouse's run.
A robin-redbreast alighting brought a gleam of
colour something brighter than a withered beech-
leaf and duller than a poppy-petal. Two tomtits
in comic motley suits disputed with tragic audac-
ity the claims of all their *biggers*, thrushes,
blackbirds, finches and sparrows. The whole
party twittered and fluttered and wrangled together, blithe and pugnacious, but the spreader
of the feast gave no heed to any of its incidents.
She smiled neither at the abrupt gobblings of the
large golden bill, nor at the absurd defiances of
the blue-and-yellow dwarfs. Her act of charity
seemed to have gained her nothing. Then all at
once, at some caprice of panic, the assembled
birds whisked themselves down from the window-
stool, onto the gravel walk below. Each one of
them bore off in his beak a bread crumb which
looked like a little white envelope, and gave him
the appearance of a letter carrier. The sudden
movement caught Lady Winifred's attention, and
she was struck by the fantastic resemblance. But
at the same moment she remembered keenly how
she had been reft of her hope for that day and
the next ; and immediately, as if the frost at her

heart were broken up, she saw the mock-letters
through a rain of tears. She had not foregone her
recompense after all.

III

Near the back gates of Lady Winifred's Big
House, the Widdy Connor's very little one makes
a white dot on the edge of the black bog-land
that widens away towards Lisconnel. She lived
in it quite alone after her son Terence 'listed on
her, which he did one winter when times were
hard and work was scarce. Everybody almost
concurred in the opinion that there "wasn't apt to
be such another grand lookin' soldier in the regiment as young Terry Connor, or in an army of
rigiments bedad." For Terry's good looks, and
good nature, and athletic prowess were celebrated
round and about Clonmalroan. Six-foot-three in
his stockings, and not a lad to stand up to him at
the wrestling; there wasn't another as big a man
in the parish unless it might be the Captain.

But of course it was not in the nature of things
that any one else should equal the extravagant
pride and pleasure in those pre-eminent qualities
evinced by Terry's mother. She made a show
of herself over him, according to the view entertained by some matrons with smaller sons;
and now and then, when the widow had exceeded
unusually in vaingloriousness, one of them might

be heard to predict that "she'd find she'd get
none the better thratement from him, for cockin'
him up wid consait; little enough he'd be thinkin'
of her, or mindin' what she bid him." The
widow for her part always declared that "the
only thing he'd ever done agin her in his life
was 'listin'; and that he'd never have thought
of, if the both of them hadn't been widin to-morra
mornin' of starvation." And perhaps the affliction which that step caused her was not so very
far from being made amends for by her exulting
delight in the splendour of his martial aspect,
when he came over to visit her on furlough, in
his scarlet with green facings, beautiful to behold. One of those carping critics declared to
goodness after mass, that she had come into
chapel with him "lookin' as sot up as if she was
after catchin' some sort of glittery angel flyin'
about wild, and had a hold of him by the wing."

But then at that time the regiment was safely
quartered at Athlone, a place no such terribly
long way off, and known to have been actually
visited by ordinary people. It was a woefully
different matter when the Connemaras were sent
off on active service to strange lands about which
all one's knowledge could be summed up in the
words "furrin'" and "fightin'"—words of limit-
less fear. Then it was that retribution might be
deemed to have lighted upon her inordinate van-

ity about her son's conspicuous stature. For this
now became a source of especial torment, as
threatening to make him the better mark, sing-
ling him out for peculiar peril.

"And you'll be plased to tell him, Mr. Mulcahy," she dictated to the schoolmaster, who
was also cobbler and scribe at Clonmalroan.
"That whatever he does he's to not be runnin'
into the fore-front of the firin', and he a head and
shoulders higher than half of the lads. He'd be
hit first thing. God be good to us. Bid him
to be croochin' down back of somethin' handy.
Or if there was ne'er a rock or a furze-bush on
the bit of bog, he might anyway keep stooped behind the others. But if he lets them get aimin'
straight at him, he's lost."

Mr. Mulcahy, who was stirring up the sedi-
ment of his lately watered ink, received these
suggestions about conduct in the field with decided disapproval. "Bedad now, Mrs. Connor,"
he said, "there'd be no sinse in tellin' him any
such things. For in the first place he wouldn't
mind a word of it, and in the next place—goodness may pity you, woman, but sure you wouldn't
be wishful to see him comin' back to you after
playin' the poltroon, and behavin' himself dis-
creditable?"

"Troth and I would," said Mrs. Connor. "If
he was twinty polthroons. All the behavin' I

want of him's to be bringin' himself home.
Who's any the betther for the killin' and
slaughterin'? The heart's weary in me doubtin'
will I ever get a sight of him agin. That's all
I'm thinkin' of, tellin' you the truth, and if I said
anythin' diff'rint, it 'ud be a lie."

"He might bring home a trifle of honour and
glory, and no harm done," Mr. Mulcahy urged.
But Mrs. Connor said: "Glory be bothered;"
and in the end he only so far modified his instructions as to substitute for her more detailed
injunctions a vague general order to "be takin'
care of himself."

It may perhaps be considered another righteous
judgment upon this most un-Spartan mother, that
while these precautions of hers were entirely
neglected, little of the honour and glory which
she had flouted did attend the fate of her Terry.
He was shot through the lungs by a rifle posted
a mile or two distant from the dusty hillock on
which he dropped, and where he lay gasping and
choking for what seemed to him a vastly long
time, before the night fell, suddenly dark and
cold, and not to pass away. As this particular
casualty was not discovered till the next morning, his name did not appear on the list which
Barney Keogh spelled over to the Widdy Connor
a few days later, and at the end of which she
said fervently: "Thanks be to the great God.

There's no sign of himself in it." But on the
very next evening, a half-line in the *Freeman*
ran: *Add to Killed: Private T. Connor;* and
when Peter Egan down below at Donnelly's,
read it out by chance, the widdy, listening, felt
as if she had just wakened up into a dim sort of
nightmare. All the more she felt so, because
everybody round her was saying: "May the
Lord have mercy on his sowl," as if anybody
could believe that Terry had really become to
them a subject for such pious ejaculations. So
she hurried back through the wide spaces of the
bleak marsh gloaming to her little, silent house,
where she shut herself in to sleep off her dream.
But it woke up with her in the grey of the early
dawning.

Lady Winifred's Captain was killed about the
same time as Terry Connor, and, like him, without anything specially glorious in the circumstances of his death. Rather the contrary. The
occasion of it was a minor disaster to the arms of
his side—a check, a reverse—over which it could
not be but that some one had blundered. In
point of fact a highly distinguished General,
dictating a draught report of the affair to his
discreet Secretary, had expressed an opinion that
the regrettable incident had been brought about
by want of judgment on the part of the com-
manding officer, the late Captain O'Reilly, when

the younger man coughed significantly, and casually remarked: " Ah, O'Reilly—he married one of Lord Astermount's daughters—the third, I think, Lady Winifred, a little fair girl. Her people didn't like the match at all, I believe, but still——" His chief appeared scarcely to notice the observation: but Captain O'Reilly's want of judgment was not mentioned in despatches.

IV

When their world came to an end for the widow, Lady Winifred O'Reilly, and the widow, Katty Connor, the bog-land was just beginning to turn springwards, and everything on it stirred under the strengthening sunshine. Round about the Big House the birds, who now despised bread crumbs, because other food wriggled abundantly in the dewy grass, sang much and gleefully in the fresh mornings, and through the long golden light as it ebbed off the lawn. But Lady Winifred, looking out no more for letters, sought a refuge from it all in the book-room, which was a dusky brown place in the brightest hours. There she sat on the floor in a corner before a far-stretching row of *Annual Registers*, and read them volume by volume. She had chosen this course of study just as she might have chosen the top of an adjacent rubbish heap in a suddenly surging flood. Steadily through she read them without skipping—*History of Europe—Chronicle—State Papers—Characters—Useful Projects*, even when they included the specification of Dr. Higgen's Patent for a new-invented water cement or Stucco—*Poetry*, even when it was by the Laureate William Whitehead. That is to say her eyes travelled down and down the double columns, where the faded ink was less distinct than the damp stains which mottled the margin. It may be doubted whether they conveyed many thoughts to her brain, but they blocked the way to others. One of the most definite impressions she received was a feeling of resentment towards those persons who were recorded to have lived a hundred years and upwards, in full possession of all their faculties.

One showery afternoon in the last days of May, Lady Winifred was interrupted in the middle of the events of the year 1783, by the entrance of Rose Ahern, the housemaid, who came to take leave of her. Rose, who was now summoned home to tend an invalided mother, had lived longer at the Big House than its mistress, and often remarked these times that "anybody'd be annoyed to see her mopin', and the two of them that gay and plisant together only a half-twelvemonth back." On this occasion, having repeatedly said: "So good-bye to you kindly, melady, and may God lave your Ladyship your

health," she continued inconsistently to linger in
her place, making small sounds and movements
designed to attract attention. But Lady Winifred had reverted to her volume Twenty-six, and
was inaccessible to any save point-blank address.
At last Rose went almost to the door, and turned
round to say: "I beg your pardon, melady—
beggin' your Ladyship's pardon—but what colour might the master's uniform be, melady?
None of us ever seen his Honour wearin' it, it so
happens."

"It was scarlet, I believe," Lady Winifred
said, continuing to look at the pages. "Oh, yes,
scarlet."

"There now, didn't I tell Thady so?" said
Rose. "And he standin' me out 'twas blue it
was, the way it couldn't ha' been him we seen;
and declarin' 'twas apter to be poor Terry Connor, thinkin' of his mother. But sure it's a good
step to her house from where we seen him—whoever he was—last night."

"*Saw him last night,*" Lady Winifred said,
looking up, ("and indeed now," Rose averred
afterwards, "'twas like openin' a crack of a
window—her eyes shinin' out of the dark corner"). "Oh Rose, what are you saying?"

"'Deed then, maybe I'm talkin' like a fool,
melady," said Rose, "and you've no call to be
mindin' me. Only when I was seein' me brother

Thady down to the back gate last night, there
was somebody in a red coat at the far end of the
Windin' Walk, there was so, and a big man too.
And this mornin' I heard several sayin' there did
be a soldier seen in it this while since, of an
evenin'. But sorra a one's stoppin' anywheres
next or nigh Clonmalroan. It's the quare long
step he's apt to ha' come—between us and harm.
And I dunno what should be bringin' poor Terry
Connor there, instead of to his own little place;
but the poor master always had a great wish for
the Windin' Walk. Many a time have I seen
him meself smokin' up and down it, before ever
he got married; and last year he was a dale in
it along wid yourself, melady, lookin' after the
wee bushes plantin'—beggin' your Ladyship's
pardon. And all the while very belike it might
ha' been just a shadow under the moonlight;
only red it was, that's sartin. But people do be
talkin' foolish, your Ladyship. And may God
lave your Ladyship your health. It was as like
as not to be nothin' at all."

"Oh, very likely," Lady Winifred said, indif-
ferently, "nothing at all."

V

But that evening she left the house once more.
She had intended to wait until dusk, but its slow
oncoming wore out her patience, and there were

still rich gleams and glows receding among the
furthest tree-trunks, when she stole forth into
the open air. It breathed freshly fragrant on
her, after her many weeks in the mouldering
mustiness of the book-room, and the blackbirds
were singing with notes clear as the gathering
dews, and mellow as the westering light. The
season was now the late autumn of spring, when
most blossoms are falling, though the young
leaves are yet in their first luminous green. On
the lawn the laburnums and thorn-bushes stood
with their outlines enameled on the grass in gold
and pearl and pink coral. Along the shaded
avenue and shrubbery paths lay softly drifts of
dimmer blossoms and blossom-dust, in faint am-
bers and russets and crimsons. But the white
plumes of the guelder roses were still glimmer-
ing ghostily above her head as she went by,
and some of the firs were studded all over with
little pale-yellow tapers like wild Christmas-
trees.

Lady Winifred was going towards the back
gate, and presently came where the Winding
Walk, under a dense canopy of evergreens, runs
parallel with the avenue, on the right hand, and
on the left within hearing of the fretted, rocky
stream in the bit of a glen below. Once between
the screening laurels and junipers, you could see,
however, only up and down short curves of the

waving path. About midway in it was a rustic
wooden seat, niched in a recess of the shrubs, and
Lady Winifred intended to sit down there, and wait
and watch. But when she reached it, she found
it already occupied by some one who had been
also watching, as was clearly seen in the look
that leaped forward to meet the newcomer, and
at sight recoiled again. In this tall woman with
a black shawl over frosted dark hair, Lady
Winifred recognised the Widow Connor, concerning whom, ages ago, before the days of the
Annual Registers, she half remembered to have
heard about the loss of a soldier son. The older
widow was rising up with many apologies for
the boldness of slipping in there, never thinking
any of the family would be coming out; and she
would have gone away, but the other hastened
to sit down beside her, and kept a hand on her
shawl. "I won't stay myself, unless you do,"
said Lady Winifred. "I only came out because
it was so warm," she explained, as she had been
explaining to herself, "and such a fine evening."

"Tellin' you the truth, melady," said the
Widdy Connor, "me poor Terry himself would
sometimes be smokin' a pipe in here of an evenin'
when there was nobody about. I was tellin'
him he'd a right to not be makin' so free—
but sure after all he done no harm. There's
great shelter under the shrubberies when the

weather does be soft—and be the same token,
we do be gettin' a little shower this minyit, melady; that's what's rustlin' in the laves. So
'twould be nathural enough if Terry was mindin'
the place. But trespassin' or annoyin' the family now, he'd never be intendin'. Just comin' of
an odd evenin' he might be, the way he used.
Anyhow Paudeen Nolan and Jim McKenna was
positive 'twas him they seen, and they all goin'
home from the hurley-match. The other lads
said diff'rint; but that Anthony Martin's a big
stookawn, and his brother's as blind as the
owls. Nor I wouldn't go be what Rose Ahern
says——"

"Rose has very good sight," said Lady Winifred.

"Ah, then you're after hearin' the talk, melady?" said the widow. "Faix now, they'd no
call to be tellin' you wrong, and bringin' you out
under the wet for nothin' to get your death of
cold. Because Terry it was, whatever they may
say. But there's wonderful foolishness in people. For some of them says they wouldn't believe any such a thing; so what *would* they believe at all? And more of them says it's a bad
sign for anybody to be walkin' that way. And
what badness is there in it, if a lad would be
takin' a look at a place he had a likin' for, and
where he might git a chance of seein' his frinds?

And it's the quare sort of unluckiness 'twould be
for one of *them* to git a sight of him, if 'twas
only goin' by, and ne'er a word out of him.
That's what I was sayin' this mornin' to ould
Theresa Joyce. For says she to me: 'It's unlucky,'
says she. 'And you'd do betther to be wishin'
he'd bide paiceable wherever he is, till yourself
comes along to him,' says she. But it's aisy for
Theresa Joyce to be talkin', and she as ould as a
crow. She can't be livin' any great while longer,
so I was sayin' to her; and it's somethin' else
she'd be wishin', if she'd no more age on her
than meself. Sure I was reckonin' up, melady,
accordin' to things that happint, and at the most
I can make it, I'm short of fifty years. That's
lavin' a terrible long time to be contintin' one-
self in."

"And I'm twenty," said Lady Winifred.

"Well, now the Lord may pity you, and may
goodness forgive me," the widow said compunc-
tiously, as if she had somehow been an accom-
plice of this cruel fate, and were all at once
smitten with remorse. She seemed to ponder
for a while deeply, and at last said: "If be any
odd chance it isn't Terry after all, and only the
Captain—I won't be grudgin' it to her; no, the
crathur, I will not."

Thereupon, silence continued long between the
two watchers, and nothing befell them, except

that their blackness was gradually softened into
the shadows as cobweb-coloured dusk enmeshed
them.

Then there came a moment when the older
woman saw the younger start, and, quivering
like a bough after it has bent to a waft of wind,
looked fixedly in one direction. "In the name of
God, do you see anythin', melady?" Widdy
Connor whispered, and as she spoke, she saw too.
For a small rent in the straggling laurel on their
right made a spy-hole, which brought within
view a curve of the Winding Walk near its gate
end, many yards away. And there, moving and
glimpsing in the twilight, from which it seemed
to have absorbed the last lingering brightness,
went a gleam of scarlet. It was coming towards
the seat, and the faces turned that way looked as
if a white moonbeam had fallen across them.
Almost immediately branches rustled close by,
and out into the path a girl hooded with a fawn-
coloured shawl, stepped warily on the left hand,
and stood poising herself for a swift dart past the
recess, unintercepted if not unobserved. Lady
Winifred could not have noticed the leap of
an ambushed tiger; but her companion sprang
up and caught the girl by the wrist. "Norah
Grehan," said the widow, "and who at all are
you watchin' for this night? Me son Terry was
spakin' to ne'er a girl, I well know. He'd have

told me, so he would. Who are you lookin' to see?"

"Och Mrs. Connor, ma'am, lave go of me," the girl said, twisting her arm and struggling, "and don't let on to anybody that you seen me, or there'll be murdher. It's Jack McDonnell that's waitin' for me below there. He that 'listed about Christmas, and now they're sendin' him to the war. He and me are spakin' this good while back, unbeknownst, be raison of me father makin' up a match for me wid some other man; I dunno who is he, but I won't have him, not if he owned all the bastes that ever ran on four legs. So I do be slippin' across the steppin'-stones of an evenin' for to get a word wid Jack, that comes over the bog from the dear knows how far beyant Lisconnel. And if they knew up at the farm, I'd be kilt."

"And maybe the best thing could happen you," said the widow.

"Ah, don't say so, woman dear. He'll be comin' back one of these days for sure, a corporal, maybe, or a sargint, wid lave to marry. And he's plannin' to conthrive for me to be livin' wid his mother's sisther in Sligo, till then, the way they won't get me married on him while he's gone—no fear. He'll be tellin' me about it to-night—and bedad there he is whistlin' to me. Ah let me go, Mrs. Connor; but whisht, like a good woman," said the girl, wrenching herself free, and speeding away between the half visible dark foliage.

Then Lady Winifred, who had heard the last part of this colloquy, got up also and said: "I think I'll go home now. It's a very pleasant evening, but the air feels rather cold."

"'Deed now you'd a right to not be out under the rain, wid nothin' on the head of you, melady, but the little muslin cap," said the widow, and added as Lady Winifred went: "And troth it's the cruel pity to see the likes of her wearin' any such a thing, ay indeed is it. Norah Grehan and Jack McDonnell, sure now the two of them's at the beginnin', and she's at the endin'. But there's an endin' in every beginnin', and maybe, plase God, there's a beginnin' in every endin'."

Lady Winifred, meanwhile, was not pitying herself. As she walked slowly back to her empty Big House, along paths odorous with the rain whose drops began to pierce their leafiest roofs, she felt again a stunned disappointment, only vaguer and more chilling than the overdue letter had caused her. And there were no little birds about now to mock her into keener consciousness. After all, things were just as they had been when she set out, no worse surely, and how could they be better, except in a dream? But a dream she might have before to-morrow came, and brought

back her long day in the brown book-room with
the companionship of the *Annual Registers*.
There were still so many unread of the dusty
volumes, clasped with blackish cobwebs, made
ghastly now and then by the shrivelled skeleton
of the dead spinster. She need not yet consider
what she should do when they were all finished.

As the Widdy Connor went towards her little
silent house, she was saying to herself: "Jack
McDonnell bedad! Sure the height of him isn't
widin the breadth of me hand of Terry; everybody knows that. It's my belief 'twasn't Jack
they seen that time at all. They couldn't ha'
mistook him for Terry, the tallest lad in this
counthryside. . . . And says I to Theresa
Joyce: 'The heart of me did be leppin' up wid
pride every time I'd see him have to stoop his
head, comin' in to me at our little low door. But
it's lower his head's lyin' now,' says I, 'low
enough it's lyin'.' And says she to me: 'If
'twas ever so low, the heart of you'll be leppin' up
twice as high wid joy and' plisure,' says she,
'the next time you behould him.' But ah sure,
it's aisy talkin'. I'll see him come stoopin' in
at it no more."

PILGRIMS FROM LISCONNEL

PILGRIMS FROM LISCONNEL

Young Mrs. Dan O'Beirne, whom the neighbours at Lisconnel still speak of as Stacey Doyne, comes up there every now and again to stay for a while with her mother. These visits generally have for their object either the giving or getting of "company." Mrs. Doyne, who is a despondently ailing person, happens to stand in especial need of heartening up, or else young Dan has undertaken a temporary job at some little distance, whither it is inconvenient to carry with him wife and child. But, of course, in so small a place as Lisconnel, "company" does not by any means confine itself to the household in which it is domiciled. Such isolation would be found practically impossible, even if it were sought. The stir of an arrival vibrates from one end of the hamlet to the other—several hundred yards—and the accompanying news penetrates as impartially as sunshine to the fireside of friend and foe. Not that Stacey has any enemies up at Lisconnel. For even Sally, the Sheridans' eldest girl, who had betrayed some touches of spleen about the time "Dan was coortin'," soon afterwards met with a sweetheart of her own, and, though she had used to describe Fergus Tighe disparagingly as "a quare little conthrivance," was presently asserting and believing him to be "worth ten of them big lumberin' fellows, wid their heads cocked up among the thatch," so had thenceforward left off fancying that she hated Mrs. Dan.

Sally's next sister, lame-footed Peg, was one of Stacey's particular friends. Peg, a person with troubles of her own, had felt much for Stacey when her prospects were, during some dreary months, darkened by young Dan's unaccountable absence and silence, which ended, after all, in a happy return, and if not literally with marriage-bells, only because the poor little chapel "down beyant" possessed none to ring. Her sympathy at that anxious time actually led her so far as to offer Stacey the loan of her two priceless old flitterjigs of volumes, "Ivanhoe," and a dilapidated song-book, her brother Larry's parting bequest. And, albeit Stacey, who was nearly as illiterate as Peg herself, did not accept, she understood how signal was the mark of friendship.

"Ah no, Peg," she had said; "I might on'y be losin' the laves on you. And sure, tellin' you the truth, it's as much as I can do to spell out a word at all, when I'm givin' me mind to it, but me mind somehow won't take a hould rightly of

anythin' these times. I wonder do there be a
great many people dhrownded in the say crossin'
over between this and Scotland—so thank you
kindly, Peg."

This trouble of Peg's could never end with
wedding-bells—that was certain. All the peals
in Christendom clashing together would fail to
scare it away.   Her lameness itself was less
incurable, though caused by an ankle "quare and
crooked ever since the day she was born"; and,
though it claimed notice at every step she took,
it probably haunted her thoughts less persistently
than the recollection of the quarrel with Larry,
which could not ever be made up in this world—
the quarrel about the pitaty planting, which had
driven him away into exile so terribly farther
than either of them had intended. Circumstances
made her peculiarly liable to the sway of such
bitter memories.   Her painful limp debarred her
from the distraction of active pursuits, and up at
Lisconnel it is very hard for a body sitting still
not to sit, as they say, "with his hands before
him."   The knitting up of coarse yarn is almost
the only manual exercise attainable, and, unluckily, the supply of the material and the de-
mand for the product are both apt to run short
long before the worker's leisure. Moreover, the
needles, under accustomed fingers, move so all
but automatically that their twinkling, regarded

as a mode of parrying heart-thrusts of regret or
remorse, is little better than just twiddling one's
thumbs. Peg used to linger over her socks and
long-hose, purposely complicating them with intricate ribbing, and double heels, and fanciful
arrangements of stitches purled and turned.

"Sure, girl alive," her stepmother would say
to her, "what for would you be botherin' yourself puttin' the like of all them diff'rint pattrons
up the legs? Tasty enough they may be, but
sorra the extra halfpenny 'll you get for them,
no more than if it grew on them be accident;
and they take double of the time doin'." And
Peg often answered, "I dunno, but maybe that's
the raison."

Not seldom, however, either wool or spirits
completely failed her, and then she would sit idle
through all the daylight on the low bank where,
a stone's-throw from the Sheridans' door, the
bog pouts up a swarded lip. From this seat she
could see, running over the Knockawn, the road
towards Duffclane, along which Larry had set
forth in the bleak grey of that sorrowful March
morning, now years past, with the thought in his
heart that he must quit out of it, because Peg
had turned agin him like all the rest. If Peg
had followed her own inclination, she would
often even now have called down the empty
road after him—so long after him—that there

was not a word of truth in it. But she only sat silent and still.

These hours of idleness made her look what the neighbours call "quare and fretted like." After a spell of them, it might have been noticed that her face grew peaked and faded, until her many freckles seemed to increase in size and deepen in hue, while her wavy red hair hung limp and lustreless, and her grey eyes widened with staring vacantly at nothing visible. A stranger would have found it hard to believe that scarcely a score of years had passed over her woe-begone head.

One of Stacey's visits happened to fall at a time when Peg was moping thus, a forlorn object in the mellow harvest sunbeams that drowsed over Lisconnel, and not to be appreciably cheered by the freshest gossip from Duffclane, nor even by the conversation of a marvellous ten-month-old Felix O'Beirne, who could say *Yah-ah-ah* quite distinctly at anybody he misliked the looks of. This struck the young matron as a singularly deplorable sign of depression, and she sometimes discussed the matter with her friends, who had no remedy to suggest. They were talking one evening at Ody Rafferty's, and Mrs. Quigley had just expressed the opinion that "poor Peg would be apt to fret herself into the next world before she was much older, for, bedad, that was the only place she had a chance of goin' aisy wid her misfort'nit fut, that had her torminted," when Stacey said, "I wish she had e'er a chance of thravellin' wid herself to Tubberbride, over away between Sallinbeg and Sallinmore. The cures people do be gettin' somewhiles at the ould well there is past belief. Mrs. O'Rourke, at our place, was tellin' me her brother-in-law gave it a thrial last Easter, and came back a diff'rint man altogether, and he that disthroyed wid the rheumatiz before he went, he'd be from this till tomorra creepin' the len'th of the house-wall. She might exparience a fine benefit yit, the crathur. There's to be a great Pattern in it, I hear tell, come Michaelmas; and I'd liefer than nine ninepennies poor Peg was goin'."

Stacey uttered this aspiration quite aimlessly, without in the least supposing that it would lead to anything, let alone to Tubberbride. But a few days afterwards old Ody Rafferty stopped at her mother's door in his donkey-cart, and thumped on the bottom of it with his blackthorn to bring somebody out. "Well, Stacey, me child," he then said, "I'm after bein' round Sallinmore ways wid a trifle of the stuff, so I made it me business to call in at the wife's sisther's place, that's livin' widin a short mile of Tubberbride. And it's as plased as anythin' they'll be herself bid me say, if you and Peg 'ud sleep the

night wid them, supposing you had e'er a notion
of thryin' the Houly Well.   Great carryin's on
they're to have in it at Michaelmas, she sez, wid
the Bishop and all manner.   I'll be goin' that
way meself agin, about then, and I could be
landin' the two of yous over there in the ould
cart, as aisy as lightin' me pipe.   The jaunt 'ud
be good for the crathur, if it was nothin' else;
sure she's niver thravelled beyond widin the roar
of an ass of this place in all the days of her life.
And I'd pick yous up agin next mornin' passin'
by."

This expedition seemed so large an undertaking to Stacey, and so widely adventurous to Peg,
that much time was needed for thinking it over,
and then one essential point had to be settled before the project could be seriously entertained.
" The child would come along wid us, in coorse?"
said Stacey.   "Me mother 'ud mind him the best
way she could, I well know, if I took and left
him behind.   But sure, then, the other childer
might get carryin' him about, or he might set off
wid himself crawlin' unbeknownst—a won'erful
quick crawl he has; there's many remarks it.
Anyway, I'd have the dread on me all the while
that he was lyin' dhrownded at the bottom of
every houle in the bog.   I wouldn't be lavin'
him."   But Ody answered, "Sure, what 'ud hinder you of takin' it along ?   A crathur that size

might as well be one place as another for any
differ it 'ud make."

So it came to pass that on a breezy September
morning Ody Rafferty's very dark-brown donkey
drew out of Lisconnel his long, narrow cart containing, among other things, Mrs. Stacey, Master
Felix, and Miss Peg; four jars of poteen, a basket
of bog-berries which Mrs. Ody was sending as a
present to her sister, and, tied up in a blue-speck-
led handkerchief, the contents of a select library,
from which its owner, somewhat to her friends'
regret, had not endured to be parted, even for a
day. The twelve-mile journey was an extraordinary experience to Peg, who had never before
gone one tithe as far, nor realised how the bog
would at last turn into fields and hedges, and
crowds of such terrible tall trees, with here and
there as many as a dozen little houses clustered
together, and two or three "grand big ones with
windows on the top of their windows, and they
the size of doors, same as in the picture on Mr.
Corr's paper bags." Ody's slow-pacing beast,
and springless cart, whose wheels were not an
exact match, made the very most of the deep-
rutted road-lengths, which led them through this
marvellous landscape; and before she reached
her destination untravelled Peg felt as if home
lay many ages behind her, across an unknown
country.

When they arrived at their journey's end,
wonders did not by any means cease, but rather
assumed a concentrated form. Their hostess,
Mrs. Kinsella, lived with an only daughter at
the back gate of Sir Francis Denroche's demesne,
that used to be a fine place entirely; and though
the family's fortune had for some time past
fallen into disrepair, the lodge was still what appeared to the girls a spacious and splendid residence. Stacey was immediately impressed by
the convenience of the hearth-fire that glowed to
greet them through polished bars, with grand
wide hobs to be standing your saucepans or ket-
tles on, and a great little oven at one side that
you could slip a cake of bread or anything into
very handy. For Mrs. Dan's cooking had to be
done mainly in a pot hung from a hook dangling
among the smoke, and on the lid inverted to
serve as a makeshift griddle. Peg's attention,
on the other hand, was at once caught by a
young woman seated in the sunset-lit window,
working with a needle and thread, a thing not
very commonly done up at Lisconnel. A rather
small slender person she was, with a clear bru-
nette complexion, and hazel eyes, and black hair,
dressed in such wonderful ways that at a first
glance it might seem doubtful whether all those
frizzes and puffs were the result of extreme un-
tidiness or supreme art. Her dress was of plain

grey linen, with a little bow of rose-coloured ribbon at the throat, so deftly tied that its loops and ends looked as precisely in their right places as the petal of a flower. The Kinsellas spoke of her as Miss Jackett, explaining that she was the sister of her ladyship's French maid, and at present their lodger.

Something about Miss Jacket interested and attracted Peg from the first; and they became better acquainted somewhat quickly during the next few days. For the visit of these pilgrims from Lisconnel was not to be so brief as they had at the outset proposed. It appeared that the grand doings of Saint Bridget's Well would not take place until the following Sunday, and nothing would their hostess hear of but that they should stay over it, Ody Rafferty fetching them home the next evening: "And plenty soon enough," she remarked, hospitably sugaring a moistened crust to propitiate the baby, who was criticising his new surroundings in no friendly spirit.

So Peg had two whole days to pass at the lodge, and spent them mostly *tête-à-tête* with the "furrin," girl, who would not accompany the Kinsellas and Stacey to the Pattern up at the Donoghues, on the ground that walking in such a desert was less supportable than the lace-making, though that might be dull to desolation.

"And I must one day finish Julie's flounce," she added. It was a puzzle to Peg how anybody could look as listlessly as Miss Jacket did upon the work of her own hands, when it took such a fascinating shape as the strip of fair-fine tracery, wherein snowy shadows of leaves and tendrils and blossoms seemed to be twined and tangled in the meshes of an elfin net. As Peg sat intently watching its growth, Miss Jacket thought there was a wistfulness in the admiring gaze.

" You shall yourself attempt it, Meess Pècque," she said, handing her a gossamer-threaded needle.

" Ah, but sure, I could never be makin' a right offer at it at all," Peg protested, taking it cautiously. " Why, the finest spriggin' ever I seen is a joke to it. A spider that was any size 'ud scarce consait he could be workin' wid that terrible thin thread —— There, it's broke on me, sure enough."

" You must commence with a grosser number," Miss Jacket said, searching among her reels and bobbins.

" Somethin' coorser might be better," said Peg.

" But certainly, coorser," said Miss Jacket, adopting the correction; " that was what I intended."

Thus Peg began her first lesson in lace-making, at which her sunburnt fingers showed a dexterity which surprised both teacher and pu-

pil. And as Miss Jacket was of a communicative disposition, Peg, although failing often to
understand, and still oftener to make herself understood, picked up along with her new stitches
sundry facts about her new acquaintance. It
seemed evident that Miss Jacket was dissatisfied
with her present situation, and thinking home-
sickly of her distant native land—a state of feeling which Peg could but too easily imagine.
Probably, however, she went widely astray in
the details of the picture which she supposed to
be occupying the stranger's memory. Her own
mind was full of a wide-sweeping brown bog-
land, with its far-away blue hills, and little fleck
of thatches huddling together on the solitude;
accordingly, when Miss Jacket said, "Do you
not find this Toubèrbride a very sad place?"
she replied, "Well, thruth to say, it does seem
to me a thrifle gathered-up like, wid all them big
trees standin' thick, and them unnathural high
walls round about; you can't git a look at anythin'. It's as if one was on'y lettin' on to be
steppin' outside. And the power of walkin' an'
dhrivin' there does be goin' by on this road has
me head moidhered, if I sit in the window."

As the traffic along Tubberbride road scarcely
exceeds on an average a couple of donkey-carts
and half-a-dozen pedestrians in an hour, Peg's
complaint would have much perplexed Miss

Jacket had its purport been intelligible to her,
which it was not.

"Ah, but it was pleasant, Meess Pècque," she
said, "in the Rue La Marck. My brother Charles
and I had a great comfort in his little chocolate
shop, before my half-sister, the widow Delande,
came with her two children. They are what
you call bozzering brats, all both of them, particularly Adolphe, a detested infant—and a glutton, *ma foi!* However, the end was that we
dispute—we quarrel—I give her impidence, as
you say. I abused her much, but very much,"
Miss Jacket said, meditatively. "So my sister
Julie, who is with a family here, got for me a
post of lace-teacher at the Convent in Water-
strand. I can make this fine lace to admiration,
but it is tedious. Far more joyfully would I tie
up the packets of *confitures*. Yes, that is a
good try at a *bride;* you are adroit, Meess
Pècque. But the Convent was horrible, with
the poor girls sitting there every morning in
rows on the benches in the whitewashed class;
and as for distraction or diversion—perhaps one
time or two times of a month, some lady comes
to see our samples in the glass-case, and says,
Ooh, exquisite, and *Oo-oh, too expensive a price,*
and goes away. Well, my dear, after a while I
give very great abuse to Sister Marie Evangel-
ista, who speaks the French. So my sister Julie

has procured me this lodging here. But you agree with me that it is *triste*, and dull inconceivably ? And as for a quarrel with Madame Kinsella, I know but a few of your bad words : and ould baste—a great rogue—a black duffel—dível —how do you say it ? But I must not think of such things yet," Miss Jacket said, regretfully, "for my sister Julie might not well be able to pay my expenses on another travel before I have the flounce finished. Then she can afford it easily. This piece is not less than two yards, and that should bring as much as five of your pounds—enough to keep one for half-a-year *chez* Madame Kinsella."

"Glory be to goodness, and would it be worth such a power of money ? " Peg said, eyeing the filmy fabric with a little awe added to her admiration.

"Surely," said Miss Jacket, measuring off between two small brown thumbs about half-an-inch of whorls and fronds. "Should not that be too expensive a price for many cups of Madame Kinsella's tay ? Bah, when shall I again taste veritable *café ?* Do you know, Meess Pècque, I think that on Sunday I shall accompany you to the holy well, and wish a wish for myself of Saint Bridget, and that will be—— But no, that I must not tell, or it will not, they say, come to pass. Yours is, of course, no secret. I hope

she will be very complaisant to you about the
weak foot. But, without doubt, she will favour
you; you are so *dévote*, Meess Pècque, with your
book of hymns always at your side," Miss Jacket
said, taking up Peg's old tattered song-book,
which lay by her on the window-seat.

"It's not hymns, so to spake, accordin' to what
I've heard read out of it," said Peg, looking a little
mistrustfully at the nimble brown fingers as they
turned over the ragged leaves, which she would
fain have reserved for her own handling. Her
statement was borne out by the fact that the
page at which Miss Jacket had opened the volume contained the stanzas beginning —

> At Shamus Flynn's the cruiskeen lawn
> Drinks deep at dusk, tastes drought at dawn,
> For draughts as bright as Delia's glance,
> Or beams that dance from dew-springs drawn.

Yet on the important Sunday this volume, despite
its secular contents, was in Peg's hand when Cornelius Dowling's car conveyed her to Saint Bridget's Well. Miss Jacket had insisted upon dress-
ing her hair to such a height of fashion that she
was thankful to hide her head beneath the heavy
folds of her brown woolen shawl. And at the
well she besought the good offices of its Patron-
ess with a fervour which to Miss Jacket, who
accompanied her, and duly presented a petition

on her own account, seemed a presage of a gracious answer.

Stacy, who had been detained at the lodge by the indisposition of her little Felix, had felt equally sanguine, and was, indeed, somewhat disappointed at first when Peg came limping in no more agile than at setting out. She could only console herself with the expectation that the case would be one of those in which the cure, starting from the time of the pilgrimage, proceeds slowly and surely. However, Stacey's hopes and fears were presently diverted into another channel, for by next morning the baby seemed so much worse that it was necessary to summon Dr. Miller, who pronounced the ailment to be scarlatina. Happily, its form was mild ; still, as it involved risks of spreading infection, it had the effect of quartering Mrs. Kinsella's guests upon her for several weeks longer. "And bedad, now," she said to them at parting, " it's kindly welcome yous are to anythin' yous got in it, barrin' the ugly sickness come on the little crathur ; and sure, he's finely betther of that, glory be to God."

Peg Sheridan used this extension of her visit as an opportunity for taking more lessons in the fascinating lace-work. So eagerly, in fact, did she grasp the chance of learning, that Miss Jacket, who at the outset only amused by her enthusiasm, ended by catching some of it herself,

and stitched away so diligently that Julie's
flounce began to approach completion. She en-
livened their industry with much vivacious chatter, from which Peg, growing accustomed to the
queer foreign accent and phrases, gathered various particulars about the defective qualities of
the Widow Delande and her children. "It
seemed an incomprehensible thing how Charles
could suffer the constant ravening of that pig
Adolphe among the assorted caramels and creams.
The loss must be ruinous. However, if Saint
Bridget ——" In the course of these conversations Miss Jacket often narrowly escaped reveal-
ing the purport of her prayer, and a very little
curiosity on the part of her companion would
have elicited it. But it was more to Peg's purpose that she acquired a thorough grounding in
the technique of the art which had charmed her.
So proficient did she become in the matter of
"knots" and "brides," and veining and tracing,
that before she left the Kinsellas' her instruct-
ress pronounced her work to be veritably ex-
cellent, and thereupon made over to her a liberal
supply of materials, folds of misty white net, and
reels and skeins of gossamer thread. Peg eyed
them somewhat as a greedy reader gloats over a
bundle of new books, and we may doubt that she
gave much heed to her friend, who was pointing
out to her that she could easily get three or four

francs a yard for the narrowest edging.   For she
only observed dreamily, reverting fondly to the
strip on which she was putting the last touches
to a tiny spray of bell-flower, "There is a look
of the rael ones on them, but they've a liker look
of some sort that I never seen yit."

"And, sure, how at all could you tell what
that sort *would* be lookin' like!" objected Lizzie
Kinsella, whose views inclined to matter-of-fact.
But Peg lacked analytic gifts, and could only
reply :

"It's just the notion I have."

Soon after this, Peg and Stacey and the convalescent Felix turned their faces from Tubberbride in the slant of mellow October sunbeams,
Peg's latest memory of Miss Jacket being her
droll grimace as she whispered with lifted eyebrows over Mrs. Kinsella's farewell cup of tea,
"Oo-ooh, exquisite!"   It was not, however, to
be a final adieu.   One dapple-grey forenoon,
when the air abroad on the Lisconnel bog-land
had begun to rumour the spring, little Mick ran
indoors to where Peg sat by the fire entertain-
ing Stacey O'Beirne, and reported that "somebody quare and grand was afther drivin' up on a
car, an' axin' where the Sheridans lived."   This
person proved to be Miss Jacket, who was standing a few yards from their dark cavernous door,
looking perplexed and rather frightened, in her

smart short cape hooded and lined with grey and
scarlet silk, a small furry cap crowning her coils
and fringes, and something wound about her
neck, not unlike a magnified specimen of the
flossy black caterpillars that Peg called woolly
bears. Mick might well be amazed.

She explained, when the girls had established
her by the hearth, that she was on her way home
to the Rue La Marck and her brother's shop,
where the obnoxious Widow Delande and family
interloped no longer. Miss Jacket's clear brown
eyes danced as fast as the flame flickers that Peg
hospitably stirred up among the embers, as she
related the manner of the enemy's rout. "Terribly Charles, my brother, and she, Victorine,
quarrelled—just as I beseeched of the good Saint
Bridget that day at the well of Touberbride. It
makes no harm now to tell my request. At
about Christmas-time it happened. Nothing
would content the detestable infant Adolphe but
to devour the most superior *nougats* and *marrons*
at three francs the pound, and because the little
glutton had lately taken an attack of the influence—you call it? his mother would give him all
that he desired. In consequence, my friends,
there was a disagreement, and they leave, and
Charles sends for me to come. So you see me
voyaging back, and in passing I call to make my
adieux, and to give you my address, Meess

Pêcque, that you may write for more of the net
and thread, should you require it. I have com-
pleted my flounce; but as for the price of it, my
sister Julie cannot expect to take it all in pay-
ment for the tay of Madame Kinsella. She will
rest satisfied with a portion, and the remainder
will be not much for the renewal of my toilets.
How goes it with your lace-work, Meess Pêcque?
Ah, ah, you are still lame of foot, I perceive.
Saint Bridget has not treated you so kindly."

"Bedad, no," Stacey said, mournfully. "Sorra
the hap'orth of good it done her at all. We'd
betther ha' sted at home." Stacey looked back
upon the Tubberbride expedition as a gloomy
failure, blotted with fears about Felix and disappointment about Peg.

"Well, now, it wasn't, so to spake, her fau't,"
said Peg, who had limped across the uneven
floor with two turf-sods on a capacious shovel.
"Truth to say," she said, leaning on its handle,
while their outer fibres twinkled into golden
threads, "that time at the well there, the ould
fut of me was gone cliver and clean out of me
head. Never a word I thought to be sayin' to
her about it whatsome'er. So how was the crathur to know? But I'll tell you what I was
thinkin' of instead. There's them couple of
books Larry went and left behind for me the
black mornin' he took off out of this to be gettin'

his death away from us all. Many's the time I
would be callin' them ould thrash to him, because I was too ignorant meself to be spellin'
them out the way he did. And more's the times
ever since I've been wishin' in me heart I could
get to tell him that I wouldn't give them out of
me hands, not for the full of them of silver and
gould. So then, when we settled we'd go to
Tubberbride, I considhered to meself that I'd
have them along wid me, and it's showin' them
to Herself at the well I'd be, an' axin' her could
she be any manes make a shift to bring him word
it was dymints and jewels worth I thought of
them, or aught else ever he owned. And that's
what I done right enough; but if I did, I disremimbered everythin' else—and no great matter.
So it's small blame to Saint Bridget. But just
the very minyit I was blessin' meself and comin'
away, the notion caught a hould of me mind that
if I could be conthrivin' some very superiligant
sort of cover for the two ould books, 'twould
hinder them of fallin' into laves the way they
was, and maybe—it *might* maybe—somehow
show Larry that 'tis the great store intirely I'm
settin' be them, let alone callin' them thrash.
And Miss Jacket's work was the purtiest thing
ever I seen, and thinkin' it 'ud look delightful on
them was the raison encouraged me to be larnin'
it. 'Deed now, workin' at it I've been all the

winther, and makin' a botch more betoken of
half me pieces of net, until I had the pattron
right. It's on'y the other day I got the girls to
bring me up a grand bit of stuff from Mr.
Corr's —— But sure, I'll fetch them out to
yous."

Peg crossed the room to a commodious wall-
cranny, and came triumphantly hobbling back,
bearing her library, which was indeed gloriously
transformed. For the stained and tattered pages
were now clad in ample bindings of glowing
scarlet, all frosted over with the most delicate
white embroideries. "There's two folds of the
glazy calico underneath the red flannen, for to
stiffen it a bit," she explained, with pride, lifting
each cover separately to show how the lace ex-
tended to the inner side.

"They're rael sumpchus," said Mrs. Stacey.
"I do declare you might think you had them
rowled up in the end of Canon O'Hanlon's
grandest vestments."

"And sorra a taste too good for them if they
was," quoth Peg.

"The quantity of lace on them," Miss Jacket
said, measuring off fingers on one of the covers,
"would trim three fifty-franc *mouchoirs;* I
could sell it for you without difficulty in Paris.
You are extravagant, Meess Pècque."

"I'm thinkin' I'll make them another couple

for fear of anythin' happenin' these ones," Peg
said, smoothing out the creased margins of the
song-book. "It's grand work, and I'd liefer be
at it than not. On'y I do be wishin'," she
added, half to herself, as she carried back her
treasures to their hole in the wall,—"wishin' I
do be that I was anyway sartin Larry knew a
mortal thing about them these times at all. But
it's just a chance; and sure, I'm thankful for that
same to Saint Bridget, or whoever of Them it
was put it into me head."

Thus, it appears that the library of Lisconnel
can hardly be termed extensive. A complete descriptive catalogue of it would run as follows :

*Ivanhoe, by Sir Walter Scott. Very cheap
edition. London: Smith & Wilson; no date.*

A song-book; title page and index missing.

But since Peg's visit to Tubberbride, it may at
least be fairly described as unique in the matter
of its bindings.

A CHRISTMAS DOLE

A CHRISTMAS DOLE

BETWEEN Julia Doherty and her fellow-serv-
ant, Rebecca Moriarty, relations had been more
or less strained for the past three years, but this
state of things still seemed to them a disagreeable innovation, because they had lived together
in amity for at least ten times as long. During
that period they had witnessed jointly and shared
many vicissitudes, the main outcome of which
had been the dwindling away of the establishment
at Lisnafrenagh House, where themselves with
their old Miss Valance now seemed a very much
shrivelled kernel in a weather-beaten nut. The
shell was indeed all worn and battered. Red
rust lay almost as thick on the whorls of the tall
entrance-gates as green moss in the crevices of
their granite piers; and the ornate lodge at the
left hand was so obviously a ruin that nobody
could think of calling for anybody to come out
of it and open them. One of the small side-
gates, however, had fallen off its hinges, and
made ingress easy for foot-passengers. So Dr.
Furlong there left his car one dingy morning a
few days before Christmas, and began to walk
up the weedy avenue. His approach could be

watched all the way from the upper storeys of
the house, which crowns a short slope, and it
was in fact at once descried by Rebecca and
Julia, cleaning windows in the front chintz room.
Julia was a tall, gaunt person, to whose long
face, straight black eyebrows, and a jaw slightly
underhung, gave a resolute expression, which
sometimes proved misleading. A heavy grey
shawl enfolded her, and she wore a black bonnet
over bands of frosted dark hair. Rebecca, in her
cold-looking bluish print gown, was a rather
dumpy figure, and her face was plump, though
its features were sharp and fine. Her sleek
flaxen hair, uncovered by a cap, was less bleached
than faded.

"There's a car stopped at us below," said Rebecca. "Dan Corish's it looks to be, and the
Doctor's on it belike. Ay, sure enough, whoever
it is he's steppin' up. I'm glad now he come so
early. I scarce thought he would for such a
thrifle."

"I'm glad," assented Julia; but her tone expressed a somewhat doubtful joy. "To be sure
he knows well enough he's a right to not be delayin' when he's called in to an ould body like
the Misthress, that might drop down any minute," she added more cheerfully.

"It was a good job, too, her gettin' the weeny
touch of rheumatics," said Rebecca. "If it

wasn't only for that we'd never have had her persuaded to see him. And why would she? and she so finely and strong in herself, and no more than the age of other people."

"I don't see any great signs of stren'th on her then," said Julia. "Failin' she is every day of her life, in my humble judgment."

"And, bedad, it's the quare things," Rebecca said, "some folks wouldn't see, if they had as many eyes as a paycock."

"They would not, thrue for you," Julia said, making an application of her own.

"You'll be takin' off of *them*, anyway, I should suppose," Rebecca said, suggestively rather than conjecturally, referring to Julia's out-of-door garb.

"That's accordin' as may happen," said Julia; "I might as like as not have to be runnin' out."

"To fetch liniment or such—oh, like enough," said Rebecca.

"Plinty besides liniment I may be fetchin'," Julia said meaningly.

"And makin' a laughin'-stock of the Family through the parish," Rebecca said bitterly. "'Twould be a pity you weren't ready time enough for that."

"What talk at all of the Family have you?" said Julia. "Isn't she all the Family there's in it? And where'd it be if she took her death frettin'?"

"Frettin' 's a quare long road for a body to be gettin' at her death by," said Rebecca. "And if she's all that's left, it's only the more raison for not lettin' her make a show of herself."

"I haven't the heart to go disappoint her, and it may be the last Christmas she'll have in th' ould place," said Julia. "That's what I'm always thinkin'."

"Once in a way 'ud be often enough, for any sinse there was in it," said Julia. "But whether or no, if it hadn't mishappint I was laid up with that maledicted ould influenza this time three year, ne'er a chance you'd have had, let me tell you, of takin' up wid playin' any such fool's tricks."

Midway in these last remarks, Julia had begun to polish a pane so energetically that the rattling of the loose window-frame might have been supposed to prevent them from reaching her ears, and she availed herself of the possibility to avoid making any reply.

"Ashamed of me life I've often been to be showin' me face in the chapel," Rebecca resumed, when the clatter had ceased. "And if it was to happen again, faix, I might as well turn haythen Turk all out. To think of that mane work, after all the family done in the days of ould."

"Ay, indeed; the Valances were always great benefactors," said Julia. "And the poor Mis-

thress is a rael charitable lady in her heart.
Sure that's why she's so set her mind on keepin'
up the Dole."

"There's a dale of pride and conthrariness in
some people's charity," said Julia. "Thick wid
them it is as a spoonful of jam wid wasps and
flies out of a pot you've left uncovered all the
summer on the dresser."

Julia's reply to this was not less evasive than
her window-rattling had been. "He'll be nigh
the hall-door by now," she said, peering out.
"Yes, bedad; there is he passin' the clump of
junipers. Saints above, but he's quare and
young-lookin'. Poor Dr. Carter's great-grandson
he might be, for any age that's on him."

"And all the betther," said Rebecca; "he'll
ha' had so much the less time to be forgettin' his
college larnin', and takin' foolish notions into his
head wid listenin' to the poor people talkin'
nonsensical."

"Thim that are so young do mostly have
plinty of nonsensical notions in their heads widout
throublin' thimselves to be listenin'—that's my
experience," said Julia.

"Well, mind you, young or no, you've under-
took to go by what he says," Rebecca said, looking sternly at her. "If he's of the opinion
there's not much ailin' her, you'll quit humourin'
her that way. It's a promise."

"Ay is it," said Julia, "and a safe one, if he's as much wit as a four-year-old. We'd a right to be steppin' down and lettin' him in. Sure enough I'll go by what he says."

So a short light-blue figure, and a tall greyish one, were waiting to receive Dr. Furlong as he crossed the wide gravel sweep, paved here and there with sodden leaves in fantastic inlaid patterns. The house which fronted him was a three-storied, basemented, stone building, with wings longer and lower. Its porched hall-door opened on a semi-circle of broken steps; upon the roof-gable immediately above it, a large ecstatic sculpture, Bacchante or Victory, seemed to dance in mockery of the surrounding decay. Dr. Furlong, young and brisk, was ushered by the two old women solemnly into a dark dismantled-looking hall, and up wide resonant stairs. "This damp weather has affected your mistress, no doubt," he said to them on the way up. But one replied, shaking her bonneted head: "We'll lave it to you, sir"; and her companion said: "I'm sayin' nothin' one way or the other." After which he desisted from further attempts at conversation.

When he had emerged from his interview with Miss Valance, however, he found them both lying in wait for him at the head of the first flight of stairs, under the big round-topped stained-glass window. Intense anxiety was stamped on their faces, and the Doctor good-naturedly hastened to relieve it by saying cheerfully: "Well, I'm glad to find that there's not much amiss here. Miss Valance is merely suffering from a slight touch of muscular rheumatism in the elbow, and should keep herself warm and out of draughts. But indeed, as she tells me that she never leaves those rooms, she runs little risk of taking cold. It's a pity, though, that she should shut herself up in such a way."

"Well, now, glory be to goodness, for that hearin'," said Rebecca. "And what was I tired tellin' you, Julia?"

But the long face in the black bonnet had lengthened at this verdict; and Julia said to the Doctor: "Yet it's rael wakely she is, at all events; cruel faible and failed like to what she was. 'Twouldn't take more than a little to make an end of her altogether."

"Really, I don't think that is the case at all," said Dr. Furlong, still wishing to reassure. "Of course, at her advanced age—over eighty, she tells me—we must expect some diminution of strength, but I should say she was in a fairly vigorous state."

"And you've promised faithful to go by what he'd say, Julia," exulted Rebecca.

To which Julia only responded under her breath: "Och, the crathur, the crathur!"

Dr. Furlong began to feel that he did not quite understand the situation. "I'll send a bottle of lotion, and I'll look in and see how she is in two or three days," he said. "I expect I shall find her well mended, as they say up in Donegal."

"You couldn't tell, sir," said Julia; "but if she was thwarted any way, or hindered of what she was used to——"

"Whist now wid that," Rebecca interrupted in a peremptory whisper. "You've no call to be puttin' your own notions in his head. 'Tisn't them we'll be mindin'."

During even his short practice, Dr. Furlong had become too familiar with the symptoms of domestic discords to lay much stress upon them, or to observe them with much curiosity; besides, his car was waiting. So he said: "Well, good-morning! I'll send the lotion;" and he had his foot on the stair, when a casual thought turned him round: "By the way," he said, "that's an uncommonly fine dog you have. But what breed is he? He might be a deerhound from his build, but his coat and colour are like a Great Dane. Is he——" He stopped suddenly, because one old woman crossed herself, and the other said with widening eyes: "*The dog?*"

"Yes, a great shaggy white and fawn-coloured fellow," said Dr. Furlong. "He met me just now outside your mistress's door, and wanted me

to let him in; but I didn't know whether that
was permissible, especially as he was dripping
wet—seemed to have been taking a bath. I left
him whining and scratching, and then he came
after me a bit downstairs, till he ran off into the
little dark passage on the right—he nearly filled
it up. I never saw such a giant."

"You've seen what shouldn't be seen by man
or baste in this house," said Rebecca; and Julia
said groaningly: "Up at her very door—the
saints be good to her!"—remarks which seemed
to the Doctor little to the purpose, so he nodded
farewell and ran downstairs.

As the sound of his steps receded, Rebecca
composed her countenance and said with some
tartness to Julia, who was continuing to ejaculate,
"Och, what ould yawpin' have you? Where's
the wit of keepin' on like th' ould weather-cock
craikin' round?"

"For the matter of that," retorted Julia,
"yourself's lookin' this minyit as if you was after
wipin' your face wid a floury apern."

"Anybody might be a thrifle took aback just
at hearin' it suddint," said Rebecca; "but that's
all I was. 'Tisn't the first time such a thing was
heard tell of here."

"'Twould be the first time if black harm wasn't
comin' of it," said Julia. "Och! and she the last
of thim all; may goodness pity us!"

"You'd do a dale better to be takin' off of thim things, and comin' down to fetch her up her cup of beef-tay, and it past twelve o'clock, instead of keenin' there like a desolit banshee; it might be about nothin' after all," said Rebecca.

"Sure I'm runnin' out this instant," said Julia.

"And what for, then?" said Rebecca.

"To bid the people be steppin' up on Christmas Eve," Julia said, as much as possible as if mentioning a matter of course.

"Is it for that same ould nonsense and blathers you'd be bringin' them?" Rebecca said with wrath and surprise, unfeigned and feigned.

"Bedad am I, what else?" Julia said, in like manner.

"God forgive you, woman!" Rebecca stormed; "and you promised faithful to go by whatever the Doctor would be sayin'."

"And what else at all am I goin' by?" said Julia.

"Didn't he say as plain as he could spake there was next to nothin' ailin' her?" demanded Rebecca.

"Is it plain?" said Julia; "and could he spake plainer than tellin' of seein' the sign? 'Twould ha' been all one if he'd said she wouldn't over the New Year."

"So then you'd have her fooled and chaited in

the last days of her life?" Rebecca said, shifting her ground.

"Liefer would I than for to have her vexed," said Julia, drawing her shawl about her shoulders. "And when she's gone, it's little I'll throuble meself to mind what any people thinks."

Rebecca, pausing, seemed to cast about for an argument against this recklessness, but apparently with small result.

"Whose bonnet is that you're wearin' of, I'd be glad to know?" she called at the last moment, as Julia was beginning to stump down. "It's long before I'd ever ha' loaned you it if——"

Julia wheeled about disdainfully: "Och! if that's all," she said, and began to fumble at the strings.

"Mercy on us, woman," Rebecca cried, more than ever aghast, "you're not runnin' out on the road in your bare head, makin' a show of us?"

But Julia had already flung the black bonnet on to the window-seat, where it alighted with ribbons widely streaming. Then as she swooped downstairs, she lifted her dark shawl over her head with a flapping spread of her arms, so that her departure was somewhat like the flight out of the house of a large black bird. Rebecca stood in consternation for a few moments, till with a start she glanced behind her, wavered affrightedly, and ran desperately upstairs. She

thought she had heard the padding of great
paws.

———

Towards dusk, on the sleety Christmas Eve,
Dr. Furlong was again walking up to the front
door of Lisnafrenagh House, and "There's one
of those queer old women," he said to himself,
recognising under the porch a capacious black
bonnet. On this occasion it contained, however,
the sleek faded hair-loops of Rebecca Moriarty.
She wore over her blue print a little knitted
shawl of flimsy texture, but an inadequate wrap
against the bleak gusts and cold drops slanting
in between the pillars. When the Doctor inquired for her mistress she replied: "I've quit
Miss Valance's service; but she's above. The
other woman can be showin' her to you."

"Perhaps I'd better ring," said he, and he
pulled a dangling bell-handle. At this moment
two old black-cloaked crones came up, and he
stood aside to let them pass. They walked in at
the door, which they left ajar, and through it
came a sound of many voices in the hall. One
of these, manly and gruff, was just then remark-
ing: "If I'd ha' thought we'd be kep' waitin'
that long, I'd ha' waited a while longer meself
before I come away from me bit of thatchin'."

"Whethen now, Joe M'Quaile," a shriller voice

said, "you might be talkin' if you was after thrampin' betther than two mile thro' the mud of the roads, that's liker ditch-bottoms, to be fetchin' home nothin' at all. 'Deed, if it wasn't only for Julia Doherty, that's a dacint poor crathur, sornin' and enthraitin' to me, sorra a fut of me'd be in it."

"Sure it hasn't the look of a place you'd be fetchin' anythin' out of," said a third voice. "The ould walls is as bare as the floor, and there's scare e'er a chair standin' on it. Stone-broke they are, whatever she may let on."

"Me pair of blankets I'm come for, and me poun' of tay, and me half-a-crown," said a quavering treble very hopefully. "And may God lave the Valances their health."

"Take care, Widdy, it's not inthrest they'll be axin' you for the loan of the bit of silver," said the gruff voice. "Quare ways the Valances have these times intirely."

"There's not been an ounce of buttcher's mate ordered up here in the last twelvemonth," said a woman's voice. "Warden was sayin' he supposed they'd be roastin' of a wood quest for th' ould lady's dinner on Christmas Day." And then several laughed and talked at once.

"Thim's the sort she has in it passin' remarks on the Family," Rebecca said, turning to the Doctor a face full of fierce bitterness. "Begor-

rah, if I had the hangin' alive of that Julia
Doherty!" Then she put her head in at the
half-open door, and called: "Bad manners to
the whole of you for a good-for-nothin' thankless
pack."

An abrupt silence followed this criticism; and
Rebecca, turning away down the steps, said to
Dr. Furlong as she passed: "The bell-wire's
broke this twinty year. You'd a right to walk
straight up."

After doubting for a moment whether to do so,
he entered the darkling hall, where were grouped
some dozen or more of poor folk, chiefly women;
all of them—so recent in date was his appoint-
ment to Lisnafrenagh Dispensary—still strangers
to him. He passed through them and upstairs,
till on the first landing he came to an open door
made conspicuous by a dim illumination. It belonged to the library, a narrow slip of a brown
room, which gave one the impression that everything wanted to be re-bound. Looking in from
the threshold, Dr. Furlong found his view limited
by a wide leathern folding-screen, set near this
end of the room, which it blocked up thoroughly.
At one corner of it old Julia Doherty, flushed
and dishevelled, was tugging violently. "Och,
sir, wud you come and lend me your assistance
to straighten out this flap of it?" she called hurriedly as she caught sight of the Doctor. He

did as requested, and helped her to extend the heavy leaf with its dainty Watteau-like groups, powdered ladies pink and white, in wide-dispread azure and peach-colour, gentlemen no less brilliant, but more succinct in drapery. The screen was placed behind a massive square-backed arm-chair, beside which stood a small spindle-legged table, with a pair of long candles burning on it to eke out the ebbing daylight, now almost swamped by the portentous gloom of an imminent hail-shower.

"I beg your pardon, sir, for makin' so free," Julia said, panting. "But the misthress might be down directly, and I'm that put about wid one thing and another. And Rebecca Moriarty's took upon herself to flounce off, and left me widout e'er a body to do a hand's turn."

"I believe I met her at the door," said Dr. Furlong.

"Ay, would you. Away is she to stop wid the Langans at the ould back lodge. Quit after five-and-thirty year, and all because I wouldn't be tormintin' and thwartin' of the poor Misthress that's took for her death."

"My goodness!" said the Doctor. "Is Miss Valance worse?"

"Oh, *you'd* stand me out there was nothin' ailin' her," Julia said upbraidingly, "and you after seein' the sign yourself. But for the matter

of that, ne'er a medical man among you all 'ud
know an atom betther. It's ignorant they aro.
Howsomever, 'twould be a cruel pity to go annoy her, the crathur, the last Christmas she'll put
in wid us; and the Blankit-dole was always what
she took a quare surprisin' plisure in. So about
play-actin' it agin we are—if Rebecca was twice
as cross."

"Play-acting?" said Dr. Furlong.

"A pair of blankits," said Julia, "and a pound
of tay, and a half-crown—that's what four-and-
twinty poor people out of this parish 'ud be getting up here every Christmas Eve time out of
mind. And the Misthress herself disthributin'
the gifts to aich one of them here in tho book-
room, and she sittin' queenly there in the big
chair. But upon me word, sir, it cost a powerful
sight of money. There was three pounds wint in
the half-crowns alone; and the tay 'ud come to
maybe half as much agin—tay's chapened these
times—and the blankits were a terrible price,
terrible. 'Twouldn't be much short of a dozen
guineas altogether. So when the Family got
ruinated a while back, how would she be af-
fordin' it at all? And she all the while, mind
you, never thinkin' of anythin' bein' diff'rint to
what they was used to, and considherin' belike
the bills got ped as natural as the laves come out
on the trees, just a while sooner or later, ac-

cordin' as may happen. But it's fairly distracted I was, schemin' and conthrivin', till this time three year I made up a sort of plan in me mind how to manage rightly. See here, sir."

She twitched the Doctor by the sleeve toward a little round table in an obscure nook behind the screen. On it stood a dark-purple grocer's parcel, with a silver coin stuck in the twine, and a white soft-looking bundle, which displayed a border of shaded brown.

"I made a shift," she said, "to get the one pair of blankits—I couldn't tell you the shillin's they stood me in—and the pound of tay, and the half-crown. And then I wint round to the people, and I explained to them the way it was wid the Family, and that the Misthress couldn't be annoyed about it, and what themselves had a right to do. So now there she does the sittin' in the big chair, wid the ould foldin'-screen behind her to keep off draughts, for 'fraid she might notice anythin'; and here I have the pair of blankits and all convenient to hand to her. And in comes, maybe, Pather Connolly, or Biddy Lynch, or the Widdy Kilkelly, and up to the front of the chair he steps, and makes his best bow, or drops her curtsey accordin'. And the Misthress gives him the bundle I'm after handin' her—sure she'd never think to ax where it come from, no more than if it was a cloud out of the sky—and then

it's 'Long life to your ladyship,' and 'Heaven be
your bed,' and 'You're very welcome, Pather,'
and this way and that way, and off wid him
round the screen. But at the back of it here, out
of sight, sure he just hands what she gave him
over to me agin, the way we'd have it ready for
the next body come, same as if we had ones
a-piece for them all, and no throuble whate'er."

"Oh! I see," said Dr. Furlong. "Then this
blanket's doing duty for the third year."

"Troth is it," Rebecca said, patting it with a
sort of furtive pride, "and nobody could tell but
it was fresh out of the shop. I folded it other side
out this mornin', and gave it a tie wid a new bit
of the pink tape. 'Have they sent the blankits
of a good quality, Rebecca?' sez the Misthress to
me only yesterday. 'Iligant, ma'am,' sez I; 'the
very same as last year.' And it's the identical
half-crown, too. But the packet of tay's new,"
she explained regretfully, "for that omadhawn
Thady Gahan last year let it fall, and burst the
bottom out of it. Be good luck there was nobody to come after him. But I thought Judy
Molloy had us desthroyed; for she come one of
the first, and if she did, she took and dhropped
the half-crown, that rowled itself into a crevice
near the door—and sorra another one in the house
I well knew—only John Egan roked it out wid
his stick. It's a good plan, bedad."

"Well, it's ingenious, no doubt," said Dr. Furlong; "but it seems rather hard on the people."

"Oh, *thim*," said Julia, "set thim up; it's the laist they may do for the poor Misthress. And willin' and raisonable enough they mostly are, I'll say that for them. It's only Rebecca Moriarty does be cross, and talkin' quare about the Family, as if I'd be doin' anythin' agin it. 'Tis the best plan of all."

"I suppose you must go through with it now, at any rate," said the Doctor, "and the sooner the better, for the people in the hall seem to be getting a little impatient."

"I'm only waitin' now for the Misthress to be callin' them up," said Julia. "She'll be here directly. 'Twas Rebecca's fantigues delayed us. But there's one thing, sir, I'm a thrifle onaisy about. It's the Widdy Langan from th' ould back lodge has come up wid herself; I heard her voice below. And she's a little ould ancient body, not over sinsible in her mind. Apt she might be to get risin' a disturbance on us, if she's axed to give up the blankit, not rightly understandin'; and then I dunno what 'ud happen at all at all. Musha, good gracious! here's the Misthress herself"—a door at the other end of the room was opening. "'Twould be a rale charity, now, sir, if you'd keep an eye on th' ould body," Julia said in a flurry, "and purvint

her by any manes of comin' up wid the first;
'twouldn't matter as much if she was nigh the
ind of thim."

"All right," Dr. Furlong said, and he took up
a position near the door, though he was puzzled
to know how he could carry out these instructions.

Meanwhile, tall and thin Miss Valance, whose
high-capped grizzled head looked the gaunter because it rose from among the softness of a fleecy
white shawl, settled herself in the big square-
outlined chair, shaking out the somewhat skimpy
folds of a black satin skirt, which the shivering
candle-light burnished gloomily; and Julia, going
to the head of the stairs, called down them:
"Come along up wid yous out of that, aisy and
quiet."

A loud clumping on the stairs, mixed with the
flip-flap of bare feet, followed this injunction immediately, as if put in motion by a spring; and
presently the procession came filing in, mostly
old women and men. Dr. Furlong watched the
proceedings from a corner near the door. They
seemed to be carried on with no serious hitch.
The presentations were made with all due forms
and ceremonies, and the gifts were promptly sur-
rendered by each recipient in turn to Julia, ambushed behind the scenes. Dinny Blake did make
some sportive feints of being about to pocket the

half-crown, but desisted at once upon Julia's pas-
sionately-whispered appeal to him to "behave
himself like a dacint Christian"; and though she
fidgeted uneasily through Miss Valance's exhortations to Joe Rea on the inadvisability of parting with any of his coin at M'Evoy's, the irony
in his undertaking to "ait ivery pinny of it that
he spint on drink" was quite unsuspected by the
person addressed. Nor was there perceptible any
false ring in Bridget Toler's fervent promise to
"be prayin' for all the Valances every night of her
life as long as she had a thraneen of thim iligant
blankits above her."

These things were interesting Dr. Furlong
when he was tardily reminded of his special commission by the sight of a small old wizened
woman pushing her way eagerly to the front,
amid encouragement from the bystanders, who
bade her "come along wid herself," and one another "be lettin' the Widdy Langan pass." He
hastily tried to interpose with some retarding
suggestions, but it was too late, and she slipped
by him at a tottering trot, in her ancestral heeded
cloak, so much too ample for her that whenever
she stood still it made a black frill round her on
the floor, towards which it seemed to be dragging
her down. Julia thus had no alternative but to
hand her mistress the Widdy's bundle, but as she
did so she made signals of distress to the Doctor,

seeming to implore his aid in counteracting the evil effects of its bestowal.

Accordingly, when the little Widdy reappeared behind the screen, gleefully hugging her parcels, she was met by two people, who were cruelly bent on inducing her to part from her newly-acquired prize. Such a proposal very sadly shocked and grieved the Widdy; nor could arguments, explanations, cajoleries, and promises aught avail to recommend it. They were all responded to by plaintive "Ah, no's!" growing shriller and more querulous with each reiteration, until at last another voice, also high-pitched and quavering, called impatiently to inquire why nobody came; whereupon Julia, with a distracted mien, ran round the screen to account for the delay as plausibly as she could. To Dr. Furlong the case had assumed a very hopeless complexion, when an ally joined him in the person of one Mrs. M'Ateere, the little Widdy's good-natured and portly niece, whose coaxing and *sluthering*, reinforced by a couple of the Doctor's not over-abundant florins, at length detached the lingering grasp lothfully from the property bundle. Yet even then she tottered away so evidently so very much less than half consoled, that he felt inhuman and remorseful as he sped to Julia with his spoil.

In the act of delivering it to her he started

violently, and all but let it drop; the cause, his having suddenly become aware, with an unaccountable degree of astonishment, that the big white and fawn-coloured dog was in the room. The beast was lying close to Miss Valance's feet, conspicuous even in that dim light against her dark gown, stretched lazily, with his heavy forepaws crossed, and his wide red mouth open.

"What is it, sir?" Julia asked.

"Oh, nothing," he answered, " only I hadn't noticed that the dog was there."

Julia flung up her hands. "The saints be good to us!—the dog!—where is it at all?"

But at this moment Miss Valance rose up stiffly and feebly. "I think, Julia," she said, "I'll now leave the rest of the distribution to you."

"Is there anythin' ailin' you, Miss Nellie?" Julia said, hurrying over to her. "Aren't you feelin' so well in yourself, ma'am dear?"

"Perfectly," replied Miss Valance. "But I'm rather tired, and my feet are cold, and I feel a chilly draught—it comes from the door, I think. Look how the lights are flickering; one can hardly see. I'm afraid to sit here any longer, so I'll make an end, and depart."

In the dimness she did not observe Dr. Furlong's presence, and she moved slowly down the room towards the door at the opposite end, Julia going with her. The Doctor at first saw the

great shaggy beast following close behind the
two old women; but about half-way he seemed
to disappear among the many shadows. From
the other direction came the sounds of the people descending the stairs. All around the wind
was moaning and howling, as it drove fitful
showers against the windows, sometimes with
the clattering slash of hail, and sometimes with
sleet in broad half-melted flakes, that came on
the swimming panes like the padding of large
soft paws.

Early on the next morning, which was wild
and wet, Dr. Furlong found himself again alighting at the gates of Lisnafrenagh. He had had
an urgent call in that direction, and took the opportunity of leaving at the old back-lodge some
tea and a roll of resplendent scarlet flannel for
the Widdy Langan, as spells by which he hoped
to lay the haunting reminiscence of her little
wizened face, all foolish and woebegone.

Dan Crilly, the driver, had been explaining to
him on the way, his shortest route to the lodge,
through the tangled shrubbery paths: "And
then, after passin' th' ould shell-house, take the
turn to the right; the other 'ud bring you to the
bit of a little lough lyin' just outside of the
demesne, that they have the quare story about."

"What's that?" asked the Doctor.

"Sure I dunno rightly," said Dan; "some ugly black work, be all accounts. The Family had some young fellow drowned in it, I've heard tell. But 'twas ould ages ago."

Not a soul did Dr. Furlong meet in the dripping overgrown shrubberies, until just at the round dilapidated arbour he saw pacing towards him the huge white dog, who stopped ever and anon to shake his shaggy coat. So narrow was the path that it seemed as if they would have hardly room to pass each other; however, before they met, the beast turned down the walk to the left, towards the ill-reputed lough. When Dr. Furlong knocked at the door of the lodge close by, a cabin smothered in sombre shrubs, it was opened at once by Rebecca Moriarty, but instead of greeting him she stood staring over his shoulders as if some other object absorbed all her attention. He faced about, and saw Julia Doherty speeding down the path, bare-headed beneath the wet and wind-tossed boughs, with her arms full of an overflowing white bundle. It was the pair of blankets, which had slipped out of their fastenings, and hung about in loosely gathered up folds. These she thrust upon Rebecca. "Widdy Langan may be havin' them now," she said; "there'll be no more givin' away up at Lisnafrenagh." With that she was rushing off again, when Rebecca caught her by the shawl. "What at all is it, woman?" she said; "sure to goodness nothin's took——" But Julia pulled herself free, still keeping her face set to the grey quivering rain-strands, and the keening gusts that carried away her words. "All alone wid herself," she said; "ne'er a hand's turn to do for her. Ah! poor Miss Nellie, the crathur, the crathur! There'll be nobody up at the House—nobody any more!"

THE FIELD OF THE FRIGHTFUL BEASTS

THE FIELD OF THE FRIGHTFUL BEASTS

MacBarry bore a heavy weight on his mind through a part of his summer at Clonmanavon, which, being only the sixth one in his life, seemed to him a season with remotest beginning and end. He was visiting his great-grandmother, Mrs. Kavanagh, who for each of his years could have given a baker's dozen of her own, and still have had several left over; and through the glowing July days the old lady worked away, steadily and swiftly, at sundry woollen garments, sometimes expressing a fear, as her needles clicked, that she would hardly have them all ready for the boys before the cold weather began. The youngest of these boys would never see fifty again, and Mrs. Kavanagh knitted the faster whenever she thought of her Johnnie's rheumatism. To Mac, on the contrary, it never occurred at this time that the days were ever going to be otherwise than warm and long, with hummings in the sunshiny air; neither did he concern himself about anybody's tendency to aches and stiffness. His cares had a quite different cause.

It was one of his great-grandmother's household laws that he should every morning take a

91

walk, attended by Kate Heron, the housemaid;
and Kate, duly carrying out this decree, would
fain have supplemented it with another, to the
effect that their walk should always bring them
along Madden's Lane. For that thick-hedged
thoroughfare ran past no less than two little
dwellings, towards whose dark half-doors her feet
instinctively turned. And on their first few
walks she met with no opposition to her wishes.
Mac, knowing nothing about the topography of
the neighbourhood, had not any alternative
routes to prefer, and was content to amuse himself with the shaggy-coated small terrier, Gaby,
while Kate's large flowery hat bobbed in deep
conference with emerging shawled heads, or vanished altogether for a few minutes, diving into
shadows beneath the shock of thatch and waver-
ing blue smoke plume. But one morning, when
they were on their way home, and had come near
the corner of the road which was only a hundred
yards or so from his great-grandmother's gate,
Mac made a very dreadful discovery.

He happened to glance up at the top of the
wall along which they were passing. A very
high old stone wall it was; three, or perhaps
four, superimposed Macs would scarcely have
reached to a level with its parapet, yet over it he
saw projecting the heads of two cows and a
sorrel pony gazing down calmly into the road.

The sight filled him with dismay; in fact, he was almost startled into betraying horrified surprise. "My goodness, Kate!" he began, forgetting his dignity so far as to pull the fringe of her amber-bordered brown shawl.

"What ails you at all, Master Mac?" Kate said, recalled from some rather far-off meditations of her own. However, he recovered his self-possession in time.

"Nothin' ails anybody," he replied stiffly. "I was only wonderin' why they can't find somethin' better to do than to stand there gapin' at everybody that passes on the road, which is no concern of theirs."

"Ah, the crathurs!" Kate responded absently.

What had really struck him was the thought of how prodigious must be the stature of the beasts to whom those prying heads appertained. For how otherwise could they look over that great immense wall, as high nearly as the house? Mac, all unversed in Rabbinical legend, had never gauged "the just dimensions of the giant Og," and recked nought of colossal storks winding with immeasurable legs; which was doubtless well for his peace of mind, since such lore would have revealed portentous abysses to his imagination. Even as it was, he stood gravely aghast. Towards all animals his sentiments had

hitherto been most friendly and fearless; but
that somehow seemed only to aggravate the
present circumstances, making more odious the
belief that the attractive and estimable tribes of
horses and cattle had stalking among them
creatures of proportions so unsightly and
grotesque. The fact, however, could not be
doubted. When he passed that way, there almost
invariably he saw ranged a row of heads fear-
somely far above his own, the more placid and
contemplative wearing immobile horns; the more
alert and observant twitching sensitive ears.
Mac wondered whether it was their legs, or their
necks, or both, that were so preternaturally
elongated; but he felt that in any case they must
be hideous to behold, and he shuddered inwardly
at the notion of what nightmare-like shapes those
interposing stones must screen. Once, indeed,
he fancied that he caught a glimpse of something
like the head of what ought to have been a very
little girl appearing over the edge in a flappy
white sunbonnet; but the figure which this com-
pelled him to imagine was so monstrous that he
hastily averted his eyes, and tried to persuade
himself that they had deceived him.

Of course, he mentioned the matter to nobody.
Self-respecting children never do confide their
haunting terrors to elders, possibly derisive of
them. No chance of gaining coveted protection

and deliverance from the torment of fear can justify one in running the risk of appearing igno-
rantly ridiculous to those who presumably know
all about everything. So Mac preserved a scru-
pulous silence, in which his alarms had ample
scope to root themselves. The nearest approach
he ever made to the subject was once, when he
remarked to Tim Brennan, the coachman, as they
were driving over Clonmanavon Bridge—he had
only just forgiven Tim's offer to let him hold the
end of the reins—"I suppose, now, you never see
cows walkin' about here who are so tall they
couldn't fit in under that arch?"

Unluckily, Tim took the question as a sort of
challenge, and replied, "Well, sir, I wouldn't say
that the most we keep hereabouts couldn't make
a shift to get through it middlin' aisy for any size
there is on them. Not but what I've seen an odd
one now and again might be very apt to stick
half-ways, unless they was after takin' a bit off
of the horns of her—ay, she would so. We've
plinty of powerful big cattle in Clonmanavon."

This answer gave cold comfort to Mac, who
had hoped to elicit an assurance that abnormally
huge quadrupeds were at any rate extremely rare
in the neighbourhood, and exclusively confined
to the one gruesome place which he called in his
thoughts "The Field of the Frightful Beasts."
Failing in this, he could not tell but that many

of them might be at large close by, and the con-
tinual likelihood of falling in with one spread a
heavy cloud over all his open-air hours. The
dread seized possession of him, and grew more
harassing every day. He was constantly peering
through gates and gaps to see whether they led
into pastures infested with uncanny herds. When
the click-clack of horses' hoofs sounded on the
road, he scarcely dared look at what was coming,
lest it should prove to be a steed with spidery
legs and snaky neck, shaped like the ungainly
shadows thrown when the low sun is drawing
caricatures.

It was quite natural that the actual sight of
the wall with its frieze of protruded heads, which
were sometimes so numerous that he could not
well count them, should have the effect of intensifying these detestable impressions ; and Mac's
experience being such, he very soon began to
shrink from turning the corner that brought them
into view. Kate Heron presently found herself
wondering: "What at all had set Master Mac
agin walkin' anywheres except Crumloughlin
ways, that was no better than an ugly boggy
ould bit of a boreen, wid nothin' in it good or
bad to bring anybody trapesin' there." But she
wondered to little purpose, as Mac did not feel
called upon to offer any explanation for his new
departure. In the course of his only childhood

he had acquired independent and masterful habits, and he now saw no reason why he should not
choose his own way.   Therefore he set a resolute
face northward every morning, calling, "Hi,
along this way," to Gaby, who generally bolted
in the wrong direction, and replying decisively to
Kate's proposed amendments, "No, my friend,
that other's a horribominable old road."   This
was, so far as it went, a simple solution of his
difficulty.   Before long, however, complications
occurred, which placed him in a serious dilemma.

One morning, just outside the gate, they met
Lizzie Egan, Colonel Hodson's nurserymaid, wheel-
ing along two fat little twin girls, whose drowsy
heads nodded in their big white-frilled bonnets
like a couple of fantastic giant blossoms.   After
a short preliminary gossip, Lizzie said: "Was you
hearin' lately how poor Mrs. Reilly is?"

"Sure, I haven't had e'er a chance since Sunday," said Kate, "and then she was only pretty
middlin'."

"'Deed, then the craythur's to be pitied.   And
had she heard a word at all from Willie?"

"At that time she hadn't; but for aught I know
she maybe might agin now."

"Well, he'd a right to be ashamed of himself,
anyway.   Takin' off like that, and lavin' the poor
ould woman frettin' in disthraction till she isn't
the size of a hedge-sparrow.   Jimmy Collins was

tellin' us he seen her one day last week, waitin' at the post office, and he said you could ha' just given her another double up, and slipped her in at the slit of the letter-box handy, she was that stooped and wizened away to nothin'. Sure, Willie might aisy throuble himself to send her a line of a letter to say where he's went. That's the laist he might do, let alone not havin' the manners so much as to ax whether the boy he was after murtherin' might be dead or alive."

"Och, for that matter," Kate said, "people say the divil takes care of his own. Sorra the notion Alec Sweeny had of dyin', nor wouldn't if it was off of ten forty-fut ladders he was shook."

"Oof, then, it's little call Mrs. Reilly has to be disthressin' herself about that Willie of hers aither; if that's the way of it, *he's* safe enough," said Lizzie. "I'd ha' called in goin' by to see how she was, only that we aren't very great these times, you know. She heard me mother passin' some remark on his conduc', and bitther as sut she's been agin us ever since. But I thought you were along be her door most days."

"Sure, not at all. What's come over Master Mac there I dunno, but pitchforks wouldn't get him along that road. Nothin'll suit him except streelin' off up the lanes at the back of the house. If he's axed to turn that corner, you might think you was offerin' to take him into disolit wilder-

nesses. He won't look the way it is," Kate said
ruefully.

"He's frightened of Molloy's big dog—him
below at the Bridge, that comes out barkin' and
leppin'—that's it, you may depind. Sure, I do
sometimes have the work of the world gettin'
Miss Carrie past him," said Lizzie. "Screechin'
she'll be like as if you was ringin' a little pig.
The baste wouldn't hurt man or mortal, but it's
the great coarse bark he has, like a door slam-
min', or a little clap of thunder, that scares the
children when they're small. And it's apt to be
what's took the young fellow."

"Very belike it is then," said Kate. "There's
no end to the foolishness of them before they've
got the wit."

"Or afterwards aither," said Lizzie. "The
more sinse they have the less raisonable they'll
behave themselves, accordin' to my experience."
And with that they parted.

Mac was positively bewildered with disgust
and indignation. He had overheard all this discussion, while apparently helping Gaby to climb
up the gate-post, and the scandalous conjecture
so coolly made by Lizzie and adopted by Kate
came to him like a sudden blast of scorching air.
Afraid of a barking dog! Placed in the same
category with a crying baby! A calumny so outrageous could not be too energetically refuted.

But how was this to be done effectually without facing the visible horror of the Frightful Beasts? —an ordeal which he could not contemplate with equanimity. One point alone was clear enough; he must modify his simple plan of merely avowing a dislike for Madden's Lane as a sufficient reason for shunning it. That would now leave him open to disgraceful imputations. Yet it was difficult to devise a better one.

All the rest of the afternoon he pondered the subject inconclusively, and was so much preoccupied with it at tea-time that his great-grandmother asked him if he was sleepy, thus crowning the insults of the day. He replied politely and reprovingly: "If a Person was sleepy, I suppose he'd have the sense to go to bed, no matter *how* early it was—even if the sun was shining straight into his cup of tea—and not think it fine to sit up blinking like an old owl."

"You see, you were so quiet, my dear," his great-grandmother said, half-apologetically, feeling herself set down, and misappropriating the old owl.

"It would be a queer thing," said Mac, "if a Person couldn't keep himself awake inside without making a noise outside, like a clock tickin' to show it was goin' on. I rather wouldn't be talkin' all the while as if I was wounded up with a key."

But next morning Mac made an important announcement on the door-steps. "Gaby's to choose where we're goin' to-day," he said. "In fact, I think I'll always let him choose. For you see, Kate, it's only a quarter as much our walk as his, because he goes it on four legs and both of us on only two. So if he chooses it will be a great deal fairer. We'll just watch which way he'll turn."

Kate, remembering what direction Gaby always seemed disposed to take, was so well satisfied with this arrangement that she felt no wish to cavil at Master Mac's logic or arithmetic; and a sparkle lit up her melancholy grey eyes as she thought to herself how surely she could call this morning at Mrs. Reilly's. It was, however, too hastily kindled, and was extinguished speedily. For when they all three reached the gate, Mac suddenly picked up a pebble, and flung it as far as he could towards Crumloughlin, indeed nearly toppling over head foremost with the vehemence of his throw. And, of course, Gaby needed no bidding to be off in a rapturous whirl upon its track. Whereupon Mac said complacently, "There, you see he wants to go this way," and set forward with the air of one acting from a strong sense of duty.

"Ah, now, Master Mac, weren't you the conthrary child to go do that?" Kate called after him remonstrantly. "Sure, how was the baste to know his own mind, and you disthractin' him wid peltin' stones about the road?"

But Mac continued to stump along inexorably. "I promised poor Gaby we'd go wherever he liked," he said in a highly moral tone, "so I wouldn't disappoint him now on any account." And Kate could only follow him with chagrin, rightly foreboding a meditated repetition of the manœuvre upon all such occasions in future. As for Mac, though he did his best to believe in his own disinterested deference to Gaby's wishes, he more than half-suspected that he was behaving somewhat meanly; and, despite his virtuous airs, his mood continued to be partly crestfallen and partly defiant, as he trudged along in brown holland suit and broad straw hat, through the hot sunshine, preceded by the cheery terrier, and followed by the reluctant maid.

The success of this stratagem was, moreover, destined to be transient. On the very next morning, when he was looking at a volume of Du Maurier's society pictures in the hall, he heard his great-grandmother's time-worn treble calling from the breakfast-room door to Kate a-scrub on the steps outside. "Oh, Kate," it said, "I find we are short of eggs. I wonder could you get some anywhere to-day when you are out with Master Mac?" and Kate replied with great alacrity: "Ay, sure, ma'am; there does be mostly a good few at the Widow Reilly's down beyond the Bridge. Grand layin' hens she has in it." And, "You might bring me a dozen, then, please," said Mrs. Kavanagh.

Mac's heart sank as he listened to this dialogue, which seemed to fix inevitably the direction of that morning's walk. He said to himself that Mrs. Reilly's hens were nasty old beasts, and he wished to goodness Gaby had ate them all the last time he was waiting there for Kate to finish, just asking what way she was, which usually took a wonderfully long while. Then they couldn't have been laying any detestful eggs for people to go and fetch. But as the hour for setting out drew near, he became alive to the futility of such aspirations, and at length he desperately determined upon a bold, practical step.

About a quarter before twelve o'clock, while he knew Kate to be still finishing her sweeping down of the back stairs, he beckoned silently to Gaby, who obeyed with his broadest grin, and they went quietly out of the house together. Mac purposed to give his attendant the slip and go his own way, which certainly should not lead to the precincts of the "Frightful Beasts." He was well aware that the proceeding would be most gravely discountenanced by the authorities, but he could

not for a moment weigh their disapproval against
that row of horrible high-reaching heads ; and he
had long regarded the assumption that he required
a caretaker at all as one of those vexatious anachro-
nisms, which a Person found himself so frequently
called upon to point out.   His independent expedition thus would subserve a twofold end, asserting a principle as well as averting a miserable
hour.

It started prosperously enough.   On his way
down the avenue Mac successfully eluded notice
by slipping behind a laurel when overtaken by
the pony-carriage in which his great-grandmother
was driving to inquire for Lady Olive Despard's
bronchitis.   But when he came to the front gate,
it happened that a fawn-coloured, sharp-nosed
collie was in the act of trotting past, upon ob-
serving whom, Gaby, inflated with a sense of being on his own premises, stood in the middle of
the gravel sweep and made contemptuous remarks.
Of these the stranger took no notice whatever,
and Gaby misconstruing this forbearance, being
himself neither conspicuously prudent nor mag-
nanimous, was ill-advised enough to venture on
a short rush towards him, with yaps of insuffer-
able import.   The natural consequence was that
in another moment he saw the collie dancing at
him open-mouthed, whereupon he lost his head,
and, instead of fleeing into the more obvious

refuge, bolted away down the road, with his enemy's nose grazing his craven heels.

Mac followed in pursuit of both, filled with
consternation, which increased as he found how
rapidly he was being left behind. Round a corner the two dogs whisked, into a grassy-rutted
cart track, and by the time he had raced through
the open field-gate at its end, they were out of
sight, and his only clue was a sound of yelping
far and farther ahead. Guided thereby, he ran
along, skirting the hedgerow with its high-grown
fringe of late summer weeds, and clamoured over
stiles, in and out of another empty hay-field, on
the margin of which something scudded away,
hopelessly beyond the reach of his shouted com-
mands and menaces. He was so bent upon the
rescue of the recreant Gaby, that he never once
thought of whither he might be going, or with
what creatures he might fall in, considerations
which would otherwise have lain uppermost.
Next there confronted him a tallish plastered
wall, with flat slabs projecting sparsely from it
for steps. Up these Mac heaved his inadequate
legs in a dislocating manner, and he plumped
down on the other side into a rustling bed of
nettles.

When he got to his feet again, he perceived
that he was in a field-corner, where, on the one
hand, wall and hedge meeting at a sharp angle,

and on the other a grassy slope swelling up, narrowly circumscribed the view. It was a place in which he had never been before, and his route thence seemed by no means clear to him. But as he stood perplexed, Gaby himself, safe and unmolested, trotted into his ken a little way up the slope. He was panting still, but had recovered sufficiently to sniff about intermittently with a business-like air, as if surmising rabbit-holes. Apparently, however, he had for the time being abandoned himself to evil ways, as when Mac called to him gleefully, he left his master's shouts unheeded, without even pretending not to hear, and after a little desultory jogging to and fro, ran quickly off out of sight over the swarded ridge. This line of conduct distressed and annoyed Mac, who, now that he was relieved about the dog, began to reflect uneasily upon his strange surroundings and possible neighbours. What if some Frightful Beast came ambling down that hill at him, or strode abruptly over the hedge close by? He did not feel by any means sure either that he recollected his way home. In short, if he would have self-confessed it, forsaken Kate's arrival at this juncture would not have been unwelcome. On the whole it seemed to him that he had better start once more in pursuit of Gaby; so he began to scamper up among the clumps of ragweed and thistles, uttering calls as he went,

which betrayed more perturbation of spirit than
he guessed.

Near the top of the slope his path was crossed
by somebody who came out from beneath the
boughs of an elm tree, in whose noon-stunted
shade he had been sitting.   It was a tall, dark-
faced young man in a labourer's dusk-coloured
suit, with a blue bundle and a blackthorn.

"Fine day, sir," he said to Mac. "Would you
be lookin' for anybody?"

"For a shaggy little disobedient wretch, that
won't ever mind a word one says to him—at least,
he sometimes won't ever—I think it's rabbits he's
hunting," Mac replied, breathlessly. In his hurry
he forgot to touch his hat until the end of his
sentence, when he supplied the omission with
much correctness.

"Maybe, now, that might be himself over
there," the young man said, taking a glance
round, and then pointing to a place where Gaby
was, in fact, skirmishing, nose to ground.

Mac suddenly climbed up on a fallen log, which
brought the truant into his field of vision as well.
"So it is, I declare," he said. "I was lookin'
the wrong way before."

"He's after the rabbits, sure enough," said the
young man; "but he'll soon tire of that. It's
only of a very odd while there does be e'er a one
down these fields. Belike you come here along wid

somebody ? " he suggested, surveying Mac, who, reassured by company, had sat down on the log to rest, and presented an appearance rather less portly than might have been expected in a person whose age lacked not more than ten months and one week of six years.

"Oh, no, I'm exercisin' Gaby quite by myself to-day," said Mac. "Kate Heron does come with us sometimes, just because it's sociabler, you see."

"Oh, Kate Heron, bedad ! " the young man said, and looked round him again.

"She isn't here to-day," said Mac. "I told you only sometimes."

"So you did, sir," said the young man.

"And because it's sociabler," said Mac.

"Ay, sir, to be sure," said the young man, "and is she gettin' her health these times ? and her sisters, and her father ? "

"I don't know about *them*," said Mac. "But to the best of my b'lief Kate's perfitly well. It's Mrs. MacQuaide, the cook that thinks she'll drop off her two feet some fine day, she's so killed with standin' over the heat of the blazin' fires."

"And is there any talk, sir, at all—of Kate gettin' married ? " the young man asked, swinging his bundle about by the knotted handkerchief ends.

"If you do that with it, it'll untie, and everything come flingin' itself out head foremost,"

Mac said warningly. "And there may be talk,
and a great deal of talk, but people don't go about
repeatin' whatever gossip they may happen to
hear downstairs."

"Sure, not at all, sir, by no manes," said the
young man. "I only axed the question of you
because—you see I'm just after trampin' over
from the town of Greenore; off in Scotland I've
been this last couple of months, and maybe I'll
be steppin' on again, and not stoppin' here any
time—it just depinds. I've met ne'er a sinsible
crathur yet to be tellin' me aught I want to
know, and I've as many as ten minds this minyit
to turn back the way I come. So I was wonderin' what news there might be in it since I quit,
such as buryin's or marryin's, or any talk of the
like."

"Oh, of course, news isn't gossip," said Mac.
"It's an entirely diff'rent thing. If it's news, I
shouldn't mind tellin' you anythin' I heard talk
about. But I think there hasn't been much about
marryin's or buryin's, at least since I came to stay
here. Let me consider"—and Mac considered
with his chin in the air, and his over-large hat
set very far back on his head. "Oh, I know
there *is* great talk about one thing, only it happened before I came, and that's the row there
was when they were buildin' Mr. Carden's rick.
It was what you may call a row, for one man

actually went and knocked another off the top of the ladder, because he got annoyed at somethin', down on the paved stones, and no thanks to him if he wasn't killed dead on the spot. They're always talkin' about that—Kate and everybody."

"Are they, sir, bedad? And what do they be sayin', everybody and Kate?"

"Oh, but Mrs. MacQuaide says nobody need mind a word of Kate Heron's, because she used to be speaking to Willie Reilly—that's the man that got annoyed—and so that's the only reason she sticks up for him now. Not that she's got any great call to be troublin' her head about him, Mrs. MacQuaide says, after his runnin' off the way he did, and never so much as sendin' home tale or tidin's of where he was gone to. Poor Alec Sweeny was worth ten of him, she says— the man who got knocked off; he was always pleasant. And she'd twice as soon be marryin' him, if it was her, as a cross-tempered firebrand like Willie Reilly. It's *news* that I'm repeatin', you know."

"Why, to be sure—not a word of gossip is there in it at all, sir. But what does Kate Heron say?"

"She says that Alec Sweeny had a right to have held his fool's tongue, instead of to be given impudence to other people, and then nothin' would have happened anybody."

" And true for her, the Lord knows," the young
man vehemently said.   " What business had he to
be blatherin' about what didn't anyways consarn
him, when he was bid keep himself quiet?   Supposin' a man did be chance put the collar on
wrongways up, and he harnessin' in the divil's
own hurry, it's no more than might aisy ha'
happint himself, or any other person, that he
need take upon himself to be bawlin' it up to
young Maggie Heron, where she was treadin' the
rick, and ready to run home wid the story to
Kate and the rest of them the next thing she
done, as he well knew, so he did; he done it
a-purpose, and the divil's cure to him," Mac's new
acquaintance asseverated, again swinging his
bundle recklessly round.

At this unexpected heat Mac felt slightly taken
aback, though he observed without discomposure:
" If I was you I'd put it down out of my hand
altogether, if I couldn't keep from flourishin' it
about.   But besides that, the woman where Kate
goes to get hairpins says that Alec Sweeny was
only jokin', the way he had, and no reasonable
person would have thought bad of it.   And Tim
Brennan says in his opinion it's likely enough
they both had drink taken, and neither the two
of them, nor the one of them, rightly knew what
they were doing.   And Dick the postman's sister
says she always had a sort of liking for poor

Willie Reilly, but there was no denyin' he had an ugly passionate temper, and you couldn't know what minute he might be flarin' up in a fury, any more than you could tell by lookin' at it when a steam-engine would be lettin' a screech out of it. And old Mrs. Walsh said she'd be long sorry to see a daughter's child of hers married to the likes of him, that might up and hit her a crack some fine day she'd never get the better of. I think old Mrs. Walsh is Kate Heron's grandmother."

"She is, sir, she is; and, begorrah, she only said very right," said the young man.

"Well, but afterwards, when we were going home, Kate was saying to a girl we met on the road that she'd dare say all the while Alec Sweeny slipped his foot by accident, and the lock of hay fallin' on him had nothin' to say to it at all; and Willie Reilly never intended him any harm; and if the truth was known he *didn't* make a wipe at him with his pitchfork.

"I'd give more than a little," said the young man, "to think that was the way of it. But I know betther."

"It was an immense high rick, I b'lieve," said Mac. "Joe Malone said anybody tumblin' off the top of it would be apt to be broke to jomethry—jomethry means somethin' like a dissected map."

"It was so; and be the same token, there it

is glimpsin' through the trees forent us," said
the young man, pointing across a breadth of pas-
ture land to where a yellow gable-end gleamed
through an opening in a cloud of round-crested
elms.

"By Jove! and is that the real one he fell
off?" said Mac, gazing with much interest and a
little awe. "And were you there too?"

"Part of the while I was, sir," said the other
gloomily. As he stood staring at the distant
rick, his memory brought him back to the noon
of a hotter day, not very long past, when he had
been at close quarters with it, pitching hay, in
fact, on the top. He recalled the glowing glare
of the June sunshine, that seemed to clutch at
anybody who stepped into it out-of-doors, and to
hold him faster and tighter the longer he stayed
under it; and the strong scent or the clovery
hay that came wobbling up to him in heavy
bundles on the end of Alec Sweeny's fork. And
then he recollected how, just when everything
was at its most scorching point, he had heard
Alec beginning with a shrill cackle of laughter
to relate the story of the ridiculous blunder
committed by Willie Reilly that morning while
hastily harnessing the cross jennet, and how he
himself, finding peremptory injunctions to desist
of no avail, and stung by the titters of Maggie
Heron, had resorted to the more vigorously re-

pressive measure of hurling down upon his too
communicative colleague a blinding and smother-
ing forkful. A spasm of rage made his thrust
of fierce-looking steel prongs so much more than
merely reckless that Alec had probably been
lucky to drop out of his reach, tumbling sheer
off the tall ladder thud upon the stones, amid
the shrieks and shouts of all beholders. "Och,
murther!—Och, mercy on us all!—Och, Holy
Virgin!—The man's kilt—he's disthroyed!" But
there the scene shifted, for a guilty consciousness
of that furious moment had prompted the assail-
ant to flee, scrambling down on the other side of
the rick, without waiting to know whether a
result so fatal had actually supervened. Before
continuing his flight over seas, he did contrive
to learn that Alec Sweeny's fall had not killed
him outright anyway; but during his two months'
absence at the Scotch harvesting he had had no
home news. Now, being just returned to Clonmanavon, whether he would there remain or
again decamp must depend upon what turn several things had taken; and he wondered how far
he might trust the report given by this queer,
old-fashioned talkative little imp of a child, who
was evidently the belonging of some Quality
staying up at old Mrs. Kavanagh's, and under
the charge of Kate Heron. Meanwhile Mac had
resumed:

"Well, then, you know, everybody declared every mortal bone in his body was broken. But were you there when Dr. Crampton came and said the most that ailed him was that he'd wranched his ankle round? So he wranched it right for him again, and Mrs. MacQuaide thinks that if Alec would have taken advice he might be well mended by this time; but he must needs go off with his foot to old Christy Hughes, the cow-doctor, and get him tinkerin' at it. And in my opinion he was a very great fool to do any such thing. For it's no business of Christy Hughes to understand about the legs of human persons; they're no more like cows' legs than the legs of chairs and tables. By the way," said Mac, sidling along the log nearer to where the young man stood, "about how high was the highest cow or horse that you ever saw any-where—near here, for instance?"

"Sure, the same as e'er a one you'd see in it, sir, I should suppose," said the young man. "But you was tellin' me the news about Alec Sweeny's fut?"

"He's got very little use of it yet, poor man!—very little at all," Mac replied, shaking his head so solemnly that his hat fell off backwards. "If you meet him on the road he's stumpin' with two sticks as slow as a snail. It isn't like any-body really walkin'; you'd think it was somethin' standin' there, and nearly tumblin' over every minute. Christy Hughes made a fine botch of it, whatever he did to him. They say it's a wonder if he's ever fit for anythin' again, and Dr. Crampton says his only chance is not to put his foot to the ground for the next couple of months. Only Tim Brennan says it's easy talkin', but how's a man to get his livin' without wages for that length of time. So Alec makes a shift to go as far as the place where they're breakin' stones; that's all he's able for now. It would be pretty detestful to get one's living by breakin' stones on the road, with a black thing on to keep the splinters out of one's eyes. Alec always takes his off when he sees us passin', but it looks ridic-'lous."

"I'm as sorry of that as anythin'," said the young man, "as sorry as anythin', supposin' that made a hair of differ. It's cruel, now, what'll take and happen in a moment of time, and no-body intendin' any great harm maybe, if you come to consider, but, och! sure the Lord knows where you'll ha' got to afore you've e'er a chance of doin' that—somewheres you never thought of bein' very belike. . . . And so you do be meetin' Alec Sweeny on the road now and again, sir? And has he and Kate Hernon anythin' to say to one another these times at all?"

"I can't be repeatin' every single thing. Peo-

ple sayin' 'What way are you?' and 'It's a fine
day,' when they're passin' isn't news," Mac said
with some sternness.

"'Deed, no, sir," assented the young man.

"Really, I don't think I remember anything
else," said Mac, reflectively. "They talk sometimes about Willie Reilly, the annoyed man's
mother; and Rose, the other housemaid, says
what she thinks baddest of, is his leavin' the
poor old woman there all this while, frettin' herself sick, and never writin' her a line to say
what's become of him."

"And did you say she was took bad?" said the
young man. "It's running over I'll be across the
fields; that's the shortest way."

"Oh, she got news yesterday from her daughter away in Chicago, who's doin' grandly, and
sent her an order of money, and that's heartened
her up finely, Rose says. But it's no thanks to
that Willie Reilly. In fact, nothin's any thanks
to him, I believe, and if he stayed out of this
altogether," Mac said, in the tone of one making a familiar quotation, "it 'ud be no great
harm."

"I'd ha' wrote fast enough, and so I would,"
said the young man; "only I thought she'd be
writin' back, and the truth is I was in dread of
what she might be tellin' me news of—somebody
after dyin', or gettin' married, that 'ud be worser

to my mind. Troth, if I'm not as good-for-
nothin' as I can stick together, get me one that
is."

At this moment a shrill alarm of barking and
yelping arose from Gaby, and he was seen to be
digging violently close under the wall at a little
distance.

"He's got one," Mac exclaimed; and ran off,
followed by the young man, passing on the way
several perfectly normal head of cattle, which
were peacefully sauntering and grazing. The
field wall was here rather low all along, and in just
one place the soil about the roots of a willow-tree
which grew against it banked it up to such a
height that standing there, a person as tall as
Mac could easily look over it. By the time they
arrived, Gaby had disappointingly abandoned his
excavations and roved farther on, leaving Mac
nothing more interesting to do than ascend this
small mound, and see what might be on the other
side of the wall. What there was gave him a
shock of surprise, for instead of merely looking
across into another field, he found himself staring
down into a road, which lay ever so far beneath.
It was a narrow road, with a sharp bend in a
short way to his left, and a long straight stretch
on the right; and he felt vaguely aware of some
familiar thing in its aspect. By and by he identi-
fied that feature as a dark stone cross standing in

a recess of the bank just opposite. Very old and
ancient it was, a block which the wild weather of
many a century had rough-hewn again into almost its primitive shapelessness. Mac remembered it quite well, and the three rude granite
steps upon which it was mounted, with a sloe-
bush sprouting from a crack in one of them; the
recollection was somehow disagreeable to him,
yet when or where he had seen it he could not
immediately think.

As he was puzzling over this point, a figure
came into sight at the farthest end of the road,
slowly approaching.

"Oh, here's Alec Sweeny himself," said Mac;
"and he's walking lamerer than ever."

The young man, who was leaning against the
willow-trunk behind him, stooped forward to
watch, and began muttering half aloud: "Ay,
bejabers, lame he is. It's the bad offer he's
makin' at gettin' along at all, and he that ought
to be keepin' himself quiet, if he's to give himself e'er a chance. Goodness forgive me, I'm
thinkin' I have the man bravely disthroyed. But
I'll halve me six pound ten wid him, I will so; or
if me mother doesn't want it, he might take the
whole of it and welcome, then he could lie up for
the winther, and he might git a sound fut under
him agin the spring. Faix, now, it's a quare
dale aisier crookenin' things than straightenin'

thim again. And sure a man's to be pitied when he's so be his nathur that he'll flare up in a blaze inside him all of a suddint minyit, till he's no more notion what he's after doin' than the flames of fire has of what they're after burnin.' Many's the time I do be thinkin', and I takin' a scythe or a rapin'-hook in me hand, the divil himself only knows what desthruction I mayn't ha' done on some mislucky body afore I quit a hold of it. But Alec Sweeny had no business to be risin' the laugh on me, if he *was* thinkin' of Kate Heron, and be hanged to him. If I thought she was thinkin' of him, it's his neck I'd as lief be breakin' as his ould ankle. And as I was sayin', sooner than get news they were marryin', I'd hear tell he was in his grave, and his murdher's sin on me sowl—I would so. That there is at the bottom of me heart I well know all the while, if I cocked twenty diff'rint lies atop of it, and the Ould Lad's got good raison to be proud of me and the likes of me. Ooh, wirra, but the man looks powerful poor and weakly in himself. Halvin' them pounds 'ill be the laist I can do, and little enough. They'd ha' set Kate and me up grand in our housekeepin' next Shrove, but sorra the bit of me'll ax her now till the year after, and afore then she's very apt to ha' took up wid somebody else; and a good job for her—and maybe it's a good job too for every bone in his

body that I dunno who he is.   Sorra a word I'll
ax her."

The young man fell silent, and shrank back a
little farther under the boughs as Alec Sweeny
came by.   He was a tall, large-framed, young
man, too, but looked gaunt and pinched; his
coat, greenishly discoloured, hung baggily from
sharp angles, and his limp was so dolorous that
the beholders felt relief when it stopped and he
sat down on the steps of the old cross, staring
drearily into the dust at his feet.   Almost at the
same moment, round the nearer corner, came
Kate Heron, in her homely brown shawl, and the
incongruous bedizened hat due to her position in
the service of Quality.   She was walking rather
hurriedly, and carrying an empty basket errand-
wise; but at the cross she hesitated, and then
halted, saying: "It's a fine mornin', Alec."

"Whethen, now, what need is there for her to
be stoppin'?" murmured a malcontent voice from
above.   "A good-day goin' by 'ud ha' been
plinty."

Kate's greeting, indeed, apparently gave satisfaction nowhere, for Alec Sweeny seemed just to
grunt in acknowledgment without raising his eyes.

"And I hope you're gettin' your health somethin' better now, Alec," Kate added after a slight
pause.

At this, Alec Sweeney not only looked up, but

scrambled abruptly with painful haste to his feet.
"See you here, Kate Heron," he said. "Do you
take me for a born fool? Or do you think I
don't know as well as I know me own name the
only raison you'd spake a civil word to me is
considherin' I'm an ould show of a cripple, that
it's a charity for a dacint body to be passin' the
time of day to? Sorra another raison have you.
Sure you wouldn't be lookin' the side of the road
I was on. And let me tell you, I'd liefer be
listenin' to me ould hammer crackin' the stones.
So you may just keep your fine talk for any that
'ud care to be pickin' it up out of the dirt, as if it
was ha'pence you were throwin' a blind beggar.
Sorra the other raison." And he hobbled away
with reckless lurches, still muttering.

"Set up himself then, bedad, and what other raison had he the impidence to be expectin'?" commented an overhearer. "Och, but he's the misfort'nit lookin' bosthoon. And if that's the way
he'll be biddin' me keep me ould pounds to meself,
what am I to do at all to set things straight and
contint me own mind?"

Kate Heron had lingered looking after the
lame man as if pondering upon this rebuff, but
had just turned to go her way, when Gaby, who
was now running to and fro along the wall-top,
barked fiercely at a robin, which caused her to
look up and recognise a well-known broad-

brimmed straw hat. "Guide me to goodness,
Master Mac, and is it up there you are? And me
lookin' for you every place, and thinkin' then the
mistress must ha' picked you up in the avenue,
and took you drivin' wid her."

"You might have *knowed* I was goin' to-day on
my walk with myself," Mac replied with dignity,
chiefly for the benefit of his new acquaintance in
the background.

"And what at all brought you up there? Ah,
now, Master Mac, you're the ungovernable child.
Don't be lanin' over the edge of the ugly high
wall, there's a darlint. How'll I get you down
out of that ever? For it's breaking your neck
you'll be if I take me eye off you to run round to
the gate."

"He's right enough, Kate; you needn't be disthressin' yourself," said the young man, stepping
forward.

"Saints above—it's not Willie Reilly?" Kate
said, doubly startled: "sure nobody'd ha' thought
of seein' you, and we all expectin' you home every
day of the week for this long while. And where
at all have you been that you weren't writin'?"

"If you'd run round to the gate below,
machree—no, I mane just plain Kate Heron—I'd
be fetchin' the little gintleman along to meet you,
and it 'ud be handier tellin'," the young man suggested, and Kate acted accordingly.

"I dare say that *would* be the best way of goin' home," said Mac. "It must be rather near lunch-time. Gaby, where've you got to?" He looked around him for the dog; and as he did so he made a remarkable discovery. Close by, a little knot of beasts were standing with their heads over the wall; the two or three cows and a sorrel pony, whose face with its white streak somehow seemed unpleasantly familiar to him. Where had he seen it before? Why, looking over a wall just like this one. But was not that the wall of the Field of the Frightful Beasts? Could it be possible that he was actually inside it? "And I declare to goodness," Mac said to himself, "we used to be passin' that stone with the steps—and there's the old white horse lookin' over too. They *aren't* Frightful; they're only standin' on the high bank. But how was a Person to know that a wall would be pretendin' it was the height of a house along the road, and then turn into a little quite lowish one on the wrong side?"

This view of the matter was such a new and agreeable light to him, that he naturally wished to flash it on; so he began: "Do you see that little black cow there?"

But his companion, who was thinking of different things, misconceived the motive of the question, and replied: "Sure you needn't mind her, sir, she wouldn't hurt anybody. It's only the

flies tormentin' her makes her put down her head
that a way."   An answer, which led Mac to keep
half the width of the field between himself and
insulting insinuations as he proceeded towards
the gate.

There Kate Heron awaited them, and one of
the first remarks that Willie Reilly made to her
was —

"I'm not axin' you, Kate; troth, nor won't I
this great while.   But d'you think, now, you'd
think entirely too bad of waitin' for me as long
as to a year from next Shrove ?   Till I get meself
a trifle broke of me outrageous temper, and till I
gather another odd few pounds instid of them
here that I'm intindin' for Alec Sweeny; and till
I've kep' the pledge for awhile, for truth it is I've
no call to be stirrin' meself up wid dhrinks, that's
deminted enough whether or no; and till I've
some sort of sartinty in me that I'm not widin
the turn of your hand every instiant whatever of
behavin' no betther than a ragin' hyenna.   I'm
not axin' you, mind you.   But if I had a notion
you wouldn't ha' took up wid anybody else agin
then ——"

"Saints and patience, Willie!" Kate said, as
airily as she could, " that's a terrible great hape
ef things you're to be gettin' done between this
and then.   You'd be hard put to it, I should say,
in a dozen twelvemonths, let alone one."

"I'd conthrive it, if that was all," he said. "But it's too long a len'th of time to be expectin' of you altogether. Somebody else'll be axin' you; and then if I keep out of the raich of doin' murdher on some one, that'll be the most I'll manage. Ay, but it's too long entirely."

"For the matter of that I'd wait a year and welcome, or ten year, or twenty, I'd wait *contint*," Kate said, with an earnestness upon which her hearer might have put a somewhat discouraging construction. But he did not, and rejoined —

"Glory be to goodness! then we'll do grand after all. It's steppin' along I'll be now to see me mother, and after that I'll go straightways and make all square wid poor Alec Sweeny. Sure a rest for his fut's all he's wantin'; dancin' jig polthogue he'll be at our weddin' one of these fine days."

He had set off, but after a few quick steps faced round to add, in a tone slightly conscience-pricked, "Mind you, Kate, I'm not axin' you, nor goin' to." Then he started again at a brisk trot, which became a positive gallop as he descended the grassy slope.

"He might have the sense to know that tearin' along like that's the very way to make them run at him, if that's what he's afraid of," Mac, watching his departure, observed with supercilious vindictiveness; "and one would suppose anybody could easily see that they're not Frightful Beasts at all."

That evening Mac and his great-grandmother had cold chicken at tea instead of eggs; for the morning's adventure had put them so completely out of Kate's mind, that she aimlessly brought home her basket, "as empty," Mrs. MacQuaide averred wrathfully upon discovering the omission, "as your own *stookawn's* head is of wit. And what am I to be poachin' now for the misthress to-night?" It was a brilliant sunset hour, and the long rays again slanted straight into Mac's creamy cup; but this time it was the old lady who seemed rather dull and abstracted. She had heard on her drive that morning how her old friend Lady Olive's chronic bronchitis had been suddenly cured, and her thoughts kept running on the news.

"We can't have been much older than you, my dear, quite small, small children, the first summer her people came to Lisanards, and that would be about the year '26. It's a long time now since she's been well enough to see any one, but it gave a sort of object to one's drive to go and ask if she had had a good night. Well, there could be no other end to that."

"You must come down the fields with me instead, great little grandmamma," said Mac.

"Oh, my dear, my days for running about in the fields were over long ago."

"I *don't* run about," said Mac; "not unless somethin' partic'lar happens. I was in a very nice one to-day, where there is a pond, and part of an old car, and a black little donkey that won't let you go very near it. You'd like it when you got inside. There's a plank across a ditch, and steps up a wall, quite easy."

"Stiles and ditches, my dear child," said his great-grandmother. "Do you want me to break all my old bones?"

"That sounds very much like just a 'scuse," Mac said, with some severity. "There's only two stiles, and you needn't tumble down into the nettles unless you put your foot on the wrong stone. And as for the Frightful Beasts, if that's what you're thinkin' of, I really can*not* imagine who put it into your head that there were any such things."

THE AUNT OF THE SAVAGES

THE AUNT OF THE BAZAARS.

THE AUNT OF THE SAVAGES

Mac Barry and his cousin Aylmer O'Sullivan, had spent a rather dreary week at Sheenagh House, to which they had been suddenly driven over from Glenamber, away beyond the other end of the lough, because in the household there, a case of measles had occurred very inopportunely just before the great occasion of their Cousin Norah's wedding. The two little boys did not like their change of quarters, for at Sheenagh House they found nobody but two elderly servants and Uncle Stephen, an old bachelor, who did not care for children, and did care for having things tidy. Mrs. Connell, the cook, and Lizzie, the parlourmaid, thought it their duty to be constantly "keeping an eye on the young gentlemen," and to the young gentlemen this seemed an inconvenient and evil eye, which discovered mischief in the most harmless occupations. So they sometimes thought the hours too long in those showery July days. Then, one morning, Uncle Stephen, on his way to breakfast, came upon them where they were making a plantation, with seedling sycamores grubbed up in the shrubbery, just at the bottom of the hall-door steps. It was not,

131

perhaps, a very suitable situation, and they certainly had scattered about a great deal of black earth, keeping a liberal supply for their own hands and faces.   Uncle Stephen seemed annoyed when he stopped to tell them that they must not make such a mess; and as he was going in, he added: "I believe your Aunt Amy is coming to see you this afternoon, so I hope by that time you will look more like civilised beings and less like young savages."

Thereupon Mac and Aylmer, who had already breakfasted, went and talked grumblingly under the big sycamore close by.

"I wonder where this old aunt is coming from *bovvering?*" said Mac. "There weren't any at Glenamber."

"I don't like aunts," said Aylmer. "Mine is always asking me seven times three times, and the dates of kings and things that are no affair of hers."

"Mine are great-aunts," said Mac; "and they talk and talk as if a person was always wanting to hear about kittens and tame tomtits."

"We might stay away outside till she's gone," suggested Aylmer.

"Let's go and live like wild savages, and never come back here any more, for one can't be let do a single thing," said Mac, with resentful reference to their interrupted plantation.

"Savages is black," Aylmer objected.

"Well," said Mac, "I dare say we might *grow* black if people let us alone." He looked hopefully at his grimy hands.

"What do savages live wild on?" Aylmer wondered.

"Oh, hunting and fishing. We could fish plenty," said Mac, "in the lake over there, that we saw the time Lizzie came screeching after us to say we'd be drowned in the bog-holes. And I've three matches in my pocket, that strike on anything, to cook them with."

"And there's a beautiful old fishing-rod in a corner in the back hall. It only wants a bit of string, and that," said Aylmer, "I can get off a parcel of oatmeal I saw in the pantry."

"Then we'll get it now," said Mac, "for Mrs. Connell's feeding the hens, and Lizzie's always making herself another cup of tea in the kitchen until she has to go up and do the rooms. Nobody won't see us."

Nobody did see them as they secured the fishing-rod, and stole out into the shrubberies—nobody but old Moriarty, who was raking at the end of the laurel-walk, and they did not mind passing him, because they knew him to be black out with Mrs. Connell and Lizzie, so that he certainly would not mention it.

"When we're savages," Mac said, as they walked along, "we mustn't ever speak to anybody, but only make signs."

"What's signs?" said Aylmer. "I don't know how to make them; and I'd rather fish."

"It's as easy as anything. You just wave your hands about a little, and crook your fingers, and waggle your head," Mac said, doing so to show how, "and those is signs."

"But what do savages make them for?" said Aylmer.

"Why, of course," said Mac, "so that people mayn't understand what they mean. Savages is uncommonly cunning."

"Oh, I see," Aylmer said. But when they had gone a few steps further he added: "If *I* wanted people not to know what I meaned, I just wouldn't say anything at all." Aylmer, who was fat and rather lazy, often considered about ways of saving trouble.

It was not far to the lough, along a path smooth under thick evergreens, and rougher presently under hazel and hawthorn-bushes, and then soft and springy where it crossed the corner of a bog. Here Mac and Aylmer luckily did not stray into any of the treacherous places where black-looking holes lurked among mossy patches sprinkled with dim white blossoms. They followed the faint track until it brought them to

the brow of a grassy slope leading down to the
lough.   One end of the long, narrow lake curved
round there and met a wide band of greensward.
Rainy weather had filled it fuller than usual, so
that the clear water came brimming up over the
gravelly rim which generally bounded it with a
sharp gleam, and it lay amongst the fine short
grass-blades in silvery-edged streaks, as if it had
been spilt on a carpet.   If you looked down into
it, you could see drowned daisies and speedwell
at the bottom, strangely mixed with the drifting
blue and snow of the sky.   A lane, overhung by
steep woods, skirted the opposite shore, but nothing was moving on it.   The little boys thought
they had come to a delightful place, especially
when Mac remembered that savages never wore
shoes and stockings, and they put theirs on the
flat top of a boulder.   It was very luxurious wading, with the soft grass under foot, and the sun-
warmed ripples lapping about their ankles, and
nobody to be shocked no matter how much they
splashed each other.   They had made their way
along the margin nearly round to the lane before
either of them had had enough of the amusement.
Then Aylmer, who was carrying the fishing-rod,
trod on a pebble, which hurt his foot slightly,
and made him think that it would be pleasant to
stop for a while.   So he said: "Do you see how
it's all ruffled up in there between those two

sticking-out rocks?   It must be crammed *full* of
troutses.   I'll begin fishing."

"That's only the wind in the water," said Mac.
"Fishes make round circles, and hop up out of
the middle of them like big shiny frogs.   I don't
believe there's any in that place; but you can
have the first turn of fishing at them."

Aylmer sat down on a grey boulder, which
looked as if it had been badly cracked long ago
and stuck together with strips of the greenest
velvet, and he began to fish steadily.   His hook
was a tin-tack, and his fly a buttercup.   "They
might think it was a yellow very fat wasp," he
said.   Mac was for a while quite content to go on
with his wading; he went in deliciously deep,
and once, falling down, partly by accident, got
thoroughly wet, which was most enjoyable; and
he hopped on one leg to and fro between several
islanded tufts of bracken and chumps of furze.
But when both his ankles began to ache, he
thought he would like a change, and standing
beside Aylmer, he said affably: "Now you're
tired holding it, I'll take it for a bit, and you can
be playing about."

Aylmer, however, only wagged his head
slowly sideways, and waved one of his hands in
the air.

"You great gaby," Mac said, "we're not going
to be savages except to other people; and you

know you were talking like anything just this minute."

Aylmer nodded three times, and kept a firm ' hold on the fishing-rod.

" Look here," said Mac, " you might be finding sticks to light the fire with when we want to cook them."

Still Aylmer said nothing, but flourished his hand in a way which evidently meant " Find them yourself." He looked fat and aggravating, and as if he did not intend to stir. So Mac said, " Give it to me, will you ? and get out of that," and made a clutch at the rod.

" You beast ! " said Aylmer, " I'd just got a beautiful bite, and you've went and shook it off."

" I wouldn't mind if I'd shook off your stupid head," Mac said. Whereupon they scuffled so violently that Aylmer's hat, which was a large straw one, fell into the water, and began to float quickly away. This accident shocked them so much that they stood still immediately, for to a small boy the loss of his head-covering seems as serious as the destruction of a roof. Aylmer lay face downwards on the flat boulder, and made a grasp at the hat as it went bobbing by, but all he did was to soak one of his jacket-sleeves right up to the shoulder. "There now," he said, turning up a countenance full of wrath, " it's swum

away to drown itself, and here am I in the blaz-
ing sun, enough to kill me."

"I don't believe savages ever do wear hats,"
Mac said, putting a bold face on the matter, "and
I won't anyway." He flung down his straw hat
so roughly that the brim cracked nearly off the
crown, and a tuft of water forget-me-not stuck
up through the chink.

"And dripping wet I am, too," Aylmer went
on, "getting my death most likely."

"He'd be welcome to a loan of the ould sack,"
a voice said startlingly close behind them, and
there stood two little girls, who had come quietly
over the grass on bare feet, though they had not
been wading. One of them held in her hand a
long rope with a small white goat grazing at the
end of it, and the other was carrying a couple of
brownish sacks and a reaping-hook. They wore
short ragged skirts, and over their heads rough
grey shawls, under the shadow of which their
narrow faces looked all eyes. The biggest of them
was perhaps as much as nine years old, so that to
Mac and Aylmer she seemed an experienced person.

"If he had it over the head of him," she said
to Mac, "he could take the little wet coateen off
of him, and let it get a chance to dry in the
sun. There's a very handy hole in the end of
this one," she said, unrolling the empty sacks,

"and there's plenty of time yet to be fillin' them wid the grass. Rosy McClonissy owns it, but she'll loan it and welcome, wouldn't you, Rosy? Say : ' Ay, bedad.' "

"Ay, bedad," Rosy said in a hoarse, shy whisper.

Aylmer, who found his drenched sleeve uncomfortable, and the unshaded sun dazzling, thought he would try this plan, and taking off his jacket, wisped himself up in the sack. Mac considered the costume so appropriate that he put on the other one; and then they did both look as uncivilised as anybody could wish, with bare legs and arms and dirty faces emerging from the rough, earth-coloured folds. The elder little girl, whose name was Matty Shanahan, spread out the blue and white jackets to dry on the flat-topped boulder.

"*Bovver*," Mac said, feeling in his pocket, "I declare my three matches has got quite wet too. I suppose now all the fire's washed out of them, and how are we to cook the troutses if we get some bites that stick on?"

"If it's a fire," Matty said, "we do be sometimes gettin' the loan of a light off a man goin' by wid a pipe. But there's no sticks, unless you look up yonder under the trees. And I never heard tell of any troutses catchin' in it at all."

"What'll we be cooking, then?" said Aylmer,

who was only half reconciled to the loss of his hat, and disposed to make difficulties.

"Oh—potatoes," Mac said cheerfully, though he did not really think this a satisfactory substitute. "Do you happen to know if there are many about here?"

"Sorra a pitaty we've in it this long while now," said Matty; "sure, we had the last of them ate before Easter."

"Then why on earth don't you get some more?" said Mac.

"How at all," said Matty, "when the rest of them wasn't fit to throw to the hins? And ne'er a one saved for seed, because where'd be the sinse, me father was sayin', of puttin' them down wid the whole of us starvin' fast while they would be growin' slow? But frettin' he is now every day, since he was took sick, sittin' on the wall to see the bit of land lyin' empty under the weeds as yella as gold—frettin' bad he is."

"Well, but one must be cooking something; and it's getting pretty late," Aylmer remarked sternly.

"Sure, it isn't hardly hungry-time yit, glory be to goodness!" said Matty, "and I was telling you me mother's had no cowld pitaties to be givin' us to take along wid us, and we grazin' the little goat, or else you s'ud be welcome to a bit. When we had them, we did be warmin' them up grand wid a fire lightin' in there under the trees. Only yous had a right to not be burnin' your fingers grabbin' at them, the way Rosy done, instead of rowlin' them out wid a stick."

"You don't explain properly; people must have enough to eat whether there are cold potatoes or not," said Mac politely but decidedly.

Matty stared at him blankly. "You are a quare one," she said. "Has any people ever enough to eat?"

"Well, if they want to go on for ever and ever and ever, they must be great *pigs*," Mac said with severity.

"When I've got joggolates," Aylmer said reflectively, "I always *do* want to go on for ever and ever and all the evers that ever were."

Matty continued to look puzzled. "Now and again," she said, after a pause, "we lights a fire, and sticks a few biggish-sized round stones in it by way of pitaties roastin'. But that's only lettin' on, and most whiles we go to the wishin' well above there in the wood for our bit of dinner."

"I didn't know there was anything except water in wells," said Aylmer.

"She said a *wishing* one, didn't you hear?" Mac said, intending to convey an entirely false impression that this made the matter quite clear to him.

"Saint Brigid owns it," said Matty. "Grand she is. I seen her picture below at Father Christy's, in an iligant white gown streelin' after her, and a sort of gould sunbonnet blowin' out flat off the back of her head. And they say that if you drop a little bit of anythin' into the wather to remind her, she'll send you whativer you're wishin' for. So Rosy and I do be wishin' a bit of dinner off of her."

"And what does she send you?" Mac inquired, with interest.

Aylmer murmured hopefully: "Joggolates, maybe."

"Nothin'," Matty replied, disappointingly. "But you never can tell she mightn't take the notion to some day. Rosy and I'll be slippin' up presently."

"We'll come along," said Mac.

"'Deed yous might better," said Matty, "than to be drownin' of yourselves fightin' on the edge of the deep pool. The bits of coateens can be dryin' here till we come back. I'll tether the little goat the way she won't get swallyin' them."

The footpath to the well wound up with a cool shade of green leaves above, and below a soft paving of dead ones, crossed here and there by roots which made irregular steps in it. Mac accounted for his tripping over them by saying that they were a different pattern from the stairs

in most places. However, all the children scrambled safely up to St. Brigid's well, niched in its
rounded rock basin under the high steep bank.
Moss, which seemed a golden-green light among
the flickering shadows, muffled its brim, and from
the creviced stones behind it harebells trembled
and hartstongue drooped. Large shining drops
swelled at the points of the long leaves, and
splashed down slowly one by one as if a string
of beads were broken into the clear water, which
they kept astir with a sliding circling ripple.
The little girls crossed themselves, and began
to say some queer-sounding words, which were
Latin, Matty explained to Mac; but she could
not answer him satisfactorily when he wanted
to know further: what they meant—a question
which might have puzzled the most scholarly—
whether savages spoke Latin; and whether Saint
Brigid was a savage. "I don't see how I'm to
order dinner that way," he said, "because I happen not to remember the Latin for anything to
eat."

"Sure, how could she help knowin' right enough
what pitaties is?" Matty said.

"And a sup of buttermilk," Rosy whispered at
her elbow.

"Is that all you're going to order?" said Mac.
"Why, that's only a little bit of a dinner—there's
lots of other things."

"Joggolates!" suggested a familiar husky voice beside him.

"I will *not* order chocolate," said Mac; "I know very well that she'd say it wasn't wholesome enough for people's dinners."

"I'd liefer have pitaties than stirabout," said Matty. "The yella male's a quare, ugly brash, and there doesn't be more than a little dab of it for everybody when it's boiled. Me mother mostly has only the pot scrapin's, but she says it's plenty. Pitaties is the best."

"Roast chicken," said Mac, "and mashed potatoes, and cold apple pie and custard might do. What shall I drop in?"

"Thim little thimbles off of the fir-tree is handy, if you haven't e'er a pin or a button," Matty said. And several small cones were found without difficulty.

Aylmer dropped one in unobserved, and as he did so murmured: "Joggolates!"

*　　*　　*　　*　　*　　*

For nearly an hour after the children had gone into the wood, nobody came next or nigh the lough. Then over the brow of the steep grassy slope, and down the same path that Mac and Aylmer had taken, came a figure all in soft white, just tinted with a delicate lilac, as are some crocus cups. Softly white, too, and plumed with faintly tinted feathers, was the large hat

which shaded her golden-brown hair. So that
she made a very high light in the strong sunshine as she passed through it. She was carrying a small hamper. Anybody who had met her
might have noticed that the lowest flounce of
her pretty dress was a little bedraggled along its
lacy edge, and that her pretty face looked a little
unhappy and perplexed. The facts were that she
had driven over from Glenamber to bring a share
of some wedding festivities to the exiles at Sheenagh House, where, arriving, she had found it
deserted, for its master was out, and the servants had slipped down to MacQueen's place, at
the crossroads, in hopes of a glimpse when the
bridal carriage drove by honeymoonwards. Only
old Moriarty was by this time scraping in front
of the house, and told her how he had seen the
young gentlemen a while ago in the shrubbery
yonder, on their way to the lough, he'd be bound,
as they were carrying the master's old fishing-
rod. "And you'll be apt to meet them comin'
back by now, miss," he added, "unless they're
after drowndin' theirselves—that's no ways too
unlikely."

"Is it far?" she asked.

"Sure not at all," he said. "You might sling
an ould cabbage-stump into it from the end of
the bit of a grove." And on the strength of this
she had started. But she was not used to bogs,

and consequently had the impudence to step on
a jewel-green mossy patch, with results harmful
to her dainty bridesmaid's attire and little silver-
buckled shoes. This accident caused her some
vexation, but she forgot all about it when she
reached the lough, for as she ran down the grass
slope the first thing she noticed was a straw hat
floating on the water, and a few steps further
brought her where she found two pairs of long
stockings and two pairs of small boots lying on
the top of a flat stone. No living creature was
in sight except a white goat tethered and grazing;
and the thought flashed into her mind that the
wearers of these things must have been the little
boys she had come to look for; a conjecture
which made old Moriarty's seem dreadfully probable. In a great fright she ran along the edge
of the water, calling "Mac—Aylmer"; and presently she was still more alarmed by a gleam of
something blue and white a little way from the
shore. It was Aylmer's jacket, which Matty had
so carefully spread to dry, and which a breeze
had whisked regardlessly into the water. But
to Amy Barry it seemed likely to be something
so terrible that she was afraid to look at it, and,
dropping her hamper on the grass, she fled panic-
stricken down the lane in search of help.

Very soon after she had gone the four children descended the shadowy path between the

tree trunks, and stepped out again upon the
sunny green margin—four as wild small figures
in their ragged wrappings as you could have met
in the width of Connaught.   The little boys had
wanted to linger up at the well, imagining their
wishes more likely to be fulfilled upon the spot,
but Matty, speaking with the authority of a
much longer experience, assured them that Saint
Brigid "was just as apt to leave them their dinners down below"; and at last persuaded them
to come and see.   She was anxious to reclaim her
sacks and resume her grass-cutting.   And, "I
declare to goodness," Mac exclaimed, as they
emerged from the wood, " she's left it in a basket.
There it is near the big stones.   Come alone,
and look what's in it."

   "Musha, good gracious, and there it is sittin'
wid itself sure enough," Matty said.   "Where's
it come from at all—unless it's from herself?   A
grand new little hamper."

   "If there's *all* our dinners in it," Aylmer remarked, discontentedly, when they had raced up
to the hamper.   "It doesn't look very big.   The
plates 'ill take up nearly all the room."

   "Of course she knows perfitly well that savages don't want plates," said Mac, who was
fumbling with the fastenings.   "Which way do
you pull the little peggy thing—do you know,
Mary?"

"Suppose somebody owns it," Matty said, hanging back; "and suppose the polis was comin' along the road there, and we meddlin' with it." Matty's eyes were visibly enlarged and darkened by the horror of the imagined situation.

"Savages and saints isn't any affair of the polis *at all*," Mac said, prescribing the constabulary their duties without hesitation, and throwing back the hamper lid with a creaky jerk: "Whoof! Is it nothing but old flowers?"

On the top, indeed, lay some sprays of white frosted blossoms, tied with wonderful silvery satiny knots and bows. Mac flung them down on the grass disdainfully, but Matty and Rosy picked them up reverentially, as if they were feathers from an angel's wing. Under them was a paper bag full of small sugary biscuits of all shapes and hues; and these the boys regarded with more respect. Then there came thick slices of dark plum cake iced and almoned, and a number of softly flushed peaches, and a heavy bunch of bloomy purple grapes. Next an oval card box of glistening crystallised fruits; and, lastly, a round one of bonbons. "Joggolates!" Aylmer said, triumphantly, on seeing these, "and it was me ordered them. But you can have ones a piece."

When all these things were spread out on the grass, Mac said: "Let's have the biscuits first.

You needn't grab them with your two hands at once, Aylmer, like a wolf." Aylmer, with his mouth full, said something indistinctly about savages. "Come along Matty and Rosy."

But Matty turned away, drawing her old shawl closer about a disconsolate face. "They're not our dinners for sartin," she said; "ne'er a pitaty is there at the bottom—ne'er a one. But belike she might send them another day, Rosy, when there's nobody in it only you and me. Themselves is some manner of Quality, so she wouldn't be mindin' the likes of us. It's time we got the grass cut. Come along, Rosy. Say 'No thankee.'"

Rosy, however, on the contrary, said: "Plase," and accepted a handful of miniature stars and crowns and crescents, pink and white and yellow, at which she looked for a minute half doubtfully. It seemed like eating up things that were almost too pretty to touch. But after she had tasted the first sparing crumb, the rest very rapidly vanished. Matty also was tempted irresistibly by a rose-and-apricot coloured cockleshell, which Mac would have her take. It held cream, flavoured with something delicious; yet before it was finished she stopped as if she had remembered a trouble, and suddenly looked ready to cry. She was thinking of some people in a dark house-room not very far off, and this made

her glance in the direction of the road leading to
it. And her glance grew into a stare, for just
then round the corner ran a figure whose white
robes swept after her over the grass—one flounce
was torn and trailing—as softly as foam, and
whose bright head had a covering not in the
least like any of the caps and hoods Matty was
used to see. The feathery brim had got pushed
far back in her haste, showing a fluff of golden
hair and a flower-tinted face. "Bedad, then it
was herself brought them their dinner," Matty
said, in an awe-stricken· tone, while Rosy edged
up to her, grasping a handful of her shawl, as if
for protection, and both little girls began to re-
treat.

It was really the bringer of the hamper, who,
having met with young Lambert May on his
bicycle, and sent him speeding to fetch assistance,
had now been drawn back by the fascination of
fear to the lough side. The sight of the four
ragged children there gave her a hope and dread
of news, as she hurried up to the little girls with
eager questions.

"Be curtseyin', Rosy, be curtseyin'," Matty
meanwhile was exhorting. "Saints is a great
sort of Quality."

"Do you know anything, please, about the
hat floating there in the water?" said the
stranger.

"Ay, miss—Saint Brigid," Matty said, curtsey-
ing extraordinarily low; "it fell off the little
boy's head, and he fightin' with the other.
There's the two of them now," and she pointed
to Mac and Aylmer squatting by the hamper in
their sacks.

"Oh," the stranger said, looking much relieved.
"And did you happen to see two other little
boys in blue and white sailor suits anywhere
about?"

"Ay, did I," said Matty.

"And where did they go to?"

"There's the two of them now at their dinners," Matty said, pointing again to the figures
by the hamper.

"Those poor children! Are you quite sure?
Why, they seem to have hardly any clothes."

"Sure, there's the little coat of one of them in
the water, too," said Matty. "It's about
drowndin' himself dead he was raichin' after the
hat, so I got him out of it, and we loaned him the
ould sack while it would be dryin', but it's fell in
again." Matty had no wish to deceive; but her
language was ambiguous, and it conveyed to her
hearer the impression that she had rescued the
child from a watery grave. She was astonished
when this beautiful young lady, "and herself a
saint," said: "Then you are a *very* good little
girl, and I'm very much obliged to you indeed."

It seemed to her that since she was in such
favour, she might perhaps venture to put in a
word about the potatoes so often bespoken in
vain. But just as she was beginning: "If you
plase, Miss—Saint Brigid, ma'am——" Saint
Brigid ran away to speak to the little boys.

Mac, when he saw her approaching, kicked
Aylmer, and said: "It's just a girl dressed up;
we needn't mind about being savages to her."
But Aylmer had too many chocolate drops in his
mouth to have room for any words.

"So you found the hamper, I see," the girl
said, which seemed to Mac such an obvious remark that he ignored it, and replied: "You're
quite welcome to some of these biscuits. I think
the white ones are the best."

"I thought you'd like them," she said. "I
hope the grapes aren't crushed; I brought the
biggest bunch I could find."

"Did Saint Brigid send you?" said Mac.

"Saint Brigid? Oh, no. What do you
mean?"

"If she didn't, I don't see how you could be
thinking anything about it," said Mac. "I
ordered our dinners up there at the well, because
we haven't caught anything yet except bites, and
we can't go back to the house until it's ever so
late in the evening. And I ordered chicken and
mashed potatoes, but I s'pose she forgot it, I wish

she hadn't, for I'm pretty hungry, and we *have* to be staying here."

"Why?" said the girl, looking puzzled.

"Because of a nasty aunt that's coming this afternoon," said Mac; "so we've went away to live wild like savages till she's gone. But I dare say the old pest will stay *bovvering* there till it's quite dark. People you don't want are always everywhere."

"And taking one to school, and asking one the dates of the kings and queens and things," came in a grumbling mumble, for Aylmer's mouth was still full. "I wish they'd all died the same time, and I wish plaguy old aunts would go and see somebody else."

"Well, I'm sorry you both think so badly of aunts," said the girl, "for I believe I am your Aunt Amy. But I don't know any dates myself."

"Nor seven times twice times?" said Aylmer.

"Not without adding up," she said.

"*She's* nobody's aunt," Aylmer said to Mac, in a very low whisper; "you needn't believe it. She *might* be Saint Brigid, for they said she had white clothes; but she's no more like an aunt than I am."

"Well, you needn't bellow at the top of your voice—she'll hear you," Mac said, giving him an indignant shove, which Aylmer returned. Their

aunt did hear and see, and to change the subject
said: "I hope you offered the little girls something."

"They're wanting potatoes," said Mac, "because they and their mother haven't had anything
this long while except pot scrapings of *yella male*
—that's what she called it, and it can't be very
nice. But they wouldn't take our things—only
a few biscuits."

"They do look half-starved, poor children," she
said. "And, by the way, which of you was it
who got so nearly drowned? You ought really
to come home and change your things."

"We weren't either of ourselves nearly drowned,
only our hats," said Mac; "people shouldn't ex-
aggelate about nothing at all."

"Oh, they've been telling tales, have they?"
Aylmer said, frowning all over his dirty round
face. "Then they may do without any of my
joggolates that I ordered. *Now* I won't keep a
single one for them."

"Pig!" said Mac.

The girl in white gathered up some slices of
plum-cake and ran off with them after Matty and
Rosy, who had gone to untether the goat. She
had scarcely reached them, when she heard shrill
voices arising behind her, and she looked round,
thinking that the threatened hostilities had broken
out. But she saw that two tall black-looking

policemen had arrived, and that one of them was
talking to the little ragged boys.   Mac seemed to
be answering him with fluent defiance; but
Aylmer suddenly jumped up, and fleeing towards her, still clutching his box of chocolate,
grasped her skirts with a hand which left its
mark and began to roar.   The policeman following him, said: "Beg pardon, miss, but did you
know them childer was making free with your
hamper of sweets?"

"They're my nephews," she said, and Alymer
made no attempt to repudiate the connection.
So the policeman withdrew, apologetic and rather
scandalised.   "That was a queer start," he said
to his comrade, as they walked away.   "A one of
them was eatin' that rapacious I thought he was
starvin,' and I come as near as anything takin'
him in charge.   They hadn't the look of belongin'
to anybody respectable."

The constables were hardly out of sight when
there appeared on the scene Lambert May, bringing with him the doctor, and several men with
ropes and poles, and Father Daly, and quite a
crowd of children and women, some of whom
had already begun to say that the poor little
crathurs' mother was to be pitied that night when
she heard what had happened them.   But their
Aunt Amy really was to be pitied, in a less trag-
ical way, when she had to explain that nothing

had happened to them at all. For she felt
ashamed of the commotion roused by her false
alarm, and did not like to think how foolish she
must appear to Lambert May. Altogether it did
seem hard that she should have given up a garden
party, and spoiled her new gown, only to frighten
and make herself ridiculous, and to be disowned
with contempt by her relations. Moreover, her
disreputable-looking nephews proceeded to behave
so badly that she felt quite abashed, and they
talked so strangely about savages and Saint Brigid
that she almost thought they must be demented.
Mac, especially, being hungry and fractious,
stamped furiously in a puddle when requested to
put on his boots and stockings, and declared that
he wasn't going to be ordered about by people
who came bothering and pretending they were
everybody's aunts. His good-humour was not
restored until he had been invited thoroughly to
inspect Lambert May's highly-polished roadster,
and even to sit on the saddle and see how entirely
out of reach the peddles were. By the time that
she had helped him to lace his boots, it is true, he
had begun to take a more tolerant view of his
aunt's character. But when he said good-bye to
her at the gate he gave her a bit of, no doubt,
mortifying intelligence.

"The man with the bicycle thinks you are very
horrid," he said.

"How do you know?" she asked.

"Because," said Mac, "when he was showing it to me, I asked him if he thought you were *his* aunt, and he said: 'Oh no, indeed, she's not my aunt, *thank goodness!*' But next time I see him, I'll tell him you aren't as nasty as most aunts—unless," Mac continued interrogatively, "you may be aren't one at all, and only letting on, the same way that we were about the savages?"

There was one person, however, to whom the afternoon seemed ending in a sudden blaze of joy. Matty Shanahan just about that time was rushing home through shade and shine at the top of her speed. Such a pace did she attain that Rosy McClonissy, following with the little goat in tow, and daring not to be left behind, tugged and panted, and called injunctions to stop, and to come on. Matty never heeded. For she was on her way to give her mother the wonderful golden sixpenny-bit that the lovely young lady—some sort of Quality or Saint—had run after her to put into her hand.

SOME JOKES OF TIMOTHY

SOME JOKES OF TIMOTHY

THE earliest of them that was memorable may be considered his first step towards the reputation he eventually reached, since, had he not played it—a practical one it was—the chances are that he would never have endured so much leisure for propounding jocular views of things on the bridge of Kilanesk. Just at the time, however, this result was quite out of sight, round many a corner, and its more immediate consequences failed to amuse anybody.

It was a sunny afternoon in March, and Timothy had been for some little time diverting himself by dropping turf-sods down the Widdy Meleady's chimney. The feat was just difficult enough to be interesting, as the black-rimmed smoke-hole opened in the end of the Widdy's mossy thatch farthest from the tall bank, against which her little house stood, with its roof slightly below the level of the lane, so that Timothy had to aim carefully and often at the delicate blue smoke-plume. He knew that the result of success would well repay his pains, experience having taught him what would follow upon the flight of a missile down the dark mouth. Open would

fling the house's door, and forth would hobble its
very ancient little old mistress, who would shriek
up to him shrill threats and reproaches and lam-
entations, and totter furiously about her small
yard below him, like a wasp with sticky wings,
while he rolled in laughter on the swarded bank,
and waited for her to go indoors that he might
resume his bombardment.   In fact, he was acting
on the penny-in-a-slot principle, albeit this March
day fell long before railway platforms were en-
livened by scarlet automatic machines.

But even the simplest machinery gets out of
gear sometimes, and now a sort of hitch occurred.
For when next the dark clod had gone skimming
true to its mark, the door did, sure enough, fling
open, but the person who came bolting out was
not the little old decrepit woman with her inef-
fectual hobble, and futile menaces.   On the contrary, it was her great-nephew, Dan M'Grena-
ghan, a renowned racer and wrestler of the
neighbourhood.   At sight of him Timothy said:
"Murdher alive," and darted off up the hill behind him, on the last run he ever took.   For in
his headlong hurry he tripped over the furze-
masked edge of a disused stone-quarry, out of
which he was drawn with a leg broken in so com-
plicated a fashion that "the docthors had to take
it off for repears, and very belike they may be
tinkerin' at it yit," as Timothy used to say after-

wards when relating his disaster. A long time elapsed, however, before he learned to turn out the facetious side of the incident.

Still, notwithstanding its woful associations, he did once again play his favourite turf-and-chimney joke. It was on the fine May morning when he first made his way on crutches as far as the Widdy Meleady's cabin, with the help of two little O'Gradys, who were several sizes smaller than himself. "Sling one down on her, Tim," urged Paddy, as they rested on the bank, and a broken sod lying handily within reach, tempted him to comply. Down it went with great precision, and out came the old Widdy. But when she saw Timothy she said: "Ooh, sure it's him divertin' himself, the craythur," and returned indoors without another word. That was, perhaps, the bitterest moment in all Timothy's life.

Then, before many months had passed, another misfortune overtook him. It had been on his track for some time, and may have literally come up with him all the sooner by reason of his lameness. For his mother's health, which was failing at the time of his accident thenceforward declined more rapidly, and her fretting over the prospect of leaving him "alone in the width of the world, without so much as his two feet to stand steady on," no doubt hastened the arrival of the dreaded parting. Not that she was so forlorn as she

might have been. The shelter of at least two
neighbouring roofs interposed between Timothy
and the grim white walls of the dreary House
at Allenstown. For in Kilanesk lived the families of her brothers-in-law Paddy O'Rourke and
Nicholas Crinion, of whom she often said self-
reassuringly, that, "at all events, neither of them
would let her own child and poor Larry's go to
loss." In this belief she remained unshaken,
practically, even when she felt most despondent;
but she could not always forbear to recollect that
her sister Biddy O'Rourke "did be sometimes as
cross as a weasel," and that Nicholas Crinion's
wife was "as near and close as she could stick
together, and so were them she came of; sorra a
one of Sheehans but was the makin's of an ould
naygur." And she knew well, that for many a
long day, seven-year-old Timothy's comfort must
depend mainly upon the disposition of the woman
of the house. To set against these disquieting
considerations, she could reflect that "Biddy's
husband was a big, soft gob of good-nature, without e'er a tint of bad temper in him, even when
he had a drop taken," and that Nicholas Crinion
"had always been a rael dacint, quiet man, and
no better brother than he had her poor Larry."
So that upon the whole she might have reviewed
her little character sketches with tolerable equanimity.

Nevertheless, it is a fact that she spent rather
a large part of her last months at Kilanesk in
scheming how to propitiate the kinsfolk with
whom she was to deposit the dearest thing she
owned. But it must not be supposed that she
sought to do so by enlarging upon the value of
this treasure. That would have been a crude and
inept device. In those days she was constantly
drawing comparisons between the qualities, mental and moral—no competition was now, alas,
possible as to physical—of Timothy and of his
cousins, the young O'Rourkes and Nicholas Crinions. "Ay, bedad, Biddy," she would say to her
sister: "It's the fool poor Timothy is at his figures compared with your little Nannie, that's
quick as lightnin' flashes, and she only a twelvemonth oulder than him. 'Deed, it's the poor offer
he'd make at sayin' his twice times the way her
father had her, when they come to see us last
Sunday."

"Her father hasn't so much sinse as you'd
crack a cockle wid," Mrs. O'Rourke would reply
grimly. But it was her habit to be grimly
pleased.

Or Mrs. Nicholas Crinion might happen to call
upon her invalid sister-in-law, and then Mrs.
Larry would not fail to point out in how many
desirable properties Timothy was excelled by his
cousins. "Sure you'll not have much throuble

gettin' *them* places, Lizzie, when they're any size
at all. It's plased people'll be to employ them,
and they that willin' and biddable. But poor
Timothy was always as foolish as if he hadn't
plinty of wit. Playin' thricks was what he'd
mostly be givin' his mind to. Not but what he's
quiet enough these times, the crathur. And
keepin' an eye on the child he could be, or goin'
on a bit of an errand, if it wasn't far to spake of,
and no great hurry about it—and not pourin'
outrageous, Lizzie, the way he would be drownded
entirely hobblin' so slow under it. And anyhow
you'd scarce notice him sittin' contint in a corner."

To which Mrs. Nicholas, unluckily, was rather
likely to rejoin: "Ah sure, my childer's brought
up to know right well that work they may git,
or hungry they may go"; a view of the matter
other than what Mrs. Larry had hoped to elicit.

On one of these occasions, Timothy, after the
visitors had departed, came and looked sternly
at her, leaning on his crutch. "There's no child
to be keepin' an eye on," he said.

"Sure, not at all, I was only supposin', be way
of a joke," said his mother.

"Where's the sinse of supposin' nonsinse?"
Timothy demanded, and withdrew, not waiting
for an answer, which would hardly have proved
satisfactory.

But his mother reserved her great stroke of policy until she felt that the time remaining at her disposal for the execution of her designs had become very strictly limited. Then she expended a long hoarded sum of "three thruppennies" upon sugar-sticks and bull's-eyes, and bade all the young O'Rourkes and Crinions to a feast. This took place in mid-wintry weather, with deep snow all round, including a small drift, like a wonderfully white pillow, just inside the wide-chinked door. The stark cold had made her cough so much worse that she was obliged to keep her bed, whence she could only issue hoarsely-whispered exhortations to Timothy to be liberal in distributing the sweets, and admonitions to behave himself like a good child. To do Timothy justice, he was quite spontaneously disposed to comply with the first part of her injunctions, and he dealt out streaky white sticks and treacly black balls in no niggard spirit. The latter and vaguer half of his instructions were not perhaps so scrupulously obeyed. At least, some parts of his behaviour did not strikingly resemble that of a conspicuously good child.

Towards the close of the entertainment, when Mrs. Larry's house was filled with an odour of peppermint that could almost be seen, and when anything one touched seemed inclined to adhere,

Nicholas Crinion looked in on his way from work to ask how his sister-in-law was, and expressing regret at finding her so indifferent altogether, sat for some time by the hearth, where the red fire-light glowed redder as the outer world grew all a colourless black and white.   The remoter parts of the room, however, were left in a dusk dim enough to cast a veil over the proceedings of Timothy and his cousin, Mick O'Rourke, who were busy at something near the door.   Pres-ently Timothy came forward, and to his mother's gratification, very politely offered his Uncle Nicholas a long white sugar-stick, one end of which was neatly wrapped up in newspaper.

"Och no, thank'ee kindly, Tim, me man," Nicholas said, blandly.   "Sure, I lost me sweet tooth ould ages ago, and I question will I ever find it again.   Ait your bit of candy yourself."

"But I'd a dale liefer you had it," Timothy persisted, affectionately.   "Put it in your pocket, anyway, and be bringin' it home."

"Sure, not at all," Nicholas said, hurriedly stuffing both hands down his pockets, to prevent a possible intrusion of the unwelcome gift.   An ill-advised move, as he found ; for Timothy, sud-denly saying : "Och, bejabers, but you must have it !" thrust the white stick, which had already begun to drip suspiciously, down the back of his uncle's neck, while his confederate, Mick, jumped

ecstatically up and down on the snowdrift at the
door, scattering moist flakes about the room.
No one who has experienced the sensation of a
lump of half-melted snow slithering along his
back like a horribly agile slug, its progress only
accelerated by the vain attempts of a groping
forefinger to arrest its downward career, will
underestimate the constraint which Timothy's
uncle put upon his feelings when he appeared to
be pleased and exhilarated by this instance of his
nephew's pretty wit, and protested with sincere-
sounding laughter that the young rapscallion had
had the better of him that time, at all events.   But
perhaps most people would have done likewise, had
they too caught a glimpse of Timothy's mother's
face, watching the scene with the expression of
one who beholds a last hope wantonly destroyed.
Nicholas's well-feigned sportiveness lulled that
fear to rest, and enabled her to breathe again as
freely as her circumstances ever permitted.   Still,
she felt that an unjustifiable risk had been run;
and later on in the evening, when they were
alone, she said remonstrantly to Timothy, who
was finishing a bull's-eye in much comfort by the
fire: "It's a terrible child you are, Tim, for
jokin' and playin' the fool, and it's too free you
make sometimes intirely."

Timothy so deeply resented what appeared to
him the injustice of this rebuke, that he hastily

swallowed his diminished sugar-ball, thriftlessly, and at some risk of choking, to retort, "And I'd like to know who was makin' jokes yourself about mindin' childer, no great while ago?" And this gibe—such is Fate's fine sense of the fitness of things—was almost the last speech that Mrs. Larry had of her son Timothy.

At his mother's wake it was settled that Timothy should be provided for conjointly by his uncle, Nicholas Crinion, and his aunt, Biddy O'Rourke, and thenceforward he had his abode under their roofs, sometimes one, and sometimes the other, "just accordin'," as they said themselves. Nobody could have foretold from one day, or even hour, to the next, among which troop of barefooted children he might be included at dinner-time or bed-time; and the tribes both of his Crinion and O'Rourke cousins were so numerous, that one more or less might be supposed to make little difference. This promiscuous arrangement had its advantages and its drawbacks. In one respect Timothy found it decidedly convenient; for the two families lived at opposite ends of the long street, and Timothy discovered that a hasty hobble down it would generally bring him from the O'Rourkes' big black pot to the Crinions' before the last steaming pitaty had been distributed; by which not scrupulously honourable means, he pleasantly supplemented his midday re-

past. He seldom inverted the order of pro-
cedure, because his Aunt Lizzie under such circumstances was apt to be embarrassingly particular in her inquiries as to whether he had already dined.   It must be said for Timothy that
only while he was at an age when people are
naturally very hungry and very selfish did he
practise this trick.   Later on, he made just the
opposite use of his opportunities, and would
sometimes come in falsely representing himself to
have had a bit down below or up above, as the
case might be.   On these occasions it was his
Aunt Biddy who felt suspicious; but she used to
think of her scanty stores and large household,
and keep her misgivings to herself.

Thus, in the matter of board and lodging, the
dual guardianship worked fairly well.   But
where clothing was concerned, it had a tendency
to introduce the principle that what is everybody's business is nobody's.   Mrs. Crinion would
be of the opinion that, " Supposing Timothy's bit
of a coateen had gone to flitters entirely, it was
a queer thing if Mrs. O' Rourke couldn't contrive
to make him up some sort of a one, and she with
three boys bigger than he growing out of their
rags every minute of the day, until cast off they
must be"; while Mrs. O'Rourke had, from just
the same premises, arrived at the conclusion
"That Mrs. Crinion, with the most of her childer

little girls, had a right to be better able to keep a
dacint stitch on him, than a body who had a
young rigiment to ready up by some manner of
means."

These conflicting views may have had a somewhat adverse influence upon the repairing and
replenishing of Timothy's wardrobe. It was, indeed, hardly possible for his tatters and flitters to
be wider and wilder than those of his cousins;
but the neighbours naturally fancied that they
were so, and when in a censorious mood, spoke to
each other about the scandalous figure his aunts
kept the poor orphan child. Mrs. Hoytes once
even went so far as to declare it was a public
show; and Judy Mullarkey, choosing a subtler
method of conveying disapproval, ostentatiously
presented Timothy with a very old knitted
scarlet comforter, all ravelling into threads. But
Mrs. Crinion promptly ravelled it a little more,
and used the wool for mending the handle of her
market-basket, where it gleamed conspicuously
on the very next Saturday—a thrifty retort
which Judy did not fail to appreciate.

Perhaps Timothy may really have been rather
unusually tatterdemalion just then, as he and his
relatives were going through a spell of hard
times. A rainy, blight-bringing summer had
conducted them to the threshold of an autumn
bleak and menacing. Illness had been infesting

them, and at that very moment a dreary chaos reigned in the O'Rourkes' household, because its mistress was laid aside with crippling rheumatism.

Timothy's other aunt was at first disposed to think it an additional misfortune when her cousin, Andy Sheehan, came driving along in his donkey-cart one of those frosty mornings. For Andy had long been considered a calamitous member of his family, having wasted his substance and come down in the world. He had started in life as the owner of a small shop and a little bit of land, which, after a few years, he found himself obliged to relinquish, setting out anew with his possessions dwindled into an old donkey and cart, and confirmed tastes for drinking and betting. Thus equipped, he adopted the ill-reputed calling of an old-clothes man which he pursued with scanty profit, and still less credit to himself. So much less, indeed, that his cousin, Lizzie Orinion, had accounted for a recent cessation of his periodical transits through Kilanesk by supposing him to have got into some especially serious trouble with the police. Now, however, it appeared that things had been looking up with him. Bits of good luck had fallen in his way. He had found a five-pound note in the lining of an ancient waistcoat, purchased for fourpence and a three half-penny mug. Also, he had made

a tidy little sum of money over a horse he backed
at the Listowel races.   And he had bought himself a new donkey, and a fine stock of crockery
wherewith to carry on his barter.

Andy related this to Mrs. Crinion at her door;
and shortly afterwards, when drinking tea by
her fire, while the children minded his property
outside, he remarked that he was looking for a
small spalpeen of a boy, to sit in the cart and
keep an eye on Nellie and his wares during the
transaction of business.   For want of such a
coadjutor, he had had a grand delft jug stolen
off him quite lately, and, furthermore, Nellie
had come near overturning the whole concern,
straying up the bank after grass.   "I suppose,
ma'am, you wouldn't think of loanin' me a
one of your little gossoons?" he concluded, half-
jocularly.

"Och, not at all, man, not at all," Mrs. Crinion hastened to reply.   "Me Pather's too big—
a fine tall fellow he's grown—and me Joe's a
delicate little crathur—och, not at all."   She
might, with perfect truth, have added that she
would be long sorry to send e'er a child of hers
travelling about the country with the likes of any
such an ould *slieveen* as Andy Sheehan, who was
drinking morning, noon, and night, if he got the
chance, and had the divil's own temper when he
had a drop taken.   At that very minute she

doubted was he altogether sober, and it scarce
ten o'clock.

"There's that one-legged child I seen along
wid them, he'd do me right enough," said Andy.

"Is it Timothy? Och, well now, sure, he
maybe might," Mrs. Crinion said, her mind in-
stantly grasping at the pitaties and farrels of
bread that his absence would leave at her disposal. "It's not much he's good for here, the
dear knows, except to be aitin'. But he's 'cute
enough, mind you, and his leg keeps him quiet.
He'd sit in the cart as steady as a rock."

"Well, then, it's comin' this way agin I am
to-morra night," said Andy—"I'm stoppin' above
for the Drumclune fair—and pickin' up the brat
I could be."

Mrs. Crinion considered for a moment. "You
might so," she said then. "But look-a, Andy,
don't be lettin' on anythin' about it to man or
baste. For, you see, be raison of his bein' poor
Larry Crinion's child, Himself as like as not might
take up wid some fantigue agin lettin' him go.
And his aunt, Biddy O'Rourke, might be talkin'.
But if he just wint off wid you promiscuous,
'twould be like as if you was only givin' him a
jaunt, and 'ud prisintly lave him back. So they'd
contint themselves wid that notion till they was
used to missin' him."

"Ay, to be sure," said Andy; "and then any

time, if I wasn't contint, or the brat wasn't contint, I do be passin' plinty of Unions in diff'rint places, and I could drop him at a one of them aisy."

"Ay could you, aisy," said Mrs. Crinion. She was still thinking of the pitaties.

Meanwhile Timothy, in complete ignorance of the arrangements that were being made for him, was on his way to do an errand at Lawlor's shop. To him, slowly halting over the bridge, Jim M'Guire, lounging there, bawled: "Och Timothy, man, just stop and tell us which of the ould scarecrows you might be after strippin' of that grand coat you have streelin' round you. Was it Mr. Kenny's? For I seen he had an iligant objic' of a one in his barley last time I was passin' through." A gibe to which Timothy's rejoinder came shrill and prompt: "Ay, bedad, had he. But it isn't there now, as you'd a right to know, when walkin' off wid itself it was—the very same way you was a-goin'." And applausive peals followed him down the street.

It would seem as if Timothy's mood must have been particularly facetious that morning. At any rate, when a few minutes afterwards Tom Crosby handed him over the counter a loaf, with the remark: "It's riz a farthin'," he was led into replying too innocently: "Arrah, now, is it any differ in the sort of yaist?"

"I'll not be long learnin' you the differ, if I

come across to you," Tom said, sternly, and with
such an apparent intention of coming that Timothy turned to flee precipitately, and in so doing
dropped the loaf, which rolled thumpingly into
an inaccessible corner behind some meal-barrels.
He was trying to fish it out with his crutch,
propping himself perilously against the counter,
when somebody came to his assistance.

This was a much smaller boy, in a grey suit,
which, unlike the garments commonly worn by
the youth of Kilanesk, did not appear to have
been originally designed for an elder and inar-
tistically curtailed. His hat alone seemed to be
somewhat a misfit, and was set so far back on
his head that its broad brim made him a sort of
halo, misleadingly, for his caretakers often considered him "a very bold child." It fell off on
the floor in his crawling among the barrels, which
drew to him the attention of Maria, the maid,
who was conversing with Mrs. Hoytes close by.
So, just as he was handing the loaf to Timothy,
she called to him reprovingly, "Ah, what are
you doing there, Master Mac? Come out of that
with yourself. It's no way to be behaving, and
you a nobleman's grandson."

"I wish to goodness," said Mac, "that you
were a nobleman's plaguey old granddaughter,
and thin you'd have to be behavin' yourself instead of *bovverin'* other people."

And Mrs. Hoytes said, soothingly: "'Deed now, it's the good nature the young gentleman has in him. And poor Timothy's a dacint little child, that's hard-set to be creepin' about. Sure, the Crinions and the O'Rourkes do be very respectable people, livin' here all the days of me life."

Mac, who was visiting his aunts up at the Grange, had presently an opportunity of making further acquaintance with this well-connected youth. For in the course of that afternoon's walk the sunny grass of a bank by the river tempted Maria to sit down and take out her crochet. It happened that Timothy was at hand, pegging pebbles at a boulder, whose ledged recesses seemed to promise "troutses," and with him Mac fell into a conversation, which Maria, on the strength of Mrs. Hoytes's testimonial, and her own wish to finish her collar, did not feel called upon to interrupt. As they were moving along to take up another position of attack, Timothy accounted for his obvious difficulty in getting over the sliding gravel by the remark that it was " very unhandy to be lame of the both of your feet in one," and he went on to explain how he had lately stepped, with painful results, on a bit of broken glass.

"Boots," suggested Mac, " would have kept the sharp edge of it off, and they aren't so much *bovver*, if you don't let her lace more than every

second hole." He glanced down with com-
placency at his own footgear, which, as the fruit
of frequent contention with Maria, were fastened
on this time-saving principle.

"The last ould brogue iver I owned," said Timothy, "went off wid itself on a swim down the
river, and it niver come back."

"But I saw plenty of them hanging up in the
shop," said Mac; "near the buckets they were,
and the legs of bacon."

"Sure, the only body I'd have a chance of
buyin' a one off of 'ud be an ould Lepracaun,"
said Timothy.

"I happen not to remember his shop," Mac
said, carelessly.

"Och, now, don't you, then?" Timothy said,
in apparent surprise. "The little ould fairy
shoemaker, that's as wizendy-up and quare-lookin'
as ever you beheld. Sure, I'd ha' thought, if you
was anywheres at all, you'd ha' been apt to see
a Lepracaun. But nobody ever seen him makin'
more than one boot at the one time—that's
sartin. So I'd ha' no throuble wid gettin' him to
break a pair for me. It's quare to be watchin'
him workin' away, tickin' tackin' wid his little
silver hammer, and his leather apern, and he in
his grand green coateen, and his red cap wid a
white feather streelin' out of it the len'th of your
arm, like a bit of a moonbame got crookened."

"Where does he live?" Mac asked, with interest.

But Timothy was surprised again—mortifyingly so. "Musha, good gracious, it is where does he live? Sure, where else would an ould fairy be livin', except it was at a fair? That's the raison of the name."

"*Of course*," Mac said, with dignity, upon receiving this piece of etymological information. "I meant where does the nearest one to you live?"

"Sure, very belike there might be a one in it to-morra at the fair in Drumclune, that's no great way off," said Timothy.

"I've drove there," said Mac. "But perhaps a person who had cut his foot with broken glass, which is very dangerous to leave lyin' about, couldn't walk so far to get anythin'."

"Anyhow," said Timothy, "thim boots th' ould Lepracaun would be sellin', does be terrible expensive. The price thim sort of crathurs do be axin' would frighten you. Keepin' his boot he may be for me."

"Would it be as expensive, I wonder, as two florins, and a sixpence, and a threepenny bit?" said Mac. "And I wonder does he make boot-laces too, or have you to get them from somebody else?"

"Ay, bedad, would it, every pinny," Timothy said. "Why, there's ne'er a Lepracaun in the

counthry but owns a big crock full up of gould
that he's got wid chaitin' thim that buys his
boots.   Look-a, sir, there was somethin' lepped in
the pool."

But Mac continued to wonder.

The next morning was all blurred with cold
mists, white on the dark hills, blue on the green
fields, and leaden-grey overhead.   Towards noon,
Timothy established himself on the parapet of
the bridge, quarters which he preferred to the
smoky gloom of a cavernous kitchen, though the
drizzle, swarming thickly about him, pricked his
face and hands chillily, as if with the alighting
of a cloud of half-thawed icy midges.   His Aunt
Lizzie, on his going out, had exhorted him with
unwonted solicitude not to stay stravading round
under the wet too late; and she had previously
been dilating, without much apparent relevance,
upon the good luck of anybody who might get
the change of jaunting through the country in a
grand little ass-cart.   But Timothy, surmising no
connection between these two facts, nor any possible bearing of them upon his own future prospects, heeded them very slightly at the time, and
gave them no further thought.

The weather and the fair having diminished
loungers, he had the bridge all to himself, until
by-and-by Felix Riley came along, driving home
three heifers, whose witless heads pointed persist-

ently in wrong directions. Felix now allowed
them to drift a bit down the road unsteered by
his blackthorn, and stopped for a word with
Timothy. "There's apt to be blue murdher up
above at the Grange to-day," he said.

"What's happint them?" inquired Timothy.

"Sure, up there, about Martin's cross-roads,
I'm after meetin' the little chap that's visitin' the
ladies—Master Mac they call him—stumpin'
along his lone, which I well know they'd niver
countenance his doin'. He slipped out, belike,
widout their knowledge. But when I made free
to axe him where he was off to, he answered me
mighty stiff that he'd business at Drumclune
fair; and that's no place, to my mind, for the
likes of him to be sthrayin' in. Sure, he isn't the
size of anythin'; and might very aisy be over-run
wid the first drove of bastes come his way. So,
if you hear anybody axin' about him, you might
just say where I seen him. I've me heifers to
git home—and, bedad, there's the red one about
steppin' into Mr. Duggan's."

"It's after the Lepracaun he's goin', I'd bet
me life," Timothy reflected, with remorse and
amusement mingled. "Sure, he thought every
word of the ould blathers I tould him was true.
'Deed, but it's quare the foolery childer'll be be-
lievin'," he said loftily to himself, from his alti-
tude of nine years.

He sat for a while longer considering in the drizzle, and then he saw George Mack approaching with a high-piled cart-load of hay. "Is it for the fair above you are?" Timothy asked.

George replied: "Ah, sure, not at all. I'm just about slingin' it in the lough over there, for fear anybody might be offerin' to buy it off of us."

"Gimme a lift," said Timothy.

"Och, but you'd niver conthrive to git up that height," said George; "and there's no room on the shaft."

"Right enough, I'd conthrive," Timothy said. And so he did, crutches and all, whereupon the load resumed its waddling way towards Drumclune.

Timothy had not been mistaken in his conjecture concerning Mac, who was about this time arriving at the fair. He found it a rather bewildering place, where many of the people one met seemed to stagger along and bawl in a strange and undignified manner, and where sudden rushes of large beasts came by, with horned heads awkwardly on a level with his own, which some persons—quite other persons, of course—might possibly have found startling. Nor did he anywhere light upon traces of the green jacket and long white feather, of which he was in quest. This gave him a foreboding of

failure, and somehow made him the more alive to
the fact, of which in his conscience he was well
aware, that he should not have set forth upon the
expedition unauthorised by his elders.

So that he was feeling slightly forlorn and
discouraged, when at last he wandered into a little back lane where nothing particular seemed to
be going on. At one end of it, into a recess
meant for holding broken stones, a donkey-cart
had been drawn—the donkey was nibbling a
grass bank close by—and converted into a
temporary old-clothes stall. Garments of various
kinds were hung from the erected shafts, and
piled on boards placed counter-wise across it, in-
terspersed with tempting clusters of the crockery,
which often played a leading part in bargains
struck for ancient coats and shawls. The pro-
prietor sat on the low wall behind it, in a weather-
beaten, greenish great-coat. He was elderly,
small, and wizened, with a deep red face, and
hair several shades lighter; and he said to Mac:
"Fine day, sir. Might you be a-wantin' anythin'?"

"A boot I was wantin'," said Mac, who by
this time had almost given up hopes of the
Lepracaun; "but the right place for gettin' it
at doesn't seem to be here to-day."

"Is it a boot?" the old man said, hopping up
with alacrity. "Sure, I've the grandest stock of

thim to-day, at all. A pair I have this minyit
'ud fit you delightful, sir, as if they was made to
your iligant measure."

"But I want only half a pair," said Mac; "and
I want it not to fit me. I don't know exactly
the size, but one that both my feet would fit into
at once would be about big enough."

"What would you say to that, honey?" the
old man said, clumping down before him a large
and heavy boot, whose travelling days were
evidently nearly done.

"It hasn't any lace in it," Mac said, being disposed to adverse criticism by the term of endear-
ment.

"A lace, sir; is it a lace? Me sowl to glory,
sure, all the gintlemen ever I knew buys their
laces sep'rit. Not but what a nice bit of string
off of a parcel looks as tasty as anythin' you
could get."

"How dear is it?" Mac inquired, beginning
to pull out his red leather purse with a silver
"M" on the flap.

Eyes expectantly twinkling watched the proc-
ess. "Why, that's accordin'," said their owner.
"But it's apt to be as much as all the shillin's a
customer would have along wid him, anyway,
and worth every one of them, and more."

"Would it be more than two florins," the customer said, laying down the coins, "and a six-

pence, and a new threepenny, and another sixpence; only it's a queer crumpled-up shape, and
Val says it looks doubtful?"

"Well, now, just to oblige you, sir, I might
contint meself to take it," said the old man; and
a bony clutch was descending upon the little
heap of silver, when another hand intercepted its
pounce, and covered its prey under a firmly-
pressed palm.

"Ay, would you, bedad, y'ould robber," the
new-comer said, "if you got the chance."

This was Timothy Crinion, whose equipage
had lumbered past just in time for him to espy
Mac at his bargaining, and to intimate a wish to
alight by dropping a crutch on George Mack's
head.

"Git out of this, you young vagabone," said
the old man, "and don't be offerin' to meddle
wid the young gintleman's money he's just after
payin' over to me."

"Och, but yourself's the notorious great chait,
ould Andy Sheehan," Timothy retorted, keeping
one hand resolutely on Mac's property. "Look
at the rubbishy bit of thrash you was takin' all
his shillin's for," he pointed a scornful finger at a
huge chasm in the upper leather of the decaying
boot. "You wouldn't give so much as a cracked
taycup for three pair of them, and that you
wouldn't."

"I'll git the pólis, and thry what *they*'ll be givin' *you*, you unchancy-lookin' spalpeen," said Andy.

"Git them, and welcome," Timothy defiantly said. But he gripped the money, and calling "Come along," to Mac, swung himself away as rapidly as he could.

Mac naturally followed, but the old man could pursue them only with maledictions and threats, being conscious that the earth was not spinning so steadily as it had done before the contents of a certain black bottle had shrunk and sunk.

Timothy had not much difficulty in convincing Mac of the worthlessness of Andy Sheehan's wares, and the advisability of deferring a purchase to a more favourable opportunity. "For," he urged, "the Lepracaun might happen to be in it some other day, and you wid ne'er a farthin' left. But if you was wishful to be gittin' a somethin' now, there's me Aunt Biddy 'ud be terrible thankful for a limon. Cruel bad she is wid the rheumatics, and sez there would be nothin' aquil to a limon, when she's chokin' wid the thirst all night." And Timothy had some trouble in halving Mac's prompt order for a dozen. His most effective argument was a whispered, "Sure, if you git that many, they'll be thinkin' you're mistakin' thim for a clutch of eggs, and buyin' thim to put under an ould hin."

Then John Harrel, from Carrickmore, the next place to the Grange, met the two boys just as he was going to drive home in the jennet-cart, and he gave them a lift back to Kilanesk, where they arrived before Mac's absence had caused any serious uneasiness.

And although he had done no business with Andy Sheehan, it seems probable that the frustrated transaction was not without its effect upon the fortunes of Timothy. All that evening Mrs. Crinion expected the arrival of her cousin's donkey-cart to carry off the interloping nephew, but it did not come. And when Andy next appeared in the village some weeks later, he merely vouchsafed a surly good-mornin', driving past her door, and was already provided with a travelling companion in the shape of a small, oppressed-looking boy. She could conjecture no cause for Andy's change of mind, and ascribed it to "some contrary fantigue," in her ignorance of how Timothy had displayed an inconvenient readiness to pick holes in the goods of his proposed employer. Yet, though she deplored the result, a more disinterested judge of the case might have been inclined to pronounce Timothy "better off stopping where he was," even if his stay promised him no more brilliant prospect than the watching of many miles of clear brown river-water slipping away beneath Kilanesk bridge.

THE VENGEANCE OF JOE MAHONY

THE VENGEANCE OF JOE MAHONY

IF you wish to put Joe Mahony, the Ballyhoy carman, into a good humour with himself, you cannot do better than ask him to tell you how he drove Constable Gatchell over to Kiltaney Petty Sessions. You may venture upon the step safely enough, for the story is not a very long one, and Joe is always in such a hurry to relate his own part in it, that he never delays over preliminary events. These happened as follows:

It was a fine afternoon in harvest-time, when Peter Daly drove Mr. Blacker's bran-new reaping machine out at the gate of the Big Long Corners, where the pale, tangled barley ears were lying low, on his way to the Little Long Corners, still glowed over with the ruddier gold of ripe wheat, which should fall next. He had to go only a short way, but unluckily it led by the entrance of Conroy the carpenter's shed, where Peter saw fit ill-advisedly to leave his horses standing, sleek and shiny, with the spick and span machine gleaming blue and scarlet behind them, while he went in and delivered a message, which got mixed up somehow interminably among several items of local gossip.

Now it chanced that little old Dan Byrne, the lame bill-sticker, with his paste-pot and a limp roll containing advertisements of a sale of sixty cocks of prime hay off the' meadow lands of Gortonagh, had just been at work on the opposite wall, whence he had torn down, among other things, a flaming yellow poster, descriptive of some bygone Portbrendan Races. This was left fluttering hither and thither in brief aimless flights at the capricious will of the passing breezes, which made waves in the grainfields and eddies in the dust indiscriminately; and one of them presently whisked it across the road right under the nose of Charlie, the fidgety young roan. For some reason best known to himself, the scrap of paper struck him as a portentous and terrific object, at which it was incumbent upon him to start with a sudden prance and clatter of hoofs, while his comrade, Major the chestnut, whose queer temper had not improved with the lapse of years, proved more than willing to take part in these demonstrations of alarm. So the next moment saw the pair bolting frantically off, and making, as ill-luck would have it, for the main thoroughfare of Ballyhoy. Peter Daly, warned by the noise outside, returning hurriedly to resume his neglected charge, arrived just in time to behold it disappear over the brow of the station-hill, at the fullest speed that could be got up in so short a space, and with no hopeful prospect of any check to its wild career.

Poor Peter is never a man of much resource or presence of mind, and at this crisis nothing more to the purpose occurred to him than to stand staring aghast, and ejaculate—"Murther-an-ages, and the masther afther payin' M'Kenzie's bill for it only yisterday—only yisterday, and pounds untould."

Upon which his friend Joe Conroy remarked consolingly, "And, bedad, it's pounds untoulder he'll be apt to be payin' afore he's done wid it now. 'Twill be a quare thing if yourself's not sacked over it, Pether, anyway; and it'll be much quarer if there isn't half a dozen people kilt, let alone the horses, wid them manner of onnathural rapin' hooks slashing wild about the road."

The onset, indeed, of an ancient scythed chariot could scarcely have been more peril-fraught than was the approach of poor Mr. Blacker's patent improved Victor-Columbia, as it came swaying and swerving along at a hand gallop, with its cruel-looking complexity of blades all fixed and revolving hungrily. By an extraordinary series of hairbreadth escapes, however, it ran amuck through the heart of the village without so much perdition as a chicken betiding the inhabitants; and thence it rushed on down Massey's lane,

whirling and whirring and flashing like some
monstrous mailed insect between the close green
hedge-rows. Here, too, good luck, if not good
guidance, warded off many seemingly imminent
casualties. A flurried cyclist congratulated himself—until he began to count his punctures—
upon having had barely time to drop with his
favourite pneumatic into a thorny ditch. The
Widdy Grehan, who is, her neighbours say, "all
the ould ages you can think of," scaled a barbed
wire fence with all the agility of sixteen. And
the Armstrongs unceremoniously turned their
croydon in at the gate of the Hunters, their
most intimate enemies.

But this chapter of accidents that did not happen could not be expected to prolong itself in-
definitely, and as the horses' pace was becoming
madder and the lane narrower there is little
doubt that some serious disasters were averted
when Joe Mahony, the carman, boldly putting
himself in their way, seized their distracted heads,
and dexterously turned them down the cart track
leading into Hart's turnip field, whereupon they
came meekly to a stand, as if relieved by release from the dominion of their own tyrannous
panic and by a sense of being once again under
rational control. Joe's action had undeniably
shown enough pluck and presence of mind to
justify him in feeling that he had played the

part of a good citizen, and deserved well of the
community. So he was naturally all the more
taken aback when a minute afterwards, while he
still stood talking reassuringly to Major and
Charlie, Constable Gatchell stepped over a neighbouring stile, and approaching him with a stern
countenance, said grimly —

"Look you here, Mahony, this won't do be any
manner of manes. I arrest you on a charge of
furious dhrivin'."

"What at all the mischief are you talkin'
about?" Joe said, glaring at him across Major's
drooping neck.

"Oh, right well you know what I'm talkin'
about," asserted Constable Gatchell, who was
newly come to Ballyhoy, or he could not have
made so ignorant a blunder; "you needn't
trouble yourself to be lettin' on. Amn't I just
after seein' that consarn tatterin' along the lane,
and I crossin' the field? At twinty mile an
hour good it was goin', fit to wreck all before it.
You might very aisy ha' slaughtered half the
parish."

"Well to goodness—me sowl to the saints.
And is it meself you was after seein' tatterin'
along wid it? You've the face on you to be
sayin' that? Troth and bedad it's the won'erful
sight you've got entirely. And me wid me own
car waitin' there under the trees, and the lad

mindin' it, till I dhrive Dr. Wilson home when he's ped his visits. Is it twinty mile an hour I'll be takin' him, should you suppose? So it's arresting me you'd be? Faith, now, I'm surprised," Joe said commiseratingly, "to hear you blatherin' that ridic'lous; but I only hope I'll be gettin' me health till *you* hear the last of it, me hayro, I do so."

Of course Joe had not the slightest difficulty, under the circumstances, in proving his case, and the mistake was rectified in a very few minutes. But none the less Joe's resentment at the affront put upon him was deep and enduring. Ardent was his thirst for a chance of being "even wid that big bosthoon"; and he may himself relate, as he loves to do, what a grand opportunity he found for taking his revenge. Seldom do the fates deal out such poetical justice.

"Is it how I dhruv Constable Gatchell? Sure now it might be a couple of months after the time he up and gev me impidence about stoppin' Mr. Blacker's yoke, and a cowld, wet, windy mornin' morebetoken it was, and the Petty Sessions day at Kiltaney. So a message comes to me from the barracks that me car was wantin' for to take a party over there at 10 o'clock sharp. Howsome'er a good quarter of an hour they kep' me waitin' at the door afore they had themselves ready; and who was it at all but me gintleman

Constable Gatchell and Constable Byrne—that's a dacint lad—and they in charge of an imp of a lost child that had been got sthrayin' on the sthrand, and the magisthrates was to settle what to do wid it. Three or four year ould the spalpeen was, wid the wits half frightened out of its misfortnit head, and too little to be walkin' a matther of five mile, and too big to be carryin'; so that was the raison of the car.

" Well and good, off we set, with the young constable and the spalpeen on the one side, and Constable Gatchell—his Honour's glory—on the other, in the pours of rain. And we just throtted on steady, till we come to the bit of hill at Cloughlavin Church, and then the mare tuk to walk aisy. And with that Constable Gatchell got up and sez, sarcastic : ' Might I throuble to ax whose funeral we was followin' ? '

" So sez I to myself, ' Och, thin, it's a hurry you're in, me boyo. Maybe it's *dhrivin' furious* you'd have me be.' And prisently after that sure the mare came to a standstill altogether.

" ' What the divil and everythin' else are you at ? ' sez he. ' You'll be havin' us late, if you don't look out and hurry up a bit, for we'd a right to get over agin eleven ? '

" ' Don't you wish you may ? ' sez I in my mind. And sez I to him, politeful—' Musha, it's more sinse th'ould crathur has in her head than to be desthroyin' herself thravellin', when she's after pickin' up a stone in her near hind fut ?'

"'Sorra the sign of a one I see in it then,' sez he, squinting over.

"'Sure,' sez I, 'it's a little, tiny splinther of a one, and thim's the worst kind, and the throublesomest to be gittin' out.'

"And, bedad, foostherin' at it I was for the best part of tin minyits, and had him ragin'. But I give you me word, we hadn't gone on above a couple of perches when she picked up another just the same sort, you percaive, and ne'er a hap'orth aisier to catch a hold of. Fit to lep out of his skin he was, let alone his ould police cape, that was flappin' up round his ears all the while, like the sails of a mill in the win', and he swearin' away in the middle of it every time he got a chance. And sure swear he might, and lep he might, for any differ it made to me or the ould mare.

"Let me see, now, what was the next thing happint us ? Ay, tubbe sure. I noticed the straddle-band lookin' uncommon quare and wake, and ne'er a bit of sthrong cord we had among us—except some in me pocket that sted there—to be tyin' it up wid, so I had to run back to Nolan's to borry the loan of a sthring. And thin, dhrivin' over Basken Bridge, if me whip didn't fly out of me hand accidental, whin I

thought to be stirrin' up the ould baste, and into
the river, delayin' us again. Bejabers, I wish I
had a pinny for every oath he had out of him
that time; and it blowin' owdacious and rainin'
polthogues.

"As well as I remimber, after that there was
somethin' wint wrong wid one of the fut-boords
that set him ragin', like one deminted. But the
sheep in Saltragh lane was the greatest obstruc-
tion at all. For, you see, it was fair day, and
ivery dhrove of them we met down I'd jump and
catch a hould of poor Rose's head to purvint her
of shying at them, and slingin' us all in the ditch.
Rael conthrary it 'ud ha' been of her to go do
such a thrick on us, considherin' all the while I've
known her, man and boy, she'd niver ha' passed
a remark if she'd met a flock of hippographs and
mad buffalo bulls, or any other outragious crathur
you could give a name to. Howane'er, that's
what I done, precautious. And, after that again,
I wint a quarter of a mile out of our way round
be Dycer's, for 'fraid she might take the notion,
for once in her life, to be scared at the thrains.

"So what wid one thing and another, goin' on
for twelve o'clock it was agin we landed up to
the coorthouse at Kiltaney, wid no less than the
Disthrict Inspector himself stravadin' about in
the wet outside, lookin' as bitther as if his gould
watch was burnin' a houle in the palm of his

hand, and awantin' to know what kep' us till that hour.

"'Well, glory be to goodness, sir,' sez I to him, 'if the constables was a thrifle late startin' from the barracks, it stands to raison the best plan was for me to be dhrivin' furious the same way I dhruv Mr. Blacker's raiper a while ago. So that's what I done, and what betther could I do?' An' sure sorra a lie I tould," Joe says, coming with an ecstatic chuckle to the point of his story, "for dhruv furious the big bosthoon was, and that's a fac'."

THE COUNSEL OF WIDDY COYLE

THE COUNSEL OF WIDDY COYLE

HER neighbours in general were of the opinion that Margaret Sheehan "thought too much of herself altogether," and it followed naturally enough that they also considered her to think less than she ought of other people, "every bit as good as she was, and maybe a bit over." They accounted for her arrogance in several different ways. Some of them ascribed it to the fact that she had been brought up by an aunt in the town of Cashalcreagh, where she had grown accustomed, as her cousin, the Widdy Coyle said, to "big shop-windies and every sort of grandeur." Others believed it was inherited rather than acquired, and reminded themselves that her mother's people, the Brennans, had "always had the name of bein' very proud." Again others explained it upon the hypothesis that "Margaret Sheehan had the notion she was the only dacint-lookin' girl in the parish—herself and her fine braided cape." These commentators, who were for the most part her contemporaries, frequently added that you "might aisy find plenty no uglier than she, if that was all that ailed her;" and as they had certainly bestowed

more attention than anybody else upon this particular point, they may have been its best quali-
fied judges.   But everybody agreed in taking it
for granted that Margaret's pride would be increased by her sister Kitty's marriage.   For
Kitty Sheehan had lately surprised Bunowen by
making a match far above its expectations, Myler
Geraghty being the son of a strong farmer, who
was actually a Poor Law Guardian, and might
one of these days become a Justice of the Peace ;
while her father, poor Jimmy Sheehan, was
merely a fisherman, with a small boat, *too* small
to accommodate the long family, for which his
few drills of pitaties sometimes proved sadly too
short between "plantin' and liftin'."   It was a
further remark of her cousin, the Widdy Coyle,
that Margaret would be a very foolish girl if she
set herself up with the notion of getting a bride-
groom equally well-to-do.   And upon this text
she was wont to relate a warning anecdote about
a family of young ladies with whom her own
mother had lived in service, and the eldest of
whom had married a lord, an alliance which led
the other sisters to entertain such exalted ideas
of their social prospects that they would not look
at a man unless he had a handle to his name.
"And what was the end of that, me dear ? " the
Widdy would conclude.   "Every single one of the
whole half dozen of them went to her buryin'

before there was any talk of her weddin'; 'deed did she—just be raison of givin' themselves airs."

The Widdy took care that this tale, with its perfectly obvious moral, should be heard repeatedly by her young cousin Margaret Sheehan; and her object herein was her nephew Dan Molloy, and the wife for whom she well knew him to be on the lookout. As Dan was a fisherman with only a fractional proprietorship in a middle-sized boat, and responsible for the support of an invalided mother, he could not be deemed a brilliant parti. But then he was, his aunt declared, "as steady as the Rock of Cashal, and near strong enough to lift it, so he'd a right to be doin' finely, no fear, if he didn't by misluck get drownded; and the crathurs must all take their chance of that, accordin' to the will of God." Moreover he was her favourite sister's son, in itself a sufficient reason to make her solicitous about his concerns. And the Widdy Coyle was not a person who would by any means be backward in endeavouring to order and settle things as she deemed expedient. Indeed neighbours had been overheard to pronounce her "fonder than she need be of meddlin' and makin' wid other people's affairs."

"But all the while, Biddy," said to her one day her sister-in-law, Eliza McFadden—in Bunowen the inhabitants are as a rule more or less con-

nected by birth or marriage—"all the while I
dunno why you should have any great call to be
settin' your mind on gettin' Margaret Sheehan for
Dan. Sorra a thraneen will her poor father be
able to give along wid her, you may depind.
Sure her mother was tellin' me herself 'twas as
much as they could conthrive to git together a
few respectable things for Kitty, the way they
wouldn't be ashamed, and she marryin' into a
rich family. So if Margaret's to have nothin'
except her stuck-up notions, apt she'll be to take
and spind every pinny she can lay her hands on,
and think it's too little into the bargain. And
that's how his earnin's ill go to loss on him, instead of savin' up a thrifle agin the bad times,
when he has the luck. It's an humble girl Dan
wants—or would, if he'd any wit."

" 'Deed now, Eliza," the Widdy explained herself, "stuck-up or no, Margaret's not the grabbin'
sort, I'll say that for her. If she's took up wid
any vagaries about marryin' grand—she may have
or she mayn't—my belief is it wouldn't be money
she'd be after. 'Twould be just her pride. And
she's a good girl wid a kind heart in her, and
clever too, mind you. Many a shillin' she makes
wid that fine crochee she does be doin'. Some
ladies in Cashalcreagh buys it off her to send up
to Dublin. Dan might do a dale worse, he might
so. More betoken he's thinkin' of her now, that's

sartin. But not any great while ago, he had some
sort of a likin' for that Ellen Mooney, and I can't
abide a bone in her body, goodness forgive me
for sayin' so. And I well know that if Margaret
won't have him, off he'll bounce, and wid Ellen
Mooney he'll take up. And that same 'ud be a bad
day for himself, and maybe a worser for his poor
mother, now she's so wakely grown, the crathur.
For Ellen hasn't e'er a bit of good-nathur in her
at all—a cross-tempered little shrimp she is."

"She is that," said Mrs. McHadden. "Like all
the rest of them Pather Mooneys. And bedad
now isn't a man a quare fool to go marry among
cross-tempered people? If he was me, he'd let
them alone till the fish comes in to warm themselves at the fire, as the sayin' is. For what's the
good of anythin', when it's heart-scalded they'll
have you from mornin' till night?"

"Well, there's the raison why I'm not wishful
Margaret would be givin' Dan the sack," said
Widdy Coyle, "and the raison why I do be warnin'
her agin thinkin' bad of marryin' a poor man.
Not that I ever make mention of Dan to her,
mind you. I've more wit. That 'ud be the right
way to set her agin him fer good and all. There's
nothin' so conthrary in their minds as most girls,
unless it's maybe some of the dumb crathurs.
If they see you're wantin' them to fancy a thing,
they won't so much as come next or nigh it. I

mind last summer we had a little red calf up at
me brother's. I was thryin' to put on cocoa, because we'd run short of skim-milk—and och to
behould the antics of her; you might ha' thought
it was black pisin I had in the bucket to choke
her wid. But the minyit I sat it down, and let
on I was goin' away and lavin' it—sure her head
was in it before I could turn round. So niver a
word of Dan do I say before Margaret good or
bad; but I just keep talkin' promiscuous about
the foolishness of folks settin' themselves up, and
the fine fortins poor people has come into now
and agin after all, and this way and that way."

In this strategy Dan's aunt and advocate per-
severed, and it must be allowed that her artfully
conveyed counsels were listened to with exem-
plary patience by her cousin Margaret Sheehan.
That Margaret was a little tired of hearing about
the perpetual spinsterhood of the six haughty Miss
O'Reillys is more than probable; but she would
go on with her crochet and say, "Och now, to
think of that!" and "Sure themselves were the
great gabies," at the proper places, quite alertly
and affably. Nor did her polite attention flag
even if the Widdy proceeded to add another favourite apologue, which turned upon a wonderful
piece of good luck met with by a poor fisher boy,
who was "that ragged lookin' 'twould ha' took
two of him to make a dacint scarecrow."

It so happened that the Widdy took occasion
to recite this very narrative one evening before a
rather large audience gathered mainly from the
youth of Bunowen. The season was summer, and
the weather was fine, so there were " a good few "
of them sitting about on the strip of sward, which
lies green betwixt the white-faced cabin-row and
the iron-grey shingle, where it makes a pleasant
basking place at the close of a warm, dry day.
As Widdy Coyle came round the turn of the
road, with her long shadow slanting away before
her nearly out to sea, and her brown, arabesque-
patterned shawl over her head, and her flashing
milk can on her arm, she noticed that the most
numerous group included her nephew Dan Molloy
and several of the young Sheehans, a circumstance
which made her bend her steps to the left, and
cross the short grass to join them. Margaret
Sheehan had found a comfortable ledge, with a
lower one for a footstool, where she could crochet
at ease; her younger sisters were perched near
her, and Dan Molloy confronted her from an opposite bank. He had placed himself there that he
might look across at her conveniently, but was a
good deal embarrassed by the beams from the
flushing west, upon which Margaret had prudently
turned her back. They dazzled his eyes, and
burnished his coppery red beard, and obliged him
to twist his face into a network of wrinkles

whenever he wanted to catch a sight of anything. Other young people lounged in the shallow little recess round which the swarded ledges ran amphitheatre-wise. It is a place where many of Bunowen's small dramas have been acted. The mistily blue sea was near enough to be heard creeping among the pebbles, and the hills beyond it were far enough off to be coloured softly like flowers—this evening they wore all the dim mauve of Marie Louise violets.

The Widdy Coyle sat down by Margaret's left hand, unceremoniously extruding Lizzie Sheehan, who thereupon slipped round to her sister's other side with a silent grimace. "Well now," said the Widdy, "if *I* was wearin' that light buff calico, I'd be afraid of me life to sit on the ground in it, gettin' it soiled—'twill show every atom of dirt. And once it's washed, it's desthroyed. Ne'er a tint of the colour will it keep; buff never does."

"The grass," Margaret said, "is as dry as the thread on a spool, and a dale claner than anythin' indoors, that's all blackened wid the ugly smoke."

"It's aisy talkin' agin the smoke, but I dunno what we'd do widout it. Them that's over-partic'lar," the Widdy said, betrayed into some inconsistency by her chronic disposition to exhort, "may be apt to have to sit in worse places before

they're a great dale oulder. Them that sets
themselves up thinkin' they're goin' to git richer,
it's poorer they may be after all, for aught they
can tell. And sometimes it's the other way round.
. . . Och Dan, is it there you are? Good
evenin' to you, me lad. I thought you'd be out
wid the Hegartys, but to be sure the tide's not
very handy for you to-night. Ye'll be makin' an
early start to-morra. And bedad, now, if you got
the same luck wid your fishin' that Thady Phelan
had, it's blessin' yourself you might be, and takin'
a holiday. Wasn't I ever tellin' you what happint Thady Phelan? Belike not."

The story of Thady Phelan was in fact by this
time familiar to all the company, but they sub-
mitted to it without a protest. Their mood was
placidly passive, and they felt that they could
listen or not listen just as they pleased either to
the murmur of the waves or the discourse of the
old woman. So she began to set forth with
much emphasis how Thady, who was a poor little
gossoon of a fisher-boy, "widout a shoe to put
his fut in on dry land," had gone out in his boat
one morning after the mackerel in Lanagawn
Bay, and how that evening late, the other lads,
who had got back before him, saw him coming
along in his old boat, without a sign of anything taken, and all settled to jeer at him about
his big haul. And how upon landing he showed

them a small, black-looking box, which he had
pulled up in his net, and which was presently discovered to contain some of the finest jewels any
one ever laid eyes on, worth mints of money, so
that Thady's fortune was made, and never another stroke of work need he put his hand to until his life's end.   It was at this point in her narrative that the Widdy introduced the comparison
already mentioned: "There was grandeur and
good luck for poor Thady now! and he that
ragged lookin' 'twould ha' took a couple of him
to make a dacint scarecrow."

Here, across the old woman's hoarser and lower-
pitched tones, a youthful voice struck clear and
shrill.   "Isn't it a rael pity then," it said, "that
Pat Kearns there can't conthrive to be gettin'
the likes of such a big haul?   For I'm sure half
a dozen of *him* wouldn't be any too many to
dress up a scarecrow wid, if it was to look anyways respectable."

The speaker was a girl of the name of Rosanne
Mooney, a cousin of the cross-tempered Ellen,
and though less reprehensible, still, in the Widdy's
opinion, over-fond of "takin' up other people's
words."   Her sarcasm was aimed at a black-
headed, brown-visaged youth, who lay with two
or three others on the sunny sod close by ; and it
reached its mark.   Certainly Pat Kearns's garments were in unusually bad repair.   A large

hole was frayed right through the elbow of his
blue woollen jersey, and the patch that had con-
cealed another rent at his knee now flapped in-
discreetly to the passing breezes.   These conspicuous defects were due less to poverty, though the
Kearns family was one of the poorest, than to
the fact that Pat had nowadays nobody at home
to be putting in a stitch for him.   His mother
had "died on him not so long ago," not so long,
at any rate, but that he remembered how she
used to darn and mend.   Perhaps Rosanne's jibe
reminded him roughly of his loss; or perhaps he
especially disliked having his rags just then held
up to ridicule; or perhaps, after all, it was only
Margaret Sheehan's imagination that made her
fancy he looked suddenly crestfallen and forlorn.
Be this as it may, it is certain that when her
younger sister Lizzie joined in the ensuing laugh,
and then chimed in with a pert reference to
Pat's "ould show of a torn cap," Margaret nudged
her reprovingly, and even went so far as to whisper: "Whist you gaby. If you don't behave
yourself, I'll bid mother be callin' you in." Now,
it is possible that the Widdy and her protégé, had
they noticed this bit of by-play, might have
drawn evil auguries therefrom; but neither of
them did.   The Widdy felt that she had improved
the occasion satisfactorily, and merely appended
a disclaimer of meaning to " pass remarks or raise

a laugh on anybody," while Dan Molloy found
an opportunity to express, in Margaret's hearing,
his opinion that "crochee was the purtiest sort
of work a girl could be doin'; a dale tastier than
knittin'." Which was so far, so good, for the
Mooneys were all great knitters. And soon after
this the group dispersed, early hours being
fashionable at Bunowen.

It had drawn towards sunset of the following
day, when Pat Kearns came rowing in along
Bunowen strand. He looked as ragged as ever,
and even more downcast, for his luck had been
bad, and his prospects in life appeared to him
very gloomy. Pondering abstractedly upon these
he was, as he leisurely rowed homeward, till a
voice hailing him near at hand startled him out
of his meditations. It was a young voice, too,
but softer than Rosanne's.

"Pat Kearns," it called, "might you happen
to have e'er a sate you could loan me aboard your
boat?"

And who should it be but Margaret Sheehan,
standing in her buff gown, which the golden sun-
glow bleached white, on the very point of the
sandy spit he was just passing by?

"Why to be sure, and in coorse I have, Margaret Sheehan, or if I hadn't, I wouldn't be long
makin' you one," Pat replied, backing water energetically to bring his black canvas bows sliding

in on the sand at Margaret's feet. But then a vague apprehension of something too good to be true crossed his mind, coupled with the remembrance of last night's scoff, which had left him a little suspicious of possible scorning, and he added: "But what at all would you be doin' in the dirty old boat? She's all fish-scales."

"And is it stayin' here you'd have me, to be drownded in the tide, if she twyste as dirty?" Margaret enquired. "Don't you see that the say's all abroad behind me?"

This statement, though an obvious exaggeration, was not quite unfounded, since a narrow blue streak had really flowed in so as to cut off the sandy spit from the mainland. It is true that Margaret could almost have jumped over the tiny straits, and might have waded across through the shallow water with perfect ease. However it was, like Mercutio's wound, of depth and width sufficient to serve a purpose. "It's not havin' anythin' hurtin' a hair of your head I'd be, let alone drowndin', Margaret astore," Pat answered; and he hastened to upholster the stern bench for her accommodation with a coil of dry net.

"So you'd took next to nothin' to-day?" Margaret said, as they glided along slowly, for Pat was in no hurry to reach the little pier. "Well, now you've picked up me, and if I was me own

weight in macker'l, or sole, or turbot, or anythin'
good for ought, you couldn't say you hadn't got
a pretty middlin' big haul. 'Deed then, it's a
pity you haven't; nor a chance of the grand
jewel box ould Biddy Coyle was tellin' about."

"Bedad if I could only be keepin' *you*," said
Pat, "I'd think 'twas the grandest haul any man
ever took, jewels or no. But sure it's landin' you
here I'll have to be directly."

"And sure landin' isn't lavin', when two people's goin' ashore at the one place," Margaret observed with the air of a person who throws out
casually some most general remark. But the
promptitude with which Pat caught it up and
twisted it into a strictly personal application did
credit to his presence of mind.

"Then would you ever think at all, macree, of
takin' me to keep?" he said, resting abruptly on
his oars, while their blades dripped chains of
diamonds in the sun. "Glory be to goodness—
sure I was always afraid of me life you'd niver
look at me. For why would you? And frettin'
I am this long while, for I well know me best
chance in this world is to be goin' out to where
me brother Johnny is in the States, that's doin'
finely; only I hadn't the heart to be settin' off
me lone, and quittin'—them I might niver lay
eyes on agin, whether they minded me or not.
But och Margaret jewel, if yourself 'ill not think

too bad of comin' along wid me, 'twill be all
grandeur entirely.   Sorra another wish I have in
the world—and you wouldn't disappoint me of
it ? "

"The States," said Margaret, "is a wonderful
far way off.   A body'd have to be considerin' a
great while about crossin' over the say."   An
answer which was so much more decisive than
Pat had dared to hope for, that he resumed his
rowing in an unspeakable elation of spirits.
"Troth and it's the proud man I am this day,
mavourneen," he said.

Margaret and he seemed, indeed, to have ex-
changed moods all at once.   For his downcast
expression had vanished, and with clear and con-
fident looks he had lifted up his head in its torn
cap ; whereas she, whose habit had been to hold
hers rather high, now fixed her eyes on the
shallows their keel was cleaving through, as if
she were busily engaged in reckoning the dancing flecks of transparent shadow and light with
which the ripples paved the sanded bottom.
This may have been partly because about the
landing-place had gathered a group of lookers on
—"and bad manners to them," she said to herself half vexed—amongst whom, as she was fully
aware, her arrival in Pat Kearns's boat would
create no small sensation.   In fact an officially
printed announcement that a marriage had been

arranged, and would shortly take place, could scarcely have made the situation plainer to Bunowen.   Before the sun had well finished setting, it was known from one end of the hamlet to the other that "Margaret Sheehan and Pat Kearns were spakin'."

The news displeased nobody except Dan Molloy and his aunt, the Widdy Coyle, the latter the more seriously of the two, inasmuch as he was likely to find consolation in what she deprecated as a domestic calamity.   Besides that, she had taken a far more active part than he in the match-making, and was correspondingly mortified by the failure of her efforts.

"I wisht to goodness, Nannie, I'd known what was in the minds of them two—the slieveens," she said, discussing the subject this time with her crony Mrs. Durkin.   "But sorra a notion had I of any such a thing.   Sure who'd ha' supposed a girl like Margaret 'ud go for to take up wid that raggety young rapscallion?   If you'd axed me, I'd ha' said he hadn't the impidence in him to be so much as thinkin' of her, no more than if she was the Queen of Connaught."

"For the matter of that," said Mrs. Durkin, "I could have tould you he was thinkin' of her fast enough.   It's my belief he niver put a stitch in her crochee-strip that Pat didn't see, if he was anywhere's widin sight of her."

"And I as good as advisin' Margaret," the Widdy went on lamenting. "To be takin' the poorest man that axed her, and *I* manin' me nephew Dan, and *she* manin' Pat Kearns—— Bad cess to them, makin' a fool of me. Many a time I might better ha' whist about the Miss O'Reillys and Thady Phelan."

"According to my experience," said Mrs. Durkin, "it's little differ one way or the other, good or bad, that advice makes, when the talk is of likin' or lovin'. You might be the whole day biddin' me to like thim boiled scallops off the rocks, and ne'er a bit would I touch, for I can't abide the thoughts and smell of them. But I might spare meself the throuble of tellin' you they was ugly things, if be chance you have a fancy for them."

"They're a nasty brash," the Widdy said with inconsequence. "But all the same," she persisted · regretfully, "all the same, if I'd known, I'd ha' held me fool's tongue about Thady Phelan and his big haul."

COCKY

COOKY

COOKY M'CANN was behaving ill, as, indeed, he had done more or less habitually all through his seven years or so. On this February morning, however, his misconduct had reached the point which his neighbours described as "beyond the beyonds altogether," and which generally led to the intervention of some one in authority.

"What at all's he at now?" his mother said, uneasily, as across her doorway gossip came a sound of shrill shrieks, mingled with a cackle of too familiar laughter.

Mrs. Walsh, who, bound for market, was passing the time of day, fell back a few steps to reconnoitre, and reported: "It's disthroyin' your bit of a shawl he is, ma'am, and tirrifyin' Mrs. Farrell's childer out of their siven sinses."

Cooky had, in fact, draped head and shoulders with a skimpy black shawl, and, thus arrayed, was reiterating short rushes towards two very little girls, who were seated on the bank close by. He approached them with flapping arms, in long hops, after the manner of the alighting crows, whom he had often seen last summer shut themselves up like pairs of black-polished shears

and drop into the green or gold of the adjacent
oat-field. His performance was rather successfully realistic, but the small children did not by
any means appreciate it, and it at length made
them break into ecstatic screams, which brought
their mother scurrying to the rescue from over
the way. While bearing them off, she hurled
many voluble reproaches at Cocky, whom they
seemed to soothe, as he shook down his mother's
shawl into a puddle and sauntered on. He was
following in the wake of a little top-knotted hen,
very white and clean, who had just picked her
steps fastidiously across the road.

"It's outrageous he is," Mrs. M'Cann said,
apologetically, looking after him. "But sure I
had him spoiled all the days of his life, thinkin'
I'd never rair him, he was that wakely, till he's
that unruly in himself he's a tormint grown to
man and baste. Chuckens is the only thing he
won't annoy if he gets the chance. He was always terrible fond of chuckens. 'Deed, when he
was littler, I did be hard set to keep e'er a weeny
one alive at all, wid the way he'd be pettin' them.
And the bawls of him whinever he found he had
the bit of life squeezed out of a one of them—
och, murdher! But now he's took up intirely
with his little white top-knotty hin. If anythin'
happint her, we'd have the quare work."

"The Widdy Goligher has the very moral of

her," Mrs. Walsh said. "Top-knot and all: you might think the two of them come out of the one egg."

But the Widow Goligher was a person at the mention of whose name Mrs. M'Cann's mouth would close suddenly as if with a strong spring, the expression of her countenance seeming to convey that it was on some disagreeably flavoured morsel. For she and the widow were black out, and had been so ever since the autumn, when the widow had seen cause to consider that Mrs. M'Cann had unfairly forestalled her in securing the promise of Mrs. Vesey's sour milk for pig-feeding. It was a feud not likely soon to die out, as its embers were fanned every week on Mondays and Fridays, when Mrs. M'Cann's supplanting bucket went by Widdy Goligher's door. So now Mrs. M'Cann chose to ignore Mrs. Walsh's remark, and proceeded: "It was be raison o' that—his bein' so fond of the chuckens—he got the name of Cocky, for be rights he's called Bernard, after Himself, poor man."

"And you've no news of him yet, ma'am?" said Mrs. Walsh.

"Sure not the sound of a word. His ship was due in Liverpool the middle of October, and here's the beginnin' ind of February—I dunno what to say to it."

Mrs. M'Cann's husband was a sailor; she said
a mate, but her neighbours said, *a mate, bedad!*
which is quite a different thing. However, for
the last month or so, in the course of which his
ship had become alarmingly over-due, they had
been saying it was much if the crathur ever set
eyes on him again, and they had temporarily
waived the question of his rank.

"If I was you," Mrs. Walsh continued, "it's
makin' inquiries I'd be meself at the shippin'
offices up in Dublin. I wouldn't let them get
the notion they was to be dhrowndin' people
promiscuous about the world, and nobody passin'
a remark."

"Sure that's the very thing I'm about doin',
ma'am," Mrs. M'Cann said. "I've sold the chest
of drawers for our fare, and we're goin' up to-
morra to stop wid me married sister in Crampton
Lane."

"Lands sakes, will you be takin' the young
chap wid you?" said Mrs. Walsh.

"Why, to be sure, ma'am. Who'd I be lavin'
him wid? He'd have their places ruinated wid
his mischief before he got me back turned, let
alone that I'd be disthracted in me mind wonderin' what villiny he was at. It's a poor case,
ma'am, to be shipwreckin' your mislucky husband
every minyit of the day and night, widout lavin'
a child behind you as well, settin' fire to other

people's houses, or conthrivin' disthruction on himself, the dear knows how."

"Ay, bedad, it is so. But you'll find him fine and throublesome to you up in Dublin, if I'm not mistook, ma'am," Mrs. Walsh said, gathering up her basket to go.

She was not at all mistaken. In fact, Mrs. M'Cann's difficulties with her travelling companion began that same evening, when Cooky said: "What'll I bring Toppy in?"

"Mercy on us all alive!" said his mother. "Is the child deminted? Takin' Toppy that far! Sure, she'd be dead twyste over before we got half-ways, and your Aunt Lizzie'd be ragin' mad if we went and brought a hin flutterin' about her house. Mrs. Murphy here says she'll keep her eye on Toppy and the rest of them for us."

"If I seen her offerin' to keep her ugly ould eyes on Toppy, I'd knock the two of them into one," Cooky said, darkly.

"Well, then, Mrs. Kavanagh would," said his mother.

"I'm thinkin' the ould male-bag 'ud do," Cooky said, deliberatively.

The ensuing stormy discussion ended in Cooky's suddenly abandoning the controversy with a cheerfulness which would have seemed suspicious to a more discerning person than his mother. Suspicious, too, next morning was his

insistence upon himself carrying the covered
market-basket, and his running back to the house
with it after they had started, on the pretext
that he had left his knife in a crevice of the wall ;
and then his lagging behind all the way to the
station, and loitering aloof on the platform until
the train came up. So successfully, however, did
he carry out all these stratagems, that not until
she had gone some distance on their long railway
journey was Mrs. M'Cann's attention caught by a
slight rustling within the basket, which she found
to contain Toppy, alert, and interrogatively peering. Cocky coolly admitted that he had made
room for her by bundling out most of its other
contents, and he listened blandly to his mother's
reproaches, while he fed Toppy with bread
crumbs. Nevertheless, retributive justice was
even then keeping time with inevitable punctual-
ity upon his track.

Within a few miles of Dublin, where night had
already fallen, a stop was made to collect tickets,
which were presently demanded at the door of
the M'Canns' compartment by a guard, lantern
in hand. Now the lid of Toppy's basket was in-
securely fastened down, leaving a chink through
which her prying head happened to bob up just
at the moment when the round yellow-glaring
eye turned its flash of light in at the open window. Perhaps she may have taken the illumina-

tion for a strange dawn in the midnight; perhaps she may have merely acted upon a sudden panic; but at any rate the result was that the stowaway all at once came fluttering forth, with a prodigious whirring of wings, and, before any one well knew what had begun to happen, had hurled herself into the blackness of the wild wet night which moaned outside. A brief white flapping across the flare of a neighbouring lamp, and a single tail feather left in his unavailing grasp at her, was the last Cocky saw, was all he retained, of his too-well-beloved Toppy. He would, of course, have followed her head foremost, but the train was already in motion, and a large-framed farmer, who sat next him, repressed him with one heavy hand as effectually as if it had been a paper-weight laid upon a rustling leaf.

"Aisy, man, aisy," said the farmer. "There's losses in every trade, and you'll readier come by another little hin than a new neck bone."

Cocky was really stunned by the magnitude of his disaster; and the big Dublin railway terminus, that vast cavern full of mysterious panting and shrieking, succeeded by clattering streets, where great luminous globes hung aloft, pearly and diamond-pierced, and ranged golden stars flung chains of light across and across the black water, all helped further to overawe and bewilder him, so that he went to bed with un-

wonted meekness, in a sort of dazed nightmare.
But next morning he awoke with all his wits
about him, and a firm conviction that he would
find Toppy as soon as he could get out-of-doors.
So, when his mother had started on her inquiries
along the Quays, strictly forbidding him to stir,
he eluded observation, and, slipping downstairs,
made his way into the streets.

To a visitor fresh from life-long residence in
Ballylogan's solitary cabin-row they would have
seemed a strange and startling experience, had
he not been pre-occupied by one engrossing purpose, which left him no leisure to marvel or fear.
He was looking out all the way for traces of
chickens, and as he went he called at intervals,
"Toppy, Toppy." In his pocket he had a crust,
filched from the breakfast-table, wherewith to
regale her on their happy meeting. But he
passed by what appeared to him endless rows of
houses, all with closed doors, and no way round
to the back, before he came upon something that
raised his hopes. This was an extraordinarily immense window, with white letters on it, and in
it a pyramidal heap of many eggs—dozens and
dozens. Evidently, therefore, hens must exist
somewhere close by, and, if so, what more likely
than that Toppy had for the time being taken up
her abode among them? Moreover, the crowning egg of the pile was a very brown one, ex-

actly like the eggs of Toppy. Cocky needed no
further evidence. Into the shop he stumped, and
confronted across the counter, an elderly, stout
woman, in a black cap with purple ribbons, who
was the wife of P. Byrne, family grocer and pro-
vision dealer.

"Where," said Cocky to her, "do you be
keepin' your hins—ma'am?" he added, on reflection that civility might be his best policy.

"What hins?" said Mrs. Byrne.

"Thim that lays your eggs, of coorse," said
Cocky.

"Och, run away wid you—we've no hins," said
Mrs. Byrne.

Cocky's eyes, which just cleared the top of the
counter, blazed angrily over it, but he had not
yet abandoned politeness. "Mind you, I don't
say you're after *stailin'* Toppy on purpose," he
said, with much self-restraint. "She might ha'
flew in among your chuckens last night unbeknownst, and got mixed up wid thim like. You
must own a power. And you're welcome to
keep the egg, though you've no call to it all the
while. I want to look through thim and see——"

"Quit," Mrs. Byrne said, drumming on the
counter. "There's nothin' for you here."

"You ould thief of the world," said Cocky,
thereupon letting himself ago, "have you no
shame in you, to be standin' up there tellin' black

lies ? Just you wait till I get in the pólis to you that I have at the door."

" Here, Pat, put the little miscreant out of it," Mrs. Byrne called to some one, who proved to be a youth big enough to hustle Cocky away with no more ado than if the black-headed, fierce-eyed urchin were an ordinary ingredient in the dust he was sweeping up.

Near the door were standing a ragged little girl and two smaller boys, interested beholders of Cocky's unceremonious expulsion. " Look you here," the little girl whispered to him, confidentially, " if it's anythin' you're after *takin'* on thim, you'd do right to run for your life. That's the pólis." She pointed to a portly uniform stationed at the nearest corner. But Cocky said : " Bejabers, I'll get him to her," and darted off, making straight for the place of peril.

The children stared after him with a sort of horror, as if watching one bent upon his own destruction ; and, still staring backwards, moved off in the opposite direction, as if from the vicinity of something probably explosive.

Constable 89 A, being twitched by the sleeve, looked down a long way, and perceiving a small, peaky face, full of fury, said : " Well, me big man ? "

" You're to come and take up herself inside there," said Cocky. " She's got Toppy's egg in

the windy, that flew out of the train last night
on me; and has her keepin' somewhere along
wid her own bastely ould hins—it's wringin' the
nêcks of thim I'll be, and givin' me impidence,
and tellin' lies in there like the ould outrageous
robber she is; and you'll know her be the top-
knot on her head."

"It's a lunatic child, begorrah," Constable 89 A
said; but before he had decided how to deal
with the matter, Cocky was seized upon by a distracted woman in a greenish plaid shawl, who
swept him off, protesting that "he had her heart-
scalded and torminted," and that it was "a
poor case to have the steamboat companies
dhrowndin' your husband or you in the rowlin'
says, and no more talk about it than if he was a
fly in a bowl of skim milk, widout your bould
brat of a child takin' upon himself to go to loss in
the streets of Dublin, where the first you'd hear of
him he'd be flattened under a one af thim jinglin'
thrams."

For Mrs. M'Cann had returned from a fruit-
less quest among puzzled clerks, to find a crown
set upon her afflictions by the disappearance of
her evil, but only son.

Travelling home next day, she felt utterly cast
down by the result of the expedition, which had
turned out all failure, from her vain inquiries
about the missing ss. *Brackenburg*, to the morti-

fying conduct of Cocky, who had been upon his
worst behaviour, and had very unfavourably impressed his Dublin relatives. But Cocky's spirits
had risen, because he was buoying them up with
the fixed idea that when he got home Toppy
would be there waiting for him. Toppy, he declared, could fly much faster and farther than the
train, and knew her way back a deal better than
the likes of whoever he happened to be address-
ing. Of course, he only brewed bitter disappointment for himself by such impossible imaginings,
and when, upon his arrival, he learned that
"sight nor light" had been seen of any little
white hen, he collapsed into a melancholy of
strange persistence. The sole hope in life to
which he clung was the possibility that Toppy
might yet return, and nothing would he do but
sit all day long on the bank beside his door looking out for this event. The tail-feather, all that
remained to him of his pet, he kept constantly
with him, and the spectacle of him crouching out
in the bleak March winds and sleet showers,
mournfully contemplating that relic, wearing
now stumpy and grimy, cast a gloom over his
end of the row. In fact, the dejection of the
M'Canns became at this time quite a weight upon
the minds of their neighbours in Ballylogan. For,
as was often remarked, "you couldn't go by their
door but there'd be poor Mrs. M'Cann standin'

lookin' the eyes out of her head for him comin'
down the road that was as like as not streelin'
about at the bottom of the say, and a step farther
you'd see that mischancy imp of a Cocky sittin'
frettin' himself into fiddle-strings over his ould
crathur of a fowl. 'Twasn't nathural; and like
enough he wouldn't be very long after his poor
father."

None of them felt sincerer commiseration than
the old Widdy Goligher from a bit down the lane,
Mrs. M'Cann's unsuccessful rival in the matter of
sour milk, and proprietress of a hen the very
moral of the so-lamented Toppy. She had petted
and prized this bird not a little, a fact which,
perhaps, sharpened the edge of her sympathy
with Cocky's tribulation; at any rate, as she
watched the moping of him and his mother in
these early spring days, she began to think of
parting with her. Her thought passed through
several stages of development until it took the
form of: "He's a mischievous little spalpeen,
but I niver seen him doin' anythin' agin anybody's chuckens, I'll say that for him. Sure, he's
frettin' himself sick for nothin'; and it's my belief the poor father's dhrownded on them all the
while. I'll be apt to let him have her." But in
the evening, when she was feeding her fowl,
second thoughts intervened: "It's his own one
he's wantin'. If I went for to offer him mine, as

like as not it's impidence he'd be givin' me. And more betoken if I send her away, what'll I do wid the settin' of Black Minorcas ould Lady Rachel's after promisin' me?"

At this point matters halted for some time, partly because her possessions were so very few. Then—it was the same day that she passed by and saw how Cocky had a little refection of cold-potato crumbs spread on the bank beside him in readiness for Toppy's return—she advanced another step: "He mightn't ever tell but she was his own one, if we put her in the bit of a shed there unbeknownst over-night. There wasn't scarce a feather's differ between the two of them. He'd be as sot up as anythin' consaitin' she was flown back after all. Anyway, we might thry it. I'll spake to Mrs. M'Cann to-morra."

Mrs. M'Cann, when spoken to, made little demur. The acceptance of a favour from the Widow Goligher was not indeed without its bitterness; but her pride had fallen with her fortunes, and she felt serious anxiety about Cocky. So she feared he would be too cute for them, but agreed to try the experiment.

It succeeded to admiration. When Cocky found the pretender roosting comfortably upon the long desolate perch, he declared with many vehement asseverations that she was his own Toppy; that there was not another hen like

her in the whole of Ireland, and that he saw
the gap in her tail where he had pulled out the
feather. His exultation was unbounded. He
could hardly be withheld from scattering to her
half his meals, and he poured derisive scorn upon
everybody who had prophesied against her resto-
ration.

A day or two later he chanced to stroll indoors, and found the Widow Goligher talking to
his mother. Whereupon he planted himself in a
defiant attitude before her and said: "Yah, hah,
ould Widdy Goligher, that thinks she's the only
one in the world owns a white hin, and Toppy
sittin' there on the roost this minyit, worth twinty
dozen of her dirty little ould ugly-looking 'scarecrow.' "

"Goodness forgive you, Cocky, but you're the
ungovernable, ungrateful child, and poor Mrs.
Goligher after bringin' you—" his mother had
begun, when the widow interrupted her, dread-
ing indiscreet disclosures.

"Here's a clutch of eggs, Cocky, *avic*," she said,
pointing to a large hay-lined basket, "for you to
be setting under your Toppy. They're a grand
sort."

"Toppy doesn't want to be bothered sittin' on
any such blamed ould thrash," replied Cocky.
"She'd a dale liefer be walkin' about wid herself.
Git along wid them."

"Ah, sure, I was thinkin'," the widow said artfully, "it 'ud be a good plan to purvint her of strayin', in case she had e'er a notion in her mind of takin' another fly off away to nobody-knows-where. The eggs 'ud be as good as a pound weight on aich fut of her, keepin' her down safe for you."

Cocky reconsidered the question for a while from this point of view. "You may lave them," he said, turning on his heel. Certainly, Mrs. M'Cann had some grounds for deploring his defective manners.

But her graver trouble was happily ended that very evening, when who should walk in at the door except Bernard McCann himself, whom nothing worse had befallen than broken-down engines, tardy tugs, and tedious repairs, causing ominous delay. So that Cocky had perhaps a somewhat narrow escape of missing the benefits which accrued to him from the Widow Goligher's condoling mood. For the sum of our neighbour's prosperity does sometimes tend rather to bake than melt us.

Be that as it may, although Cocky did acquire his hen and his clutch, the following incident makes it seem somewhat more than doubtful whether anything ever came of the latter. It happened a day or two after the return of his father, to whom Mrs. M'Cann, as she surveyed some new gaudy-hued foreign handkerchiefs, observed: " Well now, that one wid the puce-colour in the border is what you may call iligant. I declare to goodness, I think I'll be givin' it to ould Widdy Goligher. Oncommon good-natured she was about decaivin' poor Cocky wid her little hin. If I seen him anywheres about, I might be persuadin' him to run down wid it to her— or else I might be lavin' it wid her meself this evenin', and I passin' her door wid the pig's bucket. Likely enough Cocky'd only be desthroyin' it. I wonder where he is all this while so quiet ? "

Cocky was, in fact, at that very moment in the shed, impatiently watching the placid Toppy; and he might have been heard to murmur discontentedly: " It's my belief the crathur's sick and tired of sittin' on thim ould eggs. I've as good a mind as ever I had in me life to be smashin' thim wid a stone. But if it's only the hate brings thim out, maybe I could hurry thim up a bit wid givin' thim a rinse through a sup of hot wather. Bedad I will so to-night, when me mother's went after the milk, and the kettle's sittin' handy on the hob."

COCKY'S CONSCIENCE

COCKY'S CONSCIENCE

THE acquaintances of Cocky M'Cann often remarked that he had no shame in him, a statement which was not fully born out by facts; for though Cocky might indeed with truth be called "as brazen as brass" on most points, and towards most people, there were some few in relation whereto he was really capable of feeling abashed. If, for example, he found himself on any occasion convicted of lacking that knowledge of the world and experience of life which he had enjoyed nearly seven years' opportunities for acquiring, confusion visibly covered him, from the fringe of black locks cut straight above his troubled grey eyes to the bare feet shifting uneasily, as though impatient to flee the scene of his discomfiture. And when it happened to take place in the presence of anybody whom he esteemed a superior person, such confusion was naturally all the worse confounded. Now, the strictly limited number of these persons included his father, the elder Bernard M'Cann. It is to be feared that this was not caused by any recognition on Cocky's part of his duty towards his parents, whom he felt himself quite at liberty to despise. He had, in fact,

long since formed a very humble opinion of his
admiring mother's capacity. Rather it may be
taken as an exemplification of the principle that
familiarity breeds contempt, as Bernard M'Cann
was a sailor, and during much the greater portion
of Cocky's existence had been seafaring in distant climes. His returns thence with marvellous
odds and ends of foreign produce, which he, more
marvellously still, seemed to regard as careless
trifles, had marked the chief epochs in Cocky's
history, and had impressed upon him the belief
that nobody else in the parish of Ballylogan
owned "so rare a wondered father and a wise."
The tenet led him to vaunt himself with supercilious insolence over all his contemporaries in
public, exhibiting his curios with the best possible imitation of his father's matter-of-course, off-
hand manner, joined to an outspoken disparage-
ment of his audience which was his own fancy.
But in private he entertained a profound respect
for this voyager on strange seas, and would have
been most loth to betray any ignorance before
him.

Therefore, it was with no small mortification
that, shortly after one of his father's homecom-
ings, Cocky became aware of having landed himself in a tight place. It was by reason of a little
white hen, whom he called his Toppy, and iden-
tified with a cherished favourite lost to him lately

through his own headstrong misconduct.   But all
the while she was an innocent pretender, foisted
upon him by a stratagem the history of which is,
no doubt, familiar to some of our readers.   So
successful was its result that Cocky transferred
to her all, and more than all, the affections he
had concentrated upon the real Toppy, and with
them, of course, their accompanying anxieties and
cares.   His solicitude about her was such that
when, somewhat against his wishes, she had been
provided with a clutch of eggs to hatch, he kept a
resentful and unquiet eye upon her calm sittings,
apprehensive lest the task should prove injurious
or irksome to her.   At length his impatience for
her release from the dark little shed, under whose
low-browed, sodded roof he could frequent her
company only in cramped and uncomfortable at-
titudes, prompted him to take, with a view to en-
pediting matters, a step daring and irrevocable,
which he reconsidered, too late, uneasily enough.
His reflections grew more harassing as the critical
twenty-first day approached and passed, and not
a shell was chipped, "nor a sign of it on them,
no more than if they were a handful of smooth
stones off the strand," as Mrs. M'Cann reported
after investigation.   What alarmed him most was
the probability that a more searching scrutiny
might presently end in pointing him out as the
cause of the failure, and, at the same time, as the

perpetrator of something ridiculous—something
at which his father would laugh and chuckle.
His fears waxed acute when he heard his mother
say that "she'd wait a couple more days, and then
break a one of the eggs, to see was it addled they
were, for there'd be no use keepin' the crathur
on them any longer." To her surprise, Cocky,
whom she had expected to please thereby, resisted
this proposal bitterly, declaring with much grim-
ness that "he'd like to find anybody smashin' up
his eggs, and Toppy after wastin' her time sittin'
on them half the year." However, she set it
down as merely a piece of the contrariness which
she was well used to encountering in her only and
badly-spoiled child.

But Cocky, in his hobble, had a strong wish to
get his father's opinion upon the case. He could
not, of course, attempt to obtain it by any dangerous straightforward questions; so he bided his
time until he saw Bernard establish himself to
smoke an afternoon pipe on the rough stone seat
alongside their door, beneath a window where
stalky geranium leaves pressed hard against the
pane. Then he strolled up in a casual way, and,
having artfully introduced the subject of poultry,
proceeded to relate the following ingeniously-
constructed anecdote:

"One time I heard tell of a boy owned a hin—
I mane it was a girl she was all the while, a little

girl—and her mother was after puttin some eggs
under the hin—or maybe it was an ould grandmother they had in it; bedad, now I think it
was. Anyway, she was an ould black hin, wid
ne'er a white feather on her, nor a top-knot aither.
So she was a great while sittin', and the boy
thought he might as well thry could he hurry her
up a bit—the *girl*, tubbe sure I mane; Lizzie Kilkelly her name was——"

"What talk have you about Lizzie Kilkelly?"
said his father, who had hitherto bestowed more
attention upon the faint quiver of flame in the
pipe-bowl than upon his son's discourse.

"I was tellin' you what she done wid the eggs
her ould big black hin had hatchin'. It was one
day her mother, or grandmother, was wint out, I
dunno after what; it couldn't ha' been the pig's
milk, for they didn't own e'er a pig at all. So
the girl consaited that very belike the hate had a
right to help the chuckens comin' out, and she
tuk an' she slipped the eggs just for a couple of
minyits into the scaldin' wather there was boilin'
in the kettle, to thry would it hurry them up at
all—that's what the girl done."

"And she must have been a born fool to go do
any such a thing," remarked Bernard M'Cann;
"or as mad as a March hare."

"So she was," Cocky said, composedly, "ravin'."
He strolled away again with much apparent

unconcern, but, in reality, his father's comment was a serious blow to him, and his darkest forebodings were strengthened by it. During the rest of that day he was constantly expecting his mother to try her experiment upon the eggs, and he felt sure that *his* experiment would then somehow be found out; and he had ascertained that the person whose opinion he most valued would consider him a fool or a lunatic. He went to bed in a gloomy frame of mind.

The next morning was among the last of April's, and had accordingly a sort of license to deal in variable weather. But the showers which it produced at fitfully frequent intervals were by no means of the sportive, sunshiny type appropriate to the season. They came driving down, cold and fierce, on wild flurries of wind, hunting everybody who would fain wear a dry skin to seek precipitate shelter underneath dripping thatch, or on the lee-side of walls and stacks and dykes. In the course of one of the most violent *polthogues* the M'Canns' kitchen was abruptly invaded by a youngish matron who burst in on Cocky and his mother like one hotly pursued, carrying a small child and a capacious market-basket, both of which she had been trying to protect with an inadequate plaid shawl.

"Saints above, Mrs. Morissy, and is it yourself?" Mrs. M'Cann said. "Sure you're not after thrampin' over from Kilmacreagh this wild day, and wid the infant child? The teems is fit to drownd it."

"Bedad am I," said Mrs. Morissy, "and on to Stakesbridge after that again. It's a hardship on the crathur, but sorra a sowl have I to lave her wid now she's grown too lively to be lavin' wid herself. She's better off drowndin' than crawlin' into the fire like a cricket out of the pate-creel the way she would in half a minyit if she got me back turned. A rael caution she is for creepin' and crawlin', and she only goin' on for a twelvemonth. I was hopin' she might be a bit backward, for then they don't want that much mindin' to keep them off disthroyin' theirselves. But the talk she has out of her when she's in the humour would surprise you. There's nothin' she can't say if she likes—is there Biddy?" But Biddy chose to make no display of her conversational gifts, and merely stared round this strange house with blue eyes of tragic depth and darkness.

"She's a darlin' quiet child," said Mrs. M'Cann. "When my little boy here was that age he would be mimickin' the cocks and the pigs and meself; every noise he heard he made an offer at most extr'ornary. But, och, woman dear, put down your heavy basket out of your hand and sit in to the fire till I get yous a sup of milk. I didn't know there was a fair in the town to-day."

"Nor there isn't e'er a one," said Mrs. Morissy. "But I promised ould Mr. Noblett I'd bring him the butter and eggs widout fail. It's scarce enough the eggs is these times. I'm a week gadrin' a couple of dozen, and they do be short of them for the shop. Sixpence a dozen is all the ould man allows me for the eggs, and the same for the pound of me butter—lovely fresh butter and eggs; it's no price at all. But I'd be afraid of me life to disappoint him, for you see, ma'am, he's got an account agin us already long enough to paper your wall round wid, and it's to him we'll have to be lookin' for borryin' Jim's passage-money to Liverpool in June. If he can't git over to the harvest, I dunno what's to become of us at all. So I thought I'd do better to be steppin' along wid the basket, wet or dry."

"Sure, now, you maybe might so," said Mrs. M'Cann, "but sit down anyway till it takes up. Your basket's all right where it is, ma'am, behind the door. There's not a drop comes in under it now ever since himself made the grand little trinch over to the gripe for runnin' off the wather. He's a terrible handy man about the place when he's at home. You needn't be afeard of anythin' happ'nin' it."

As far as danger from inundations went Mrs. M'Cann was justified in her confidence, and yet she gave her guest a very false feeling of security. Cocky withdrew from the apartment almost immediately after the visitor's arrival. His mother said he was shy. In point of fact he was generally irked by the society of small children, unless they had sense enough to be tormented. He did pull several ugly faces at Miss Biddy Morissy, but for any effect they produced he might as well have made grimaces at the solemn eastern blue before sunrise. So he slipped away, and stood in the little passage with its door opening into the rain.

There his attention presently turned to Mrs. Morissy's big market basket, which was set against the half-high partition wall, out of view from the room within. Naturally he poked up the loosely tied-down lid to observe its contents. "Musha, good gracious," he said to himself as they appeared, "but she has a great power of eggs." To this colourless reflection, however, succeeded another of a complexion quite different. The sudden thought occurred to him that it would be a grand thing if he could exchange some of those fine fresh eggs for Toppy's unlucky clutch, because then their parboiled condition would never be discovered, by any of his belongings at least, nor, consequently, would his piece of folly ever be brought home to him. It was Cocky's habit to execute with dispatch his boldly-conceived designs, and before many moments elapsed he had staggered cautiously out, bearing the heavy basket, to Toppy's narrow shed. His operations there seemed to be supervised by some singularly handy good luck, as he accomplished the transfer of the eggs very rapidly, without any breakages, and had safely restored the basket to its former place several minutes before Mrs. Morissy finished recounting the latest vicissitudes of her life, and was ready to start again in a treacherous gleam of sunshine. Nothing did she surmise of any tampering with her wares.

On this occasion Cocky behaved so nicely, lifting the basket, and pushing back the packing-case gate for their visitor, that his mother was rapt in proud admiration of his polished manners. His amiability was simply due to his satisfaction at the trick he had played, but Mrs. M'Cann fondly took his unwonted courtesy for a sign that he proposed to be "a rael good child entirely," wherein she, too, was much mistaken, and promptly set to rights.

The temporary clearing up appeared to her a suitable opportunity for prosecuting her inquiry into the condition of Toppy's eggs, off which she therefore enticed that patient sitter to flop after a lure of potato parings. She was just tapping a warm egg warily on the edge of the metal dish that had held these, when a shrill shout of re-

monstrance startled her.   Cocky had been swimming his cap in a large adjacent puddle, and
pleasing himself with the thought that now he
and Toppy might have a brood of little fluffety
chickens after all, when he espied his mother's
approach to the shed, and at once sped in hot
haste to stay her proceedings.   "You've smashed
it," he howled, perceiving that he had come too
late, "you've smashed it on me, and I after
biddin' you to let thim be."

Mrs. M'Cann, however, was for the instant
deafened by amazement at what she saw.
"Why, I declare to the great goodness," she
said, "it looks to ha' been laid only this minyit
of time.   Saw you ever the like?   And she over
three weeks sittin'—as fresh as anythin' it is."

"Of coorse it is, and you've tuk and bruck it;
the biggest one of thim all.   Disthroyed the best
of me chuckens—that's what you've done,"
Cocky clamoured, kicking up in his fury large
splashes of liquid mud against the front of the
shed, out of which his mother was awkwardly
backing.

"Och, thin, stop that, child dear," she entreated
him; "you'll have me a mask of dirt—your
father 'ill hear you—and you're terrifyin' the
hin."   Cocky upon this last consideration stopped
short in the act of hurling a stray turf-sod with
the mien of an angry monkey.   "But as for

chuckens, what chance is there of e'er a one after all this while? Ne'er an atom of use it is to be keepin' her any longer on such unnathural ould eggs. But sure, sure honey, I won't be touching them at all." She hastened to add, finding that she had touched unseen springs which set him dancing again like a belligerent ostrich, "she has tin left yet, and that's plinty." Cocky yelled: "Plinty, is it?" and, jumping high, flung down the sod into the pigsty amid profuse spattering.

"I'll tell you what I'll do, doaty darlin'," she urged. "If you'll be a good boy, and whisht, and not let your poor father see you behavin' yourself bold, I'll fry you the cracked egg for your dinner wid a taste of his fat bacon. It'll make a lovely bit of kitchen to your pitaties, and the little hin can be sittin' as long as you plase; I won't meddle or make wid her. There, jewel."

Upon these terms peace was patched up. At dinner-time Cocky enjoyed the fried egg with an injured air, and replied with aggrieved forbearance when his father joked about his luxurious meal. Later on he attempted to exhort from his mother a further concession of pitaty-cake for his tea; but as she was out of buttermilk, he had to content himself with an unsatisfying bounty of sugar on his crust of bread.

The following fortnight was a somewhat uneventful one for Cocky. He spent a large part of

it in keeping jealous watch and ward over Toppy,
against whose continued sitting he was well
aware that his mother had received much neigh-
bourly advice, especially from the old Widow
Goligher, the original proprietress, if he had but
known, of the white, top-knotted bird, which he
had been beguiled into accepting as his lost
favourite. That circumstance now gave all the
more unseemliness to the taunts and threats with
which he assailed her one day when he had un-
fortunately overheard her recommending the re-
moval of the clutch.

"You'd take them away unbeknownst you
wud, wud you, you ould tormint?" he said, pop-
ping up from behind the dandelion-studded bank
to glare furiously at her, as she stood by her
own door in converse with Mrs. M'Cann. "Bedad, now you're the quare ould impident woman
to be managin' other people's hins. What's gone
wrong wid your own little white one, I'd like to
know, that was as ugly as sin to Toppy? If it's
died she is on you, it's my belief you starved the
life out of her wid never feedin' her rightly at
all, that's what *you* done; and now if you don't
keep your tongue off interfering wid Toppy,
that's no business of yours, I'll be very apt to let
out your ould skinny pig there, and hunt him till
he drops down."

The Widdy might well reiterate that poor

Mrs. M'Cann was to be pitied with him, the
dacint woman. But she had neighbours who
were even more pitiable.

One morning, soon after, Mrs. Morissy paid
the M'Canns another visit. This time she
brought neither baby nor basket, and had a story
to tell, according to which the state of her affairs
was truly commiserable. For she related in the
first place how little Biddy was took bad, the
crathur. The doctor couldn't rightly say what
it was ailed her; some sort of wakeness like
and she seemed to be just dwindlin' away, and
their fine young cow was after dyin' on them,
indeed yes. And then there had been terrible
work about that last basket of eggs she'd brought
into the shop. "Sure, ma'am, the next time I
looked in there, I found Mr. Noblett ragin' mad
with me. For, sez he, the one half of them two
dozen eggs was the most awful things he'd ever
witnessed; and he had a couple kep to show me,
and bedad I'd niver seen or smelt the aquil of
them. I dunno what they were like at all. But
divil aught amiss was there wid me own eggs I
well know. So, sorra a pinny would I get for
the good ones itself, and he bid me not to be
bringin' butter or eggs or anythin' else next or
nigh his place the longest day I'd live. 'Twas
no fault of mine, that's certain, but it's on'y impidence and abuse I got when I passed a remark

about them to the women I'd gad'red some of
them from, bedad did I." Mrs. Morissy's insin-
uated suspicions had, indeed, made havoc of her
amity with her neighbours, and had left her an
estranged and resourceless woman. "And now
I'm just after thrampin' over to Noblett's to thry
would they be anyways more raisonable," she
continued, "but not a bit of it. Bawlin' to me
to quit he was, like as if he was scarin' crows.
Afeard I was to so much as ax him for the thrifle
of groats I wanted bad for the child, and the big
tin full of them starin' at me off of the shelf
fornint the counter. I'm bothered what to say
to it all."

Mrs. M'Cann could say nothing more to the
purpose than:—"Well, now that was quare and
conthrary, and that ould Noblett's an ould lad.
I declare you might think there was some manner of *pishtrogues* put on the eggs this year, for
they beat everythin'. But if I was you, ma'am,
I'd be apt to give the little crathur a spoonful of
applemint tay. I heard tell not so long ago of a
poor man was cured with it, that was bad with
paliasses. Them herbs do be very lucky things
sometimes." So Mrs. Morissy by and by departed, faintly cheered, bearing this prescription
in her mind, and in a quaint patterned mug a
drop of new milk for Biddy.

Now Cocky had been present during her tale

of woes, and as he listened to it, there had crept
over him an unusual and uncomfortable feeling,
which was nothing more nor less than self-re-
proach.   He had always taken it for granted
that the loss of the spoiled eggs would fall upon
Mr. Noblett, whom nobody liked, and whom
everybody called an ould naygur, so that to do
him a bad turn might be considered rather praise-
worthy than otherwise, not that Cocky was wont
to concern himself greatly about the meritorious-
ness of his actions.   The discovery of the misfor-
tunes which his method of extricating himself
from his embarrassment had incidentally drawn
down upon the Morissys, came to him, therefore,
with something of a shock, and set the seldom
used machinery of his conscience going.   It
worked without much force, yet with a disagreeable amount of friction.   He did not reach the
point of wishing that he had not taken the eggs;
but he did somehow wish that he had not made
faces at the big-eyed baby.

Wishes of that sort are a weak relief for remorseful twinges, and these continued to molest
him intermittently throughout the rest of the
day, until towards bed-time a more efficacious
remedy suggested itself.   It occurred to him that
when Toppy's chickens were hatched, he might
present Mrs. Morissy with one of them.   This
would be a handsome reparation, he thought, as

he knew that she would have had no more than sixpence for the dozen eggs, while he had heard his mother say that you would get as much as ninepence for a good chicken.

"Be the hokey I will so," he said to himself as he began to fall asleep.

And as if to reward this virtuous resolve, on the very next morning he found that the chickens had come out. Ten of them there were, for not a single one had perished, or was even a laggard, and such splendid chuckens had never, of course, been seen in Ballylogan. They were, it must be admitted, a mixed lot, all uniformly downy and pipy-voiced, but as to size and colour and shape varying in degrees which became more perceptible day by day. Cocky's joy in them was extreme, and the sole inevitable drop of bitterness that mingled with it came from the thought that one of the lovely brood must go as a gift to Kilmacreagh. He spent a good deal of his leisure in choosing "Mrs. Morissy's chucken," and the task seemed to get only more difficult as time went on. For a while he had almost fixed upon a black one, because he had three of that hue; but they all throve so grandly that he had to abandon the idea. Then a little white one that had got its eye hurt seemed an appropriate offering, until its eye was cured, and he fancied he saw signs of an incipient top-knot, which again

altered his views.   Later on an ungainly, long-
legged, specklety bird, which walked over its
brethren with enormous feet, promised to be the
least precious of the brood; but it grew so very
tame and cute, and developed such an engaging
way of galloping to meet him whenever he came
near, that he felt himself really quite unable to
face the prospect of a parting.   Moreover, as he
often reflected, he would have only *nine* chuckens left, and somehow or other—he could not
have given any definite reason—still he certainly
did especially wish to have *ten*.   The matter
worried him not a little, nor could he see any
way of shaking off the self-imposed obligation.
But at last a new light flashed upon him.

It was a softly fading pink June sunset, and
Cocky, leaning half dreamily against the door of
the pigsty, had not been thinking particularly
about the chickens or anything else, when all at
once he stood up straight with a gleam of
triumph in his eyes.   " Musha long life to it," he
said, " but meself's the quare gaby to not have
remimbered it sooner.   Why, the big egg mother
tuk and bruck on me—why tubbe sure in coorse
that one was Mrs. Morissy's chucken."

AS LUCK WOULD HAVE IT

AS LUCK WOULD HAVE IT

SOME of you may have heard how,[1] last St. Patrick's Day was a year, very old Mrs. Rea, who had fully determined to celebrate it by an excursion from Letterowen to Dublin, found herself, almost at the last moment, obliged to put off her travels for a twelvemonth, and let Dinny Fitzpatrick go instead. Of course, so long a postponement made the ultimate carrying out of the project more or less doubtful, a fact of which her friend and contemporary, Julia Carroll, did not fail to keep her in mind, often dwelling upon the many odd things that might happen, that would send ould bodies like them thravellin' a dale farther than Dublin, a long while sooner than next March. Julia was led to repeat such remarks partly by disapproval of Mrs. Rea's plan, and partly by a certain pleasure which she herself took in the prospect of that longer journey. "If one had e'er a notion at all," her friend would sometimes grumble, "what manner of road they'll be taking a body." But Julia would rejoin serenely: "Ah, sure, 'twill be quare if it's not more

[1] The Stay-at-Homes (*A Creel of Irish Stories*).

agreeable at all evints than them rackety ould
thrains."

However, when St. Patrick's Day came round
again, on her long-meditated expedition Mrs.
Rae did go, in a way. But *in a way* it was, as
people say, meaning, in a way not of their own.
For she went less on pleasure than on business,
and rather melancholy business too. It was connected with a very deplorable accident which
had befallen Dan Fitzpatrick about a month before. Dan was the oldest of the young Fitzpat-
ricks, and the best liked of his family, who were
generally regarded as persons to be respected for
their quick wits and upright dealing, and mis-
trusted for the crossness of their tempers. Hot
they unquestionably were, some in a flaring, some
in a smouldering fashion, both detrimental to
friendliness and good-fellowship. Only Dan was
an exception, being a big, soft-hearted, easy-going
man, not over-clever, a safe subject for pleasant-
ries, and a maker and mender of peace. So there
were regrets both at home and abroad, when
during the past summer Dan went away to work
in the city of Dublin, at the other end of the
country. The neighbours said about this proceeding that Dan was a great fool to do any
such thing; that Dublin was a place where you
couldn't tell what might be after happening to a
person before you'd hear a word of it, no more

than if they were in the States; that Maggie
M'Grehan was at the bottom of it for sartin—
you might depend sorra aught else would have
made Dan, that thought such a heap of his own
people, go take off with himself away from them
all, high wages or low wages. They also said, in
selecter conversations, that Maggie would liefer
have got Dan's brother Dinny, and only when
she saw that he would have nobody but her sister Norah, she settled her mind to put up with
Dan—who was too good for her, they often
added.

There was some truth in this gossip. At any
rate, it was true that Dan's departure to Dublin
had been caused by a conditional half-promise
from Maggie M'Grehan. She would have nothing to say, she declared, to ten shillings a week
and living in an ugly little hole like Letterowen,
that she was sick of the sight of; but if a man
was earning decent wages, and in a place where
you were not apt to get moped to death entirely,
it would be a different pair of brogues. Furthermore, she admitted that the man might be Dan
Fitzpatrick. Whereupon, off one August morning he went to look for a job of well-paid work
which was offered on a Dublin railway. His
hope was that by Shrovetide he would be in a
position to fetch home a wife, and for some time
this seemed likely enough. But now the latest

news of him that had reached Letterowen was
the woeful story of his being run over on the
North Wall by a dray, with the resulting loss of
his right arm. This calamity, having trampled
all Dan's prospects into the dust, cast a shadow
over the festivities with which the wedding of
his brother Dinny and Maggie's sister, Norah
M'Grehan, was attended at Shrovetide, just a
fortnight before St. Patrick's Day. Everybody
supposed at first that the occasion would be a
specially trying one to Maggie, with her bride-
groom that was to have been lying maimed in hospital, and people wondering how at all he would
contrive now to keep himself, let alone a wife.
They were quite ready to bestow sympathy and
condolence; but Maggie lost no time in making
it plain that these would be completely thrown
away upon her. So prompt was she indeed about
disclaiming any personal concern in the disaster,
that Letterowen presently buzzed and clacked
with reports of her heartless demeanour.

"Would you like to know what I heard her
sayin' meself on'y this mornin'?" to the Widdy
Cornish said Mrs. Hannigan, on the Sunday after
the sad tidings had arrived. "Kate M'Grehan
was telling Mrs. M'Cann, from Ballylogan, and
they goin' in to eleven o'clock mass, and, sez Mrs.
M'Cann, ' Och, but is it his *right* arm the poor
man's afther losin'?'

"'Deed is it,' sez Kate.

"'Ay, bedad,' sez Maggie, 'you may trust Dan Fitzpatrick to make a rael botch of a thing when he's about it. That's most all he was ever good for,' sez she. And a grand blue scarf round the throat of her that minyit that the crathur sent her in a prisint at the new year."

"She'll be takin' up wid somebody else before Easter, you'll see," the Widdy predicted.

"It's quare, now, the differ there is in the same people," said Mrs. Hannigan. "For Norah and Kate are kind-hearted girls, the both of them, and Maggie herself's friendly-spoken enough when she plases. A pretty slip of a crathur she is, too. You'd never think, to look at her, that she'd be apt to talk so unfeelin'."

"Ah, she's no nathur in her, sorra a bit; that's what ails her," said the Widdy Cornish. "And if *she* was all that poor Dan's got shut of, maybe he'd ha' no great loss. But his hand—och, the unlucky bosthoon, what 'ill he do at all?"

This question was often asked just then in Letterowen, and as often left unanswered. It seemed so puzzling, in fact, that the neighbours commonly gave it up, falling back upon commiserations of Dan and censure of Maggie, neither of which was much to the purpose. There was one person, however, who could find no relief in such unpractical measures for the sorrow of her heart,

and that was the mother of Dan, an infirm old
woman, with few resources at her command.
She came creeping up to Mrs. Rea's door two or
three sunsets before St. Patrick's Day, and
quickly made it clear that the object of her call
was to ascertain whether Mrs. Rea still kept her
purpose of going on the cheap railway excursion
up to Dublin. "They're advertisin' it this good
while below at the station, you might ha' noticed,
ma'am," she said. "So I suppose you'll be off
fine and early the way you was intendin'."

Last year Mrs. Fitzpatrick had been among the
most earnest of Mrs. Rea's advisers against the
venture, on the ground that it was no thing for
an ould body at her time of life to think of doing. But now, inconsistently enough, she added
suggestively, watching Mrs. Rea's face with anxious eyes: "The fare's oncommon raisonable
enough, that's the truth ; it's a great chance. If
I was able for it at all I wouldn't be long runnin'
up," and her expression grew piteously woe-begone when Mrs. Rea replied : " 'Deed, then,
ma'am, I've as many as twenty minds to not stir
a fut. You was all tellin' me last time I was
too ould for jiggettin' about the world, and very
belike I am so. I'd git more wid less goin', as
the cow said, and they drivin' her to the fair."

Several circumstances had combined of late to
make Mrs. Rea less energetic and enterprising

than usual. To begin with, she had, in the course of poetical justice, caught "a rael bad could intirely," no make-believe like what she had feigned that time twelvemonth, that Dinny Fitzpatrick might visit Dublin in her stead; and this had left her depressed and languid. Poor Dan's mishap, too, had a discouraging effect; and the weather threatened to be unkind.

"Ah, to be sure, you must plase yourself, ma'am; it's nothin' to me," Mrs. Fitzpatrick said, in deep dejection. "I was only thinkin'—you'r threatenin' it so long—you might have the notion yit. And I was only thinkin', if bechance you had happened to ha' wint, you might maybe ha' left an odd thrifle of a few things for me wid that poor child up at the hospital, and brought me word what way he was lookin' at all, and if there was e'er a chance they'd be lettin' him home to me any time. It's ould ages since I seen a sight of him. Ne'er another one there is I could be axin'; they're all took up at home wid themselves and their foolery and no talk of goin'. But sure what matter at all about it? I'd ha' ped anybody's fare and welcome."

But after all she was not going to be disappointed in that way. Mrs. Rea's ardour for roving, though it had flagged somewhat, was by no means extinct, and now this proposed errand stirred it up and gave it fresh fuel, at which it kindled again as warmly as ever, so that to Mrs. Fitzpatrick's great relief she answered —

"Pay the fare to your great-grandmother's cat. Sure, ma'am, dear, it's as plased as anythin' I'll be to go see poor Dan. He and I was always great since he wasn't the size of a frog-hopper. And anythin' you was wantin' to send him, I could be takin' along in me basket as aisy as lookin' at them."

So Dan's mother went home half-comforted, and spent the evening in packing up and unpacking some small parcels, that would certainly be ready in good time. It seemed to her a step towards getting back her son, who was twice as valuable now that everybody had begun to say he would never be fit for anything again. "Glory be to God, he has his two feet on him yet," she said to herself, as she folded up a pair of socks.

By the time that Mrs. Rea was setting off in the early grey of St. Patrick's morning, her big, old, much-battered market-basket had grown more than half-full of different things. For, when Letterowen heard of her mission, many of the neighbours entrusted her with various little presents, chiefly fair-complexioned fresh eggs, and swarthy lumps of tobacco, but including an old, long-treasured Christmas card from the Widdy Cornish, and a postage-stamp, which Joe

M'Keown had kept in an empty match-box for the last five years without finding occasion to affix it. The Christmas card was ironically extravagant in its gilt good wishes, and Mrs. Rea had been charged with dozens of others that Dan's well-wishers could send only in a still more portable form. Yet notwithstanding that, when she had added her own substantial round of girdle cake, there remained but little spare room in her basket, and though her memory was stored with many a " And Mrs. Carroll bid me say," and " Your brother Dinny tould me to tell you," she felt as if something important lacked. Maggie M'Grehan had given her no message, not a word ; " And," thought Mrs. Rea, " the crathur up there'll be lookin' out for a one, that I know right well."

She was careful, accordingly, to introduce the subject of her expedition whenever she fell in with Maggie, and, on St. Patrick's eve, meeting her at the shop, and finding that hints, broad and broader, produced no effect, asked her point blank whether she had e'er a message for Dan.

" And what at all have I to say to sendin' messages to Dan Fitzpatrick ? " Maggie demanded, with ostentatious surprise.

" You'd plenty to say to his goin' up to Dublin and gettin' himself destroyed," said Mrs. Rea.

" Did anybody ever hear such blathers and non-

sense? As if I was after biddin' the man take
and rowl himself under the ould cart-wheels,"
Maggie protested, flouncing angrily away.

But a bit later on that same evening she presented herself in Mrs. Rea's kitchen, with some
little shame in her face, and in her hand a pink-
glazed cardboard box, with a strip of looking-
glass in the lid. "'Twas Dan Fitzpatrick sent
it to me awhile ago for houldin' hair-pins," she
said, laying it on the table, "so I was wonderin',
Mrs. Rea, as you had talk of carrying messages,
if you'd think bad of takin' it back to him, and
just tellin' him I've no use for it. I don't want
people to be passin' remarks about me gettin'
prisints from him these times."

Maggie had tried very hard to put her new
blue scarf into the box; but she possessed so
few others, and this one had such a lovely satiny
gloss and was of so becoming a colour that she
really could not.

Evidently Mrs. Rea did think very badly indeed of the proposal. If she had been requested
to swallow the box whole, she could scarcely
have eyed it with more disfavour. "Troth and
bedad, will I do no such a thing," she said, waving it off her table as though it were red-hot.
"If that's the only word of kindness you have
for him, you may thravel off and be takin' it
to him yourself. And it's my belief you might

thravel a dale farther after that agin before you find e'er a body little-good-for enough to match wid you—a heartless baggage as ever I set my eyes on," she commented, as Maggie retired hastily with her rejected commission.

But Mrs. Rea had again to set disapproving eyes upon Maggie M'Grehan only a few hours afterwards, when, the bustle of bundling into the early morning excursion train having subsided, they found themselves seated opposite to one another in the same compartment, and along with Maggie was Con Goligher, affable and insinuating; obviously she had taken up with somebody else. Perhaps they would have the face to go and see Dan, Mrs. Rea thought; however, it appeared that they were going no farther than Powerstown Junction, where they alighted, and relieved her for the latter half of her journey from the duty of staring stonily over their heads.

The first thing Mrs. Rea did upon arriving towards noon in Dublin was to lose her way completely, or rather utterly fail to find it. For a very long hour she was astray in the bewildering streets, and not before she had been grievously affronted by a lady, who interrupted her preliminary "I beg your pardon, ma'am," with a glum "I've nothing for you," and not until she had begun to feel hopeless, as she desperately clutched her basket's worn handles, of ever again beholding another familiar object, did the wide hall of the right hospital receive her, and a wonderfully pleasant-spoken young nurse assure her that Daniel Fitzpatrick might be seen in a ward close by.

It was, on the whole, a joyful meeting. Her pleasure at the almost despaired-of sight of a friend, and the unexpected discovery that he was well enough to be up and dressed, took the edge off Mrs. Rea's melancholy observations of how gaunt he looked "wid the face of him gone to nothin' in his beard," and then that woeful empty sleeve. Dan, on his part, was delighted at a glimpse of Letterowen; and he had, moreover, good news to communicate—no less than that he had just got his discharge, and would be setting off for home in another hour or so. "Great argufyin' I had wid Dr. Clare," he said, "before he was contint to give me lave. But I tould him of the terrible chape fares there would be on the thrains runnin' this day, so the end of it was I had him persuaded I might, and I'm goin' on the two-thirty from the Broadstone."

"Glory be to goodness, Dan; then I'll go along wid you, and we might have a better chance of findin' our ways out of it," Mrs. Rea said, hopefully. They were sitting at a window by the head of Dan's bed in the long bleak ward, and she looked out over the grey roof ridges with a doubtful expression, as if she were contemplating the billows of a perilous sea which had to be crossed.

"Ooh, that'll be grand," said Dan; "only then, ma'am, you'll ha' seen scarce a sight of Dublin at all—the Phanix, and the Pillar, and——"

"Man alive," said Mrs. Rea, "it's the quare sights of this place I'll be behouldin' wid my good will. Sure, wasn't I thrapesin' thro' it and thro' it and round about it just now like a sthrayed heifer, wid me head in and out of a dozen big doors till me heart was broke, and sorra the dacint-lookin' thing I seen in the whole of it, only a fine hape of turf they have sittin' beside the canal, close be the edge of the wather there, wid the little ripples tug-tuggin' at the image of it, like as if they was tryin' to pull it in pieces and wash it away back to wherever it come from. Rael nathural it looked. I was sayin' to meself I'd give a dale meself to be stookin' sods that minyit on our ould bog at home."

"Ne'er a one 'ill I be cuttin' this year," Dan said, with a sudden droop of his head, as if something had fallen on it. "Bedad, it's the quare bad offer I'd be makin' at it now, ma'am, wouldn't it?"

"Oh, boy, dear, maybe you might be doin' somethin' betther," Mrs. Rea said, feeling the vagueness of her encouragement.

"I dunno what at all it's apt to be, thin," said
Dan.   "There's such a power of things you want
to take your two hands to, let alone a left one
that needn't set up to be the half of a pair, not
be any manner of manes.   I'd ha' had more of a
chance if they'd took one of these ould brogues
on me," he said, looking down at his feet.   "For
I might ha' conthrived to stump about after me
work in some sort of a way.   But, sure, now I
may thramp to the world's end, and what 'ud I
do when I got there?   Walkin's no more use to
me than it 'ud be to this ould chair.   Howan'e'er,
'twas as luck would have it, ma'am, and that's all
can be said.   And, well now, yourself was the
rael dacint woman to come see me.   And what
way did you lave them all at home?"

Mrs. Rea was more than willing that their discussion should turn upon the news of Letterowen
and the contents of her basket, and at first the
distribution and display of them went on glibly
and satisfactorily.   "Grandly your mother is
looking, ay is she so, *considerin'*.   And them's
the socks she knit you; and she bid me tell you
not to be frettin' about anythin' but come straightways home to her the first minyit you could.
Och, it's quarely plased the crathur'll be this
night.   And your brother Dinny and Norah
M'Grehan are doin' finely.   He's sendin' you a
bit of rael Irish twist.   They've got Martin

O'Connor's little house at the turn in Brierly's
boreen, and Mr. Hamilton's just after givin' Dinny
another shillin' a-week to do the odd jobs of car-
penterin' up about the place."

"Ay, bedad, Dinny was oncommon handy wid
the tools," said Dan.   "It's lucky 'twasn't him it
happint to anyway.   That would ha' been a pity
and a half."

But after a short while Mrs. Rea began to feel
that they had not changed the subject for the
better.   It would have been easier to deal with
Dan's gloomiest forecasts of his future than with
the wistful glances that watched the parcels coming out of her basket, and the expectant pauses
which lengthened after each of his leading questions.   "And how's poor Johnny M'Grehan gettin' on these times?   I haven't any news of them
this great while.   He would be disthressed wid
the sevare weather last month. . . .   But it's
plased he'll be to have Norah settled so near.
. . .   Did you say there was any talk about
Kate's goin' out to service?   It was rael good-
nathured of her to be sending me the bunch of
coltsfoot; an iligant smell it has off of it.   And
Kate it was that sent it, ma'am?"   Once she
caught him in the act of stealthily groping round
the inside of the basket with his clumsy single
hand, and although he, with a sort of laugh, declared himself to be only counting how many eggs

she had brought him, she knew only too well
that he was really trying to feel whether there
still remained some little packet overlooked.
But everything had been delivered, even the
postage stamps, and Mrs. Rea, with that in her
mind which made her garbled statements sound
as false to herself as they were disappointing to
their hearer, rejoiced when it was suddenly found
that the time for starting had arrived, and they
had to bustle away from the hospital to the terminus.

On his way home Dan was silent, and seemed
to be meditating. Their crowded train was a
slow one, that stopped wherever it could find an
excuse, and Mrs. Rea noticed that at all the sta-
tions which were large enough to own a bookstall Dan emerged from his reveries, and kept
eager eyes upon it as long as it was in sight.
The garish litter on counter and shelves evidently
had some fascination for him. Yet Dan's tastes
were by no means studious. At length, as they
were steaming slowly out of Ballylavin, he mut-
tered, half-aloud: "They had a one in it there,
right enough; I seen it hangin' up, if the ould
naygurs would but stop aisy and give you a
chance to be gittin' it. But, sure, you never
can tell that they won't be slitherin' off
agin wid themselves on you before your feet's
firm on the platform. They've no more consid-

eration now than a blast of win' goin' by," Dan grumbled, with the querulousness of a convalescent.

"What ails you then, man," Mrs. Rea said, partly overhearing, "that you're murmurin' there like an ould pitaty-pot on the boil? What at all was you wantin' to git? If it's a newspaper, there's very apt to be one of thim little chaps wid the baskets yellin' past the windy the next place we come to, and you might have a chance thin."

"'Twas just one of them sixpenny purses I'd a mind to be gittin' they have on the stalls," said Dan. "Mostly there do be plenty of them hangin' up along with the straps and other conthraptions."

"And what for would you be throwin' away your sixpinnies buyin' purses, wid little enough to put in thim?" Mrs. Rea said, thriftily reproving.

"Well, I was thinkin'—thinkin' I was," said Dan. "I'd like to be bringin' one home to— Maggie." He tried to take the name out of its long silence naturally and unconcernedly, but did not quite succeed. "I haven't got her e'er a hap'orth," he said. "Nor anybody else for the matter of that. But you see, ma'am, she wasn't sendin' me anythin' be you, and she might be takin' it into her head 'twas be raison of that I didn't, so I'm not wishful she would. 'Twould ha' been diff'rint if you was after bringin' anythin' at all. But I'll tell you the notion I have, ma'am. Very belike she was thinkin' bad to be annoyin' you wid carryin' parcels thravellin' that far, though, 'deed, now rememberin' a word in your head wouldn't ha' throubled you much—and she has a little prisint keepin' for me all this while, the crathur, at home. I'll find it when I git there. Mightn't that be the way of it, ma'am, wouldn't you think?"

"Och, I do be thinkin' many a thing," Mrs. Rea replied; and, though her words were vague, she had before her so distinct a vision of a shiny pink cardboard box no doubt waiting ready, that she added, with some bitterness in her tone: "If them that was good for nought got lost, and them that was little good for went to find them, there'd be a dale of empty sates in chapel of a Sunday mornin'," a cynical sentiment of which Dan was too much pre-occupied to make any particular application.

Soon after this the two travellers found themselves at Powerstown Junction, with half-an-hour to wait for the train which should bring them to Letterowen. This station is not a large or much frequented one, yet to Mrs. Rea, despite her Dublin experiences, it seemed an imposing scene, full of bewildering bustle, at which she preferred to look on from a bench somewhat secluded, niched between a lamp-post and an automatic machine. The grey day was nearly done, and the west, clearing for sunset behind her, flung over her head a sheaf of long ruddy rays, which slanted across to the opposite platform, and glanced at the many-tinted literature displayed upon Messrs. Eason's stall. "Bejabers, ma'am," Dan said, catching sight of it as he sat, "I'll be steppin' over there and thryin' have they e'er a purse in it at all. We've plenty of time, no fear."

"But how'll you git across all thim, lad?" she said, pointing to the network of shining metals by which their strip of platform seemed to be enisled. "Don't you go for to be settin' your feet on a one af thim rails, whatever else you may do; you niver can tell the instant or the minyit there mightn't be an ingin comin' up threacherous at the back of you, and sendin' you to desthruction. The accidents there do be in the papers is enough to terrify you."

"Sure, I'll go be the bridge," said Dan. "Sorra the accident there'll be. I've had enough of thim, bedad, to last me for the rest of me life."

Accordingly, Mrs. Rea watched the tall gaunt figure of Dan, in his loose-grown old coat, glimpsing away up and down the latticed bridge. And the next thing she saw was the gleam of a brilliant blue scarf, and there at her elbow stood

Maggie M'Grehan, with Con Goligher close by.
"Musha, good gracious, and is it yourself, Mrs.
Rea?" said Maggie. "You're early back from
Dublin!"

"Ay, it's meself," Mrs. Rea said, stiffly, "and
there's more than me back to-night from Dublin,
too. Lookit, d'you see yonder?" She nodded
towards the bookstall, where Dan, with his back
turned to them, was bargaining.

' "Och to goodness, if it isn't Dan Fitzpatrick,"
Maggie exclaimed, so loudly that Mrs. Rea, notwithstanding the broad expanse of rails said,
"Whist," apprehensively. "Don't have him to
be seein' you now the first thing, and he comin'
home wid his misfortin, if you've settled in your
mind you'll have no more to say to him. Be
steppin' on wid yourselves, you and Con, before
he turns round and gets a sight of you, there's a
good girl," Mrs. Rea said, in her anxiety conde-
scending to entreaty.

But Maggie, tired and disappointed, and dissatisfied with herself and her holiday, was as per-
verse as a fractious child; so she replied, "Musha,
cock him up. What's Dan Fitzpatrick that I
should be botherin' meself gettin' out of his way?"
And, instead of moving on, she plumped down
on the bench, saying—"There's room for you,
too, Con Goligher."

"Well, then, you Con," Mrs. Rea said, desperately, "you're a good-nathured fellow I believe; git along wid yourself anyway, and that 'ill be the next best thing."

"I don't see why at all," said Con, who, to do him justice, would have been less obtuse if he had not taken the edge off his sensibilities with too many glasses of whiskey. "Let Dan Fitzpatrick go where he plases. I'm not afraid of him, or any man in the county Cork."

Mrs. Rea uttered a despairing "wirrasthrue." The time for saying anything more to the purpose had gone by. For Dan had concluded his purchase, and, whether allured by that gleam of blue, or merely acting with the recklessness of a railway man, was coming, in disregard of all rules and bye-laws, straight back across the line. The low sun's rays blinked dazzlingly into his eyes, and may have blinded him to the fact that the down express was just going to run through; or he may have miscalculated the distance; or perhaps he did not allow for the drawback that his empty sleeve and one hand full of a little parcel would be to him in scrambling up on the platform. At all events, he was a second or so too late to elude the sliding swoop, which swept him as far away as if it had been a wave from a shoreless sea.

Maggie M'Grehan, shocked and sorry and remorseful, wailed lamentably on the twilit plat-

form. "Och, poor Dan, the saints may pity him.
There wasn't anythin' he wouldn't ha' done for
me, I well know.   Och, I wisht he'd never gone
off to Dublin.   I wisht I'd sint him e'er a bit of
a word—I wisht I had."

Con Goligher was trying to pacify her. "Sure
'twas no one's fault," he said; "it couldn't be
helped.   'Twas as luck would have it."

"Ay, to be sure," said Mrs. Rea, who was
standing by.   She could not keep out of her mind
the thought of that little pink box, and she
added : "As luck would have it, for sartin.   But
I dunno if his luck isn't as good as yours, Con,
me man."

AN OULD TORMENT

AN OULD TORMENT

THE long car which runs on Tuesdays and Fridays from Barlesky to Glenmoran seldom goes fast, and is generally at its very slowest about half-way up the tedious ascent beginning where the plantations of Castlereval over-arch the road, but emerging upon a barely bleak plateau, with a sea view ahead, partly intercepted by the nearer roofs of Ardowney village. In soft weather, when the roads "do be cruel heavy goin'," our drivers say, apologetically, the hill is climbed at such a leisurely pace that there would be time to relate fully and discuss between the foot and the top the most involved piece of gossip, and the opportunity is not often let slip. It was not so on the rather dreary autumn afternoon which found Miss Debby Rourke that far on her long day's journey from Kilclashan, a little place "the dear knows how many mile up beyond Barlesky," to Drumbeg, "a good step on the other side of Glenmoran," as Mrs. Fahy, who at this stage had become her neighbouring fellow-passenger, took occasion to explain. "And the tiresome thramp it is for a body, after one's bones has been jogglin' the best part of the day on these weary ould conthraptions of cars," she added with commiseration, for Miss Debby looked small and decrepit in a coarse grey shawl of the cheapest quality. But "No doubt me niece's conveyance will meet me in the town—Mrs. Kinsella, that is, of Shinogue Farm," Miss Debby said, with such an intolerably lofty air that the current of Mrs. Fahy's sympathy was turned all awry, and she replied, "Ay sure, the poor woman might happen to be sendin' th' ould garron in to be fetchin' some thrifle she might want, now that she's through with thrashin' her little bit of oats."

But Miss Debby's satisfaction on this day was proof against any trivial nips and pricks. The main root of it was that she felt herself to be so successfully carrying out a long-cherished design. Her journey southward from the remotest corner of the county Donegal had been the object of several years' planning and saving up, during which her actual enjoyments had been scanty in the extreme; and now, unlike many much-premeditated pleasures, this expedition promised to take place under peculiarly happy circumstances. Its immediate occasion was highly auspicious. Mrs. Kinsella, a widowed niece, struggling with an unmanageable holding, had written to announce the engagement of her only daughter to Francis McEnery, a thriving young farmer in the neighbourhood, which, she said, was more

than ever Lizzie could have looked for, poor girl!
and would be the making of her brothers, poor
boys! Francis owned a good little bit of land,
and had no parents nor brethren living, nor any
drawback except a father's sister that kept house
for him, and was warranted to clear out of it
when he brought home his wife. The letter was
full of exultation undisguised save by eccentric
spelling. Miss Debby chose to accept it as an
invitation to attend the wedding. Few things,
indeed, could have been further from the writer's
intentions or wishes; but it fell in exactly with
those of the reader, and in such cases the reader
has sometimes a terrible power to construe *ad
lib*.

It seemed to her a splendid chance. Miss
Debby liked society and variety, but had experienced little of either, as early in life she
had quitted Drumbeg to rough it along with a
needy brother on a lonesome mountainy farm,
and since his death had lived even poorlier as
lodge-keeper of a derelict demesne on five shillings a week, eked out by knitting and poultry.
No doubt it may be considered unfortunate that
on the few occasions when she had met with her
relatives at Shinogue Farm she had impressed
them unfavourably as a prying sort of person,
prone to make and publish ungratifying notes.
For unkindly observation is sometimes resented

almost as deeply by one's neighbours as inoffen-
sive indifference. Nevertheless, Miss Debby was
now fully determined to pay a long-threatened
visit, and she made arrangements for an absence
which she hoped might extend up to Christmas,
if not beyond it. She expected to put in at least
a month with her niece Nannie Kinsella, and she
had sundry old acquaintanceships in the district,
which she counted upon as likely to be value for
a certain amount of board and lodging. Sentiment and a strictly commercial spirit mixed
themselves queerly in her forecasts of her prospects. Early in November was the date mentioned for the wedding by Mrs. Kinsella, and
October had not yet run out. But Miss Debby
quoted to herself: *It is better to hinder folk at
the setting on than help them with the readying
up;* a proverb intended as a warning against
belated arrival at a feast; and she had resolved
to allow herself an ample margin. As a further
precaution, she had been careful not to post the
announcement of her coming until there was no
time left for her niece to write and put her
off, even if so disposed. "They'll be bound to
take me in, like it or lump it," she reflected
with triumph whenever she recalled this bit of
strategy.

Therefore she was not in the least abashed by
Mrs. Fahy's studiously disparaging tone, and re-

plied with unabated self-importance: "Ay, bedad, it's themselves 'ill be bound to have plinty of sendin' and fetchin' these times, wid the weddin' comin' on."

But Miss Debby's pride had indeed reached its destined falling place; and another shove from her travelling companion brought it heavily down. "'Deed now, it's to be pitied are they, the poor people!" Mrs. Fahy said not uncomplacently. "Greatly knocked about they must be wid young McEnery takin' and breakin' off the match."

"What talk have you, woman?" Miss Debby said, with a jump which so nearly toppled her off the car that she had to recover her balance by a strangling clutch at Mrs. Fahy's shawl. "Sure it's only a fortnight last Thursday since I got the letter from me niece, tellin' me all the news of how it was settled at Michaelmas. If you've heard anythin' diff'rent, somebody's after makin' a fool of you."

Her obvious perturbation, mocking her professed incredulity, was exceedingly agreeable to Mrs. Fahy, who replied with a calm assumption of the facts, more convincing than any argument: "In coorse it's been a terrible upset to them. And it's not as if there was a word agin poor Lizzie. Everybody's sayin' they ought to have the law of him. But sure two lone women

like her and her mother has no chance of doin'
anythin' widout e'er a man to look after the law-
yers. It's losin' money they'd be. If her brother
Patrick was a couple of year or so oulder, he'd
have a right to be cloutin' McEnery over the
head, but he's only a spalpeen yet. Bedad now,
I think we're all talkin' about it these last three
weeks, or very near, ma'am, letter or no."

So at Glenmoran, where the car stopped, and no
conveyance met her, Miss Debby started on her
long walk to Drumbeg in a disconcerted mood.
She had slightly relieved her feelings by remark-
ing to Mrs. Fahy when assisting her to alight with
a flop: "An ould body that's gettin' as mighty
clumsy as you are, ma'am, has no business to
be thravellin' on these awkward ould cars. You
might as aisy as not twist your ankle round gettin' off, and niver put your fut straight under
you agin, the way it happint to a poor woman I
knew." But this gave her only a passing gratification. The effect which this sudden deplorable over-clouding of her grand-niece's future
would probably have upon her own reception and
entertainment at Shinogue Farm was naturally
what chiefly occupied her mind, not, however,
entirely to the exclusion of some impersonal interest about the details of the event, and a wish
to ascertain the correctness of various theories
as touching its cause, which had been put for-

ward during her past half-hour's gossip with stout
Mrs. Fahy.

Her hopes of, at any rate, satisfying her curiosity upon reaching the farm might have been
smaller if she had known how things were going
on there. A dead silence, in fact, prevailed between mother and daughter upon the subject
which occupied their thoughts, and Mrs. Kinsella
would have had to own herself as ignorant almost
as the speculating neighbours about the ins and
outs of the matter. From the first onset of the
trouble, Lizzie had been unapproachably incom-
municative; and a brief statement that she would
have nothing more to say to Francis McEnery
was the only account she gave of the abrupt
change of plans which had all at once transformed her glowing vivacity into a dumb and
gloomy study in black and white. One day Mrs.
Kinsella, after long, wistful watching, ventured
to say, but dared not address the remark to anybody in particular: "It's better off many a girl
is at home than she would be in e'er a place else,
when all's said and done. And, anyway, the dear
knows her mother's better off to get the chance
to be keepin' her awhile—and the longer the better—instead of to be lonesome and fretted wid
missin' the pleasant face of her about the house."

From Lizzie, who, truth to say, was at that moment dismally scowling, this declaration elicited

no response, unless we should count as such the
fact that in the course of the same afternoon she
spontaneously remarked upon the fineness of the
young pig Mrs. Kinsella was rearing, and said he
looked real beautiful.   If she did, in truth, think
him so, he was the one agreeable object she beheld
in a world all grown waste and ugly ever since that
morning a long fortnight ago when a certain
letter had arrived, to which she had replied by
hurriedly making up a parcel of small miscellaneous articles, and running down to post it
herself at Killoughal post-office, near the cross-
roads.   It was of trifling bulk, and weighed
only fourpence-worth of stamps, yet the absence
of its contents left a terrible gap in her life, and
had somehow given whatever she met with an
ill-favoured aspect. Consequently, it seemed only
"all of a piece with the rest" when another
letter came bearing the singularly unwelcome
news that they must expect to see Aunt Debby
Rourke before night.   Lizzie, indeed, had received the tidings of this fresh calamity in total
silence.   Mrs. Kinsella, stricken with remorse at
having incurred it by a superfluous bit of vain-
glory, and a subsequent faint-hearted suppression
of the mortifying latest intelligence, offered,
though not without evident twinges of scruple,
to "go meet th' ould torment at Glenmoran, and
tell her they couldn't conthrive to put her up by

any manner of manes." But Lizzie had said,
"Och, no; let it alone; sure it's all one," and
continued to fling her few small possessions dis-
regardfully out of her bedroom into a tiny closet
adjoining, as a preliminary to the preparation of
the chamber for this self-invited guest.

So brief was the notice she had given that before these hurried operations were well accomplished, the sons of the house, who had been
acting as scouts, tumbled over one another in
their haste to report: "She's comin' along up the
lane." And two or three minutes afterwards
Mrs. Kinsella said despondently from a front
window: "Sure enough, there's herself stumpin'
in at the gate, and the dear knows, I don't, when
we'll be apt to see her stumpin' out agin. Mercy
on us all! but it's the quare show she does be
makin' of herself, wid her shawl over her head,
as if she belonged to nobody respectable in the
world . . .   and a bit of an ould sack like in
her hand, as if she was some tinker's wife out
pickin' up other people's pitaties and chuckens.
It's meself was the fool to put pen in ink to be
writin' to her. I might ha' known 'twas as good
as stirrin' up a wasp's nest wid a bit of stick."
So she descended repiningly to express her joy
and felicity.

With a characteristic fine tact Miss Debby replied: "Well now, Nannie, I only heard tell of

your upset, as I come along on me way here;
the people was all talkin' about it. But sure, sez
I, why should everybody be disappointed because
the young man's took and went off his bargain
wid your daughter — no fault of hers, very belike. And I thought I'd a right to be keepin' me
word wid yous, weddin' or no. I'm bringin' her
a pair of lovely brown woollen stockin's in a
prisent, that she can be wearin' as well single as
married, if she never gets another chance itself."

As she seemed disposed. to enlarge upon this
theme, Mrs. Kinsella desperately despatched Lizzie upstairs, by way of seeing to the lighting of a
fire, while she herself conducted Miss Debby into
the kitchen for a cup of tea, and seized the opportunity to insist that there must be no allusions
to Francis McEnery. Lizzie, she said, had never
uttered a word about him ever since the day a
letter had come from him — nobody except herself had seen it — and she had just bundled up
every little present that ever he gave her in a
parcel, and sent it away by the post. It was
most mysterious. But the girl couldn't be annoyed about the matter; and, with Mrs. Kinsella's
good-will, the young villain's name should never
be mentioned in that house. Otherwise, of
course, her Aunt Debby would be welcome to
stop the week's end out, "and she after comin'
that far for as good as nothin' at all."

"The week's end, bedad!" Miss Debby commented in her mind, with much dissatisfaction at such a limit to her stay. But for the present she judged it discreet only to say: "Sure, then, how'll you hinder her of hearin' the neighbours clackin' about him? Let alone her bein' apt to be meetin' himself continyal, goin' to chapel and market, and all manner? 'Twill be awkward enough."

"Och, for the matter of that," said Mrs. Kinsella, "we might be worse off, for, as it so happens, because of we ever goin' Killoughal ways, which is north, and the McEnerys Duncorry ways, which is south, we do be walkin' out of the other's road every step we set, and so they're not like to lay eyes on one another in half a dozen months of Sundays, unless it was by oncommon bad luck. But here's Lizzie herself comin' down again. Aunt Debby — we'd betther whist."

Miss Debby's curiosity was scarcely more than whetted when she found herself left alone for the night in her little room. There were dozens of questions about the quarrel which she earnestly desired to ask; but she felt that her niece's injunctions could not, under the circumstances, safely be disregarded. So she sought some solace in spying round and about the apartment. It did not at first sight promise to produce anything of great interest; but Miss Debby's inquisitiveness was as deft as an ant-eater's tongue

at thrusting itself into improbable crannies, and
her researches were at length repaid by a find.
Out of a crack at one corner of the old dressing-
table she poked a small bit of crumpled paper,
which seemed to have been crushed in somebody's
hand, and then stuffed into a crevice out of sight.
There was large pen-and-ink writing on it. That
this presumably had never been intended for her
perusal did not trouble her at all, and hardly
even occurred to her, as she smoothed out the
sheet with the back of her hair-brush, and began
to decipher a letter: "Moneyhill Farm," it ran,
"October 7th. My dear Lizzie,—My Aunt Rose
was asking me to meet her sister-in-law, Miss
Kelly, coming on the eleven o'clock train, and
that was the reason of my not getting out to you
on last Sunday ; and every day since that I have
had to be showing her the sights of the place,
when I could spare the time from the turnips
and mangolds, for me aunt's cold is no better yet.
And little enough there is to be showing anybody
in a little old dog-hole of a place, which is what
I call this. But you have no call to be so cross
over it, for I might slip over the fields for an
hour next Sunday, or maybe on Sunday week.
And if I knew you was on the road with your
mother, and we passing on the car, I would stop
right enough, but they never told me till we wor
round the turn. But I mean to let you know

that if any person was passing the remark that
Miss Kelly was wearing a gold-jewelled brooch,
the same as the one I am after giving to yourself,
that hers is twice as little as yours. And, according to my reckoning, it is not three weeks
all out since I was at your place with the silk
coachineel scarf, that cost the double of the
brooch. So no more at present from yours truly,
Francis McEnery."

"And with that she must needs take and
flounce off to send him back his brooches and all,
just because he happint to write in a bit of an
ugly temper. The same as herself done very
belike," Miss Debby moralised, as she finished
her spelling out. "And when that ould Aunt
Rose of his is as sure as anythin' wishful all the
while to be makin' up the match for the sister-in-
law—Miss Kelly, bedad. Och, the young gaby
—Lizzie! She's as good as made him a prisent
to the two of them now. And no more sign of a
weddin' than if I was after landin' on a black
rock in the middle of the wild says; and I dunno
what excuse I have, if themselves here make up
e'er a raison agin my stoppin' in it."

On the verge of sleep Miss Debby's last co-
herent thought clung to a vague sense that the
bringing on again of the match would surely be
to her own, if nobody else's advantage, and next
morning she woke up to a clearer and stronger

perception of this truth. She considered it, one
must admit, very exclusively from her own point
of view. To the many inconvenient and mortifying circumstances that would attend her pre-
mature return to Kilclashan without any grand
doings to brag about she was keenly alive,
while the changed fortunes of the persons most
concerned scarcely roused her sympathy at all.
Perhaps the best-defined of her sentiments, other
than purely self-regarding, was a wish for the
frustration of the designs on behalf of " the sister-
in-law, Miss Kelly," which she had promptly assumed in Francis McEnery's Aunt Rose. However, the result of her meditations was that she
appeared at breakfast with a secret plan ready
made, which impelled her to announce her purpose of going towards Glenmoran after the meal,
in quest of a cousin of hers, one Patrick McAnliffe,
whose family she had known in her younger days.
Seeing that so many " ould ages" had elapsed
since then, and that Patrick McAnliffes were
perplexingly plentiful all over the countryside,
Miss Debby's chances of lighting upon this particular kinsman seemed rather remote. Mrs.
Kinsella and Lizzie remarked on hearing of her
project, "that liker than not there was no talk
about any such ould crathur bein' in it these
times, for if he was one of the McAnliffes of
Rochestown, he must be the age of seven people

by now." But they did not discourage her from
the enterprise by any manner of means. On the
contrary, they promoted it, by arranging for her
to travel the greater part of the way in a cart
which was taking a calf to market, and as the
vehicle bumped out of the yard, they said and
assented with congratulatory grumbling that
they'd be well shut of her for the rest of the
morning, at all events—the ould torment!

Now, all the while, Miss Debby had no real
intention of prosecuting researches among the
Patrick McAnliffes of her youth, and to what
was the true object of her little jaunt she at-
tained without much trouble, though she found
it expedient when making enquiries to take a
few precautions, lest she should endanger the in-
cognito which she chose to preserve. Accordingly, in the course of that mild moth-grey
October forenoon, young Francis McEnery, busy
with the pulling of his ruddy, crisp-leaved man-
gel-wurzels, was interrupted, embarrassed, and
bewildered by the appearance to him of a little
old, very poor-looking woman, who claimed a
most intimate friendship with his deceased parents and grandparents, and who proceeded to
trace with himself a cousinship so intricate that
at the end of twice up and down the cow-lane he
only understood something dimly about a marriage between Ody Heffernan, that was one of

the Ballyfottrel Caseys, and as big a rogue as
ever saw crooked, and Biddy Doherty, that was
a one of the red-headed daughters of Matty Byrne
of Chapelmacottal, and sister's child to Peter
Riordan, the same that had a right to have
owned the townland of Rathgormley, if his wife
got fairity from them she ought in her stepmother's faction.

This unlooked-for family connection, whose
talk was as voluble as it was puzzling, chanced to
descend upon Francis in an unusually defenceless
plight, because his housekeeping aunt had accompanied her sister-in-law, Miss Kelly, home
to Derry, for a little change of air after her bad
cold; so that he had no ally indoors to back him
up in the repulse of a persistent invader. His
gawky unreadiness left him an easy prey to Miss
Debby's encroaching approaches. She got without difficulty into the kitchen, where she established herself by the hearth, and made it plain
that she would not depart thence until she had
been refreshed with tea; and while the kettle was
boiling she pursued her investigations into his
domestic affairs with considerable success, pick-
ing up two or three bits of information that she
regarded as valuable. One of these, for instance,
related to Miss Kelly, and might have been
thought by a superficial observer of but little
seeming substance. But Miss Debby deemed it

worth while to make a mental note of the fact
that Francis McEnery would have been glad to
clear away the big bunch of quiver-grass Maggie
Kelly was after sticking in the corner of the
dresser—an ugly, littery thing, he hated the
sight of it !—only he was afraid she'd be mad if
she found he'd moved it, supposing she came back
again, he couldn't tell would she or no, but he
misdoubted his Aunt Rose had a notion of bringing her along.

"The man's a *noony-nawny*, and 'ill be just as
bad or good as whoever gets him," Miss Debby
said to herself; and then she became more boldly
personal than ever, and as she sweetened her hot
tea she said to him point-blank, "And so yourself and Lizzie Kinsella's apt to not be makin' a
match of it, after all ? "

Her host at this home-thrust could only glow
in a deeper confusion, and stammer out self-
betrayals. "What's a chap to do when a girl
takes and slings every iotum he's ever gave her
back in his face in a parcel in the post, like as if
they was so much ould cabbage-leaves ? And
has him openin' it at the breakfast-table, unbe-
known, to set people passin' remarks, and risin'
a laugh on him. But there's as good as she that
'ud ha' thought them worth keepin', and sayin'
thank'ee for civil—and better than she, after that
again; unless anybody's of the opinion that a

saller skin and a big head of black hair's the only
thing fit to be lookin' at." Francis was so evidently quoting that Miss Debby knew Miss Kelly,
the sister-in-law, must be a blonde.

"Well, but Lizzie Kinsella's a fine slip of a
girl, mind you," she said. "You might look for
her acquils for a long while among them that's
gingery coloured, or yellery, and cross-tempered.
You see, she was pointed out to me one day, and
I goin' the road wid the people I'm stoppin' at,
that was how I seen her," Miss Debby added artfully. "They do say she'll marry Thady Fanning
now. I dunno, but anyway he's after her."

"That's how she served me presents—the way
I was tellin' you—every single one of them,"
Francis said in a tone of rueful resentment.

"And every single one of them 'ud I serve
straight back to her agin, if I was in your coat,
ay, would I, bedad," Miss Debby said, her eyes
following his to where the edges of a brown-paper
parcel protruded from behind a hung-up tin dish
cover.

"Maggie Kelly's got the cornelian pin out of
it now," he said despondingly. "Nothing 'ud
suit me aunt but I must let her have it : she as
good as made me give it."

"Sure you might very aisy be gettin' Lizzie a
somethin' else in place of it," said Miss Debby,
"any day you was in town at market. You'll be

dhrivin' the bit of a sorrel mare I seen in the field there, under the ould yoke of a side car you have in the shed, plenty of times in the week, I'll bet you twopence."

"Of an odd while I do," said Francis.

"Are you apt to be dhrivin' by Killoughal cross-roads any time to-morra or next day?" Miss Debby inquired.

"Sure I've got to be passin' there about noon to-morra, bringin' his reverence at Rathbrian a barrel of bruised oats I was after promisin' him."

"Bedad then, that's as handy as if it was bespoke," said Miss Debby with glee, "for you can be lendin' me a lift a long step down them lanes. It's wishful I am to go see me Uncle Willie's married son's nephew and his childer. I was tellin' you about them—och yis, you remimber. So I'll be ready there waitin' for you before twelve right enough."

"The *somethin'* you will, y'ould torment!" Francis said to himself. Still, she was showing symptoms of immediate departure, and, in his eagerness to hail these, he agreed to her arrangement about the car with an apparent alacrity, all the while inwardly deploring the fact that the shortest round by which he could avoid the cross-roads would take him better than three miles out of his way—a detour too wide even for the circumvention of so annoying an ambush.

At breakfast next morning Miss Debby again
had a programme to announce. This was Thursday, so, as she knew full well that she would be
expected to take the returning long-car home on
the Saturday, it behoved her to use despatch, if
her actions should have any influence upon the
posture of affairs. Her cousin, one of those
McAnliffes, she said—relying upon an ancient
intermarriage between the families for justifica-
tion in thus misleadingly describing Lizzie's
recalcitrant bachelor—had promised to meet her
that morning at the cross-roads, not far from
Shinogue Farm, and bring her with him on his
yoke, the way she could get to go see Katty Der-
mody, that was married to ould Nicholas Keogh
livin' out beyond Cloughduffy. And again Mrs.
Kinsella and Lizzie entirely approved of her intentions. But would Lizzie, Miss Debby wondered, think bad of showing her the short cut to
the cross-roads over the fields, so that she needn't
be killin' herself thrampin' further than there
was any occasion. Miss Debby put forward this
speculation in a casual, promiscuous sort of way,
and yet the point was a cardinal one—the very
pivot upon which her whole plot turned. And
at first a ruinous hitch seemed to threaten, for
Mrs. Kinsella said sure Jimmy and Bobby could
run along with their aunt. There was no school
that morning, and it would be a charity to keep

them out of mischief ; and the two boys, perhaps
seeing different possibilities, expressed a most
inconvenient willingness to oblige. Miss Debby
had to protest vehemently against an escort which
would lead to the ould legs being raced off of her
by a pair of young miscreants, and even so she
might hardly have carried her point if she had
not contrived to drop into Mrs. Kinsella's ear,
the opinion of a certain renowned Dr. O'Dwyer
to the effect that walks abroad in the fresh air
were the only certain means of preventing a girl
who had had a disappointment the way Lizzie
had from being a great deal more likely than
not to go into a decline.

Carry it she did, however, and when she set out
not long before noon, her grand-niece Lizzie was
her companion through the pleasant autumn fields.
They were a silent couple, slipping their skimpy
shadows along past the briar-bushes, bright
with berries and dew-drops and frost-painted
leaves. Both looked with pre-occupied eyes.
Lizzie was thinking how, not many days ago,
the shine and shadow had been weaving itself
into a marvellous vista, at the end of which
gleamed her wedding morning ; whereas now
nothing lay before her but the common-place
dreariness of a joyless winter. Miss Debby, on
her part, was forecasting all the vexations that
would attend her own untimely return to the

lonely, dilapidated gate-lodge away at Kilclashan. "Biddy 'll be ragin' mad when she be-
houlds me," she said to herself. "And she consaitin' I was quit for a couple of months. Leppin' she'll be." Biddy was her *locum tenens*.
"Falix now, if the match be good luck was on
agin, I'd make it me business to stop over the
weddin', one way or the other, I would so. It's
no better than robbin' me of me car-fare."

But by this time they had reached a stile
leading into a narrow, hedge-muffled cart-track,
across the further end of which glimpsed the
high-road. And here Lizzie spoke. "Well now,
Aunt Debby," she said, "you can't be missin'
your way. There's the road before you, and a
couple of perch to the right 'ill bring you to the
cross. So I'll run back to me mother, that's about
churnin'. I think I hear wheels."

Sure enough, they sounded unseen, driving behind the hedgerows. Everything would be destroyed at the most critical moment by Lizzie's
turning back.

"Och no, jewel, don't lave me for your life,"
said Miss Debby. "I want you to help me over
this and up on the car."

"To be sure I'll give you a heft over," said
Lizzie: "but it's the quare bosthoon your cousin
'ud be if he couldn't lend you a hand up on his
car." She raised Miss Debby as she spoke under

the elbows with a vigorous shove; but the old
woman dropped back with an ungainly stumble,
and then sat down with screeches on the steps of
the stile. "Och murdher!" she said, "I'm desthroyed! I'm after wranchin' me unfortunate
ankle. I couldn't put me fut under me for the
worth of everythin' in Ireland. What at all 'ill
I do? Och, Lizzie, girl dear, you must—I dunno
what else you can do but just skyte down now
straight to the car, and bid himself—me cousin
—step up and fetch me. Make haste, for the
sake of goodness; don't let him be passin' out of
call."

Thus did it come about that Lizzie Kinsella
sped in headlong haste out of Neil's Lane, and
was barely in time to catch up with Francis
McEnery's car, as the sorrel mare jogged out of
sight round the corner, driven by some one who
thought fit to be very hard of hearing. But,
"The saints look up and down on the whole of
us!" he said, jumping off with a wide-sweeping
curve, when at last he had turned his head and
recognised the person calling after him. "Is it
yourself, Lizzie Kinsella? And what at all's took
you then these times whatever?"

Lizzie was so long explaining that sorrel Sally
enjoyed a most satisfactory browse up and down
the deep grass-border, undisturbed save by an oc-
casional twitch of the bridle in her master's ab-

sent-minded hand. In fact, explanations were
still in progress when the two young people became aware of a third person shuffling towards
them out of the lane, which caused Francis Mc-
Enery to observe: "Och, botheration to it! whatever's bringin' the ould woman about? Bad luck
to it! I'd forgotten her cliver and clane."

To which Lizzie replied: "Bedad now, and so
had I. And she lettin' on she couldn't stir a step
wid a wranch she'd gave her ancle. Little enough
ails her, anyway, to keep her of comin' botherin'
where she isn't wanted."

The fact was that Miss Debby had been in-
cited by curiosity, and a fear of ferrets, which
always beset her when among hedges and
ditches, to take an observation of this long-pro-
tracted interview. She had hoped to do so unseen, but perceiving herself to be detected, she
began to approach with an ostentatious hobble
and loud groans.

"Never mind, Francey," ungrateful Lizzie
said in a diminishing whisper. "She'll be quittin' out of it, body and bones, to-morra or next
day, I hope to goodness; and then, when you
slip over, we might get a couple of minyits' talk
and no fear of her comin' meddlin' and makin'
wid us—the ould torment!"

MOGGY GOGGIN

MOGGY GOGGIN

IF Moggy Goggin had lived among genteeler people her name would probably have been smoothed out into Margaret Geoghegan; but Society in and about Lettercrum made small pretensions, and Moggy Goggin, with roughly-compressed gutterals, she was to her neighbours, except when they spoke of her as an "ould crathur." This they were rather apt to do, as she was a person of no social importance, dwelling all alone in a very tumble-down shanty, formerly a shepherd's, huddled under the bank at the end of Long Leg, one of Matt M'Cormack's fields. She had been established there for several years, yet nobody seemed to know much about her, beyond that her near relations had all died or otherwise "quit out of it." Her cousins, the M'Cormacks, were, indeed, better informed, better than they cared to let on, being fairly prosperous farming folk, and disposed to resent the circumstances that connected them with such an extremely poor old woman. As a matter of fact, Mrs. M'Cormack was her half-sister's daughter, but they never owned anything more than a vaguely remote cousinship; and Moggy, who was

313

not an encroaching person, advanced no claim to
closer kindred.   Although only two or three
fields lay between her and the farmhouse, her ap-
pearances at it were few, and would have been
fewer, had not Sally, the youngest girl, had certain looks and tricks of speech that reminded her
of her own favourite sister, Norah, in a way
which made her feel young again for a minute,
as she sometimes did when the birds all began to
sing together very suddenly, after a spring
shower, under the eaves of a low-flashing sunset.

One early autumn morning, however, Mrs.
M'Cormack, looking out from her back door, said
with dismay : " Och to goodness, if there isn't
that ould torment of an ould Moggy Goggin
comin' through the field.   What at all's bringin'
her at this hour of the day, and it not ten
o'clock ?   I declare she's never from under one's
feet.   Annie, girl—och, she's not here—Sally,
then, run and see what she's wantin', and maybe
she might turn back.   But I'm afraid of me life
she'll be meeting himself and me nephew that's
out and about somewheres—and Matt's no more
gumption than a three-year-old ; he'd let out who
she was as soon as look at her ! "

Mrs. M'Cormack had special reasons for dread-
ing such a disclosure.   They had partly arrived
a few days before in a letter from this stranger
nephew, Thomas Martin, of Archmount, Illinois,

U. S. A., just returned on a brief visit to the old country. It said, among other things: "Perhaps you may not have had the news that poor Aunt Norah Jackson died of pneumonia last Thanksgiving Day at Lambertville. I saw her a week previous, when she entrusted me with her savings to bring home to this country, which I was then about visiting shortly. Her wish was that her sister Margaret, if still living, should have the money; but otherwise her late sister Sarah's daughter Julia, or, namely, I take it, yourself. A friend of the family informs me that he believes old Margaret Goggin is lately deceased, and likely she is, as being the eldest sister she must have reached a great age, but doubtless you can let me know. If this is so, I can hand over the cash to you when I come to your place. It amounts to a trifle over two hundred pounds."

As Mrs. M'Cormack had read the last words her eyes gleamed wistfully. The handing over of two hundred pounds struck her at this time as such a particularly desirable transaction. For then her favourite son, Dick, could make a match of it with Kate Neligan, who had a fine fortune, and they might settle down comfortably close by Tullyglen, instead of which it seemed as if the poor lad would have to take off to the States and seek a fortune for himself before the new year.

It was provoking to think that only the superfluous existence of old Moggy Goggin rendered
the better arrangement impossible. "Lately di-
saised, bedad!" Mrs. M'Cormack said to herself
bitterly; "ne'er a much she is, or sorra the sign
of it on her. Sure if she was good for anythin'
she'd ha' been dead these twenty years. But
them's the sort of people that live for ever and
ever, like a fish in the well. And what at all
would the likes of her do wid a couple of hundred
pounds?" As Moggy's livelihood depended
mainly upon the precarious weekly sales of her
poultry's eggs, she would no doubt have thought
it not impracticable to find a use for the sum;
but Mrs. M'Cormack answered the question in
her own way: "She wouldn't know what to be at
wid it. You might as well be trowin' it in the
river. I wonder, now, who was tellin' Thomas
she was dead? Aisy enough she might be, and
nobody the wiser—and she livin' away in a bit
of corner, out of the world."

To this question no answer was forthcoming;
but the result of her meditation upon it was that
in replying to her nephew's letter she made no
mention of old Moggy—it would be time enough
to tell him when he came—and that to her family
she said nothing about the tantalising nearly-ac-
quired bequest. On the morning before Thomas
Martin's arrival, however, she remarked during

breakfast: "And you needn't be talkin' about
ould Moggy Goggin before your cousin. Maybe
she'll keep out of this, be good luck, the few days
he's here, and I hope she may, for the dear knows
she's no credit comin' about any place, the show
she is in her ould rag of a shawl, and th' ould
shoes of her lookin' ready to drop off her feet;
it's barefut I'm always expeckin' to see her
comin' streelin' over one of these days."

The young M'Cormacks carried out this injunction dutifully, and the subject of Moggy
Goggin was avoided in the presence of their
visitor. But one of the first things he said to his
hostess next day, when, fortunately, nobody else
happened to be within hearing, was: "And so
me ould grand-aunt Margaret Goggin's dead!"
Mrs. M'Cormack set down the bowl she had in
her hand with a clatter, which left it uncertain
whether she assented to the statement, and he
went on: "Well, it seems more reasonable that
the bit of money should come to you. With
your fine family growing up, you'll find plenty
of uses for it. Anyway, there it is, and I can pay
it over to you whenever you like."

Mrs. M'Cormack hesitated for a moment.
Something she must say, and she felt that what
she said must be of fateful import. She was just
beginning to speak when she heard her husband's
step approaching, and her speech turned into:

"Don't—don't say anything about it to him."
Her nephew stared at her with surprise, which
grew into comprehension, as he nodded know-
ingly, and said: "All right, Aunt Julia." And
next morning she had a delightful roll of bank
notes in her possession. Moreover, she had
learned, with loud regret and mute relief, that
her nephew and his two little boys must depart
on the Saturday, and as here was Wednesday, she
could look forward to her anxiety being soon
safely ended.

Therefore it was now most contrary that just
when matters were proceeding so smoothly the
old woman's perilous presence should intrude itself upon the scene. "She's comin' along—ay,
the mischief doubt her, she is," Mrs. M'Cormack
said, looking out with disgust. "If Sally had
the wit of a blind beetle, she might ha' contrived
to turn the ould torment back. The Lord knows
how long she'll stop here blatherin', and those
two may be landin' in on top of her every minit
of time."

Old Moggy, it appeared, had come to report
that her heart was broke wid the brindled bull up
in Long Leg. "I thought I'd just tell you the
way he's carryin' on," she said apologetically.
"For when he come out first into the field he
was paiceable anough. But this last week or so
it's outrageous he's been. Times and again he's

run at me; and, you know, ma'am, I have to be crossin' the strame and the corner of the Mount Field to get to the road gate, and it's thereabouts he's keepin' continyal. Bedad, I believe he has his eye on the house watchin' till I come out. Yesterday he had me afeared to stir a step the whole day, and I wantin' to get down to town wid me few eggs. They're sittin' in the basket yet."

"Sure he's only a young baste, scarce full-grown," Mrs. M'Cormack replied, testily unsympathetic to this complaint.

"Young he is," said old Moggy. "'Deed, now, it seems only the other day I would be seein' him in the yard here, not the size of anything. But he always was a passionate little crathur, and more betoken, I distrust them brindly-coloured bastes. Never a one of them I knew but was quare in its temper, and quare's no name for him. This mornin' he stravaded away wid himself off beyont the mount. John Cleary was tellin' me he seen him above there, or else I wouldn't ha' got the chance to slip over here at all, for it's in dread of me life of him I am."

If Moggy had but known, she could scarcely have put forward an unluckier fact, so far as her own purpose was concerned. For upon hearing it, Mrs. M'Cormack said to herself: "More power to him then; it's a charity, there's something to keep her out of this." And she immediately re-

solved that no matter how the brindled bull might
see fit to conduct himself, he should remain at
large until her nephew had fairly gone.   But to
Moggy she said suavely enough : " Ah, well, I'll
spake to Matthew about it, and he'll regulate
him.   He's busy these times wid the last of the
oats.   But if that's the way he is, it's home wid
yourself you ought to be runnin', or else you
couldn't tell where the baste might be agin you
got back."

"Thrue for you—faix, and I ought to," said
Moggy, taking the hint as she was intended to
do, if not altogether as it was meant, and she
turned ruefully to face her homeward way.   "I'll
go along wid you," said Sally.   But Moggy declined the offer, saying, " Sure not at all, child.
Where'd be the sinse of havin' him runnin' at two
of us instead of one ? "   And her mother, having
sent her off to wash up the dairy things, stood
watching the old woman out of sight with anxious hopes that she might meet nothing on her
journey back; but she was not thinking of the
bull.   Now that she had that roll of bank notes
stowed away upstairs, she somehow found the
aspect of "ould Moggy Goggin," doubled up in
her ragged grey shawl and greenish black gown,
more repellant than ever, the possession of wealth
having, no doubt, endowed her with finer sensibilities.

Moggy herself fared on with hopes and fears, which grew acuter as she approached Long Leg. It is a long narrow field with a bend in the middle of it, and flowed through by a stream, beside which there are thorn and briar-bushes. The bull, she thought, might be waiting for her round the corner; and when it was safely turned, her cottage looked dreadfully far off across the stretch of green, while danger might lurk behind every clump. And, in fact, she was at least fifty long yards from her door when the ominous shrill roar sounded, and the bull came trotting gaily through the gap in the hedge out of the adjoining field. She was only just in time to shut herself in before the rushing tramp went by outside, with a baffled bellow that scared her even in her security.

All the rest of the day she remained in a state of siege, her enemy choosing to graze so close by that to strew her hens their supper seemed quite a hazardous venture, and the gathering of their eggs was an impossibility. On the morrow he gave no signs of changing his quarters, and from hour to hour she looked out, vainly hoping for the approach of relief in the shape of men sent to drive him off. Nobody came, and she was left a prisoner, fretting over the impracticability of reaching the town, where she might replenish her small store of provisions, for not only her dwin-

dling grain of tea and sugar, but her heel of a
stale loaf, and her flaccid bag of meal had begun
to look poor indeed. The September sun went
down in an amber glory on her alarmed vexation, and rose again on the same posture of affairs.
Apparently the brindled bull found the herbage
in that corner of Long Leg very much to his
taste, and by noon Moggy had grown so desperate that she sometimes said "Shoots" faintly,
and flapped her apron in his direction as she stood
at her door.

But when the shadows had stretched into a
deep border along by the hedge, the beast, who
for some time past had been stalking restlessly
to and fro, crossing and re-crossing the stream
with querulous roars, began to move steadily
towards the Mount Field, and presently disap-
peared from view. Moggy was just wondering
whether she dared set forth on her expedition,
when something new came in sight. A party of
three people were walking up Long Leg. It
consisted of a fair-bearded man, in a light brown
suit, with hat and boots which were both black
and glossy (rale iligant), and two small boys, in
a sort of fanciful sailor costume, more iligant
still. These were Thomas Martin and his youngest sons, who had come out for a stroll. It was
churning day at the farm, and the master had
given his hand a rather nasty cut with a reap-

ing-hook in the course of the morning, which
caused much bustle and confusion in the household, and made Thomas think it advisable to
take the children out of the way. Their presence was reassuring to old Moggy, and she resolved upon going. "I'll caution the strange
man about that baste," she said to herself, as
she went into the house to get ready. But she
found that the handle of her basket was broken,
and dim eyes and tremulous hands made its repair a work of time, and when she emerged
again, it was to stand aghast; for the interval
had brought back the bull with aggravated circumstances. Something had wrought the natural arrogance of his temper to a pitch of frenzy,
which transformed him in demeanour from a
hectoring bully to an example, half-terrible, half-
grotesque, of the tyrant in his rage. He advanced with rapid strides, lashing his tail and
lunging aimlessly with his wide horns at invisible
objects by the way. The gravest feature of the
case was that he seemed to be making straight
for the smallest of the children, little Jack, who
had strayed off while his father's thoughts were
occupied with vague reminiscences of a place
seen at five years old, half a lifetime ago. The
child had become horribly aware of the beast
just as Moggy appeared, and she sent a quavering call, bidding him run to her, much the near-

est refuge. Jack's panic, however, was blind and
deaf, and he evidently meant to rush after his
father and brother in the opposite direction, de-
stroying his chances of escape. So she risked a
bold sally, captured him and began to tug him,
heavy and resistant, towards her house. It was
a terrifying race, with the thud of hoofs gaining
on them so fast, that she felt as if her feet were
taking root. Once, at least, all seemed lost, only
the pursuer paused to demolish with swinging
strokes, a clump of ragweed, which gave them a
fresh start. But a little farther on they were
hopelessly overtaken; and, as a last resource,
Moggy, snatching off her old shawl, flung it in
the bull's face. By good luck, one of the largest
of its many holes caught on a horn, so that the
folds hung down blindingly; and while they were
being furiously rent and tossed and trampled into
shreds, the old woman and the child escaped
safely indoors, where they were joined by the
other two fleeing from the opposite direction.

Thomas Martin was volubly grateful for Jack's
rescue, but old Moggy said: " Ah, sure, not at
all. It's sorry I'd ha' been if anythin' happened
the little crathur. I declare now the two eyes
he has in his head is the livin' image of me poor
brother Johnny, the time he was the same size.
And for the matther of that, it was only the ould
shawl kep' the baste off him. Saints above! look

at the quare work himself there's havin' wid it, tatterin' it he is into nothin' you could give a name to."

"Well, ma'am, you shall have the best to replace it that money can buy," averred her visitor; "and you must tell me who I'm to send it to."

"Why, Moggy Goggin's what they do be callin' me," said the old woman. "But I mind me mother sayin' it was Margaret I was christened be rights."

"Margaret Goggin—well, now, that's extro'nary. And are you anything then," he said, "to the M'Cormacks here, at the farm?"

"Sure, Julia M'Cormack was daughter to me half-sister, Sarah Finny, she that died a few years ago at the ould place in Westmeath," said Moggy. "But it's cousins we are these times, and not much talk of that, for, you see, they're getting on finely, and I'm diff'rint."

"There's bound to be talk of it, though," said Thomas. "To think now of Aunt Julia playin' such a trick on me, and takin' the money." He thought of it for a while perplexedly, and then began to compare with Moggy notes upon family history, which soon placed her identity beyond a doubt.

"'Deed, but the States is a great place for people to be gettin' their deaths in," she said;

for her grand-nephew's news had been largely
obituary. "It was there me poor sister Norah
went out to, and married David Jackson, but
she'll be gone this long and long ago—never a
word I've heard from her."

"Not a great while," he said; "something
under a twelvemonth, anyway."

"Glory be to goodness!" said Moggy, looking
relieved; "frettin' I was thinkin' of all the time
I was delayed of follyin' her, but sure I won't be
long after all."

"Oh, come now, Aunt Moggy! I hope you'll
be here many a year yet," Thomas said, meaning
encouragement, "and she's left you a legacy—a
handsome one, too—something over two hundred
pounds. So you've every reason to take a new
lease of life."

"'Deed, has she? That was very good of the
crathur," said Moggy, rather abstractedly.

"A very tidy sum indeed: it will set you up
in fine style," he went on expatiating. "You
haven't any great shakes of a place here, but
you'll be able to move out of it now, and fix
yourself comfortable," he said, critically surveying the dark little room, with its mud floor and
smoky rafters.

"Ah! sure, it's terrible work movin'," said
Moggy; "I'd liefer not be gettin' that sort of a
legicy. And, plase goodness, it's scarce worth

me while to be settlin' meself too comfortable
anywhere hereabouts.

"But, bedad now," she said, after reflecting
for a few moments; "if I had as much as a
couple of odd pennies in the week, that I could
be givin' little Larry Flynn for doin' me messages in the town, 'twould be a great thing entirely, for the road's gettin' a weary long length
wid itself. And then I needn't be troublin' me
head aither about the bull. Ay, rael grand it
'ud be," she said, with a gleam of satisfaction.
"But here I am, forgettin' the tay all this while;
sure the childer'll be starved," she exclaimed,
and started into a bustle of preparation, against
which Thomas Martin protested in vain.

The tea itself, although the very last pinch of
black dust went into the pot, had not much
strength to boast of; but there was still enough
brown sugar left to make it quite to the taste of
her great-grandnephews at all events. While
they were drinking it, three men appeared in the
field armed with pitchforks, ropes, and other im-
plements, evidently designed for the coercion of
the brindled bull, who was presently seen being
led away in captivity. Old Moggy stood at the
door to watch the departure of her enemy through
the pleasant green field, which the sunsetting
light had strewn with spangles of clear gold and
flecks of soft shadow. "I declare now," she said,

"I'm sorry the crathur's to be put out of it be raison of meself. Only it's a pity he couldn't ha' kep' himself paiceable. What call had he to be runnin' at a body that wasn't makin' or meddlin' with him, and plinty of room for the both of us? But some quare notion he'd got into his head of the whole place belongin' to himself; and that's naither nathur nor raison," concluded Moggy Goggin.

When the Martins returned to the farm, Mrs. M'Cormack was looking out for them with some anxiety, which had been aroused by hearing in what direction they had gone, and which had made her send the men after the bull. But worse than her worst fears were confirmed, when her nephew replied with marked coolness to her greeting: "Thank'ee, Aunt Julia, the children aren't hungry. They're just after having their tea with their old aunt, Moggy Goggin. The bull drove us into her little place down there." She knew at once that the discovery had been made, and it was hardly necessary for him to add: "I find that I was under a misapprehension about that legacy, and needn't be troublin' you to take charge of the money any longer." In great bitterness of spirit she mumbled something about fetching it down, and went upstairs to do so. As she came back along the passage with the notes in her hand, her husband called at her through

an open door, "I seen them drivin' in the young
bull. I've a notion of sendin' him to the fair at
Bagnalstown on Thursday; cattle's goin' well
this week." But she said to herself, going on
her way regretful and unrepentant: "Troth,
thin, it's the quare price you'll have to get for
him, me good man, or else he'll be the dear baste
to us, an' himself the raison of better than two
hundred pounds goin' off us to that ould pest of
an ould Moggy Goggin."

A STORY ON STICKS

A STORY ON STICKS

THOSE tall, bare, tarry poles made a wonderful difference, everybody remarked, in the look of the country, and well they might, as hardly anything grows higher on it than a stunted furze-bush. That part of it is in fact simply a sweeping expanse of dull olive-green bog, which seems as if it must have been much trampled, anciently, under the hoofs of huge primeval cattle, on so large a scale are its endless round-topped tussocks, each one moated about by the network of narrow fissures in the black peat. Water lies deep at the bottom of them all. You see it glimmer as you stride squelching, or spring splashing, from spongy cushion to cushion. For this is "a very wet bog entirely." It shivers all over if even an empty turf-cart comes jiggeting along one of its intersecting tracks, and the passage of a heavy load is attended by shocks of really formidable violence. In stormy times, when the ponderous Atlantic rollers are swinging themselves against the many-buttressed cliffs, and seething over smooth-floored recesses of sand, every assault with its foam and thunder will start vibrations felt underfoot far inland;

as far, that is to say, as one can get on the little
Inish of Anashee. Its excessive wetness makes
this corner of the wide bogland, Meenmore, an
extremely lonesome place. Nobody can work on
it; still less on it can anybody live, except where
a stray fleck of drier ground emerging here and
there gives room for a single little white cabin to
be set down in a skimpy patch of vivid green.
Even for sporting purposes it is too sodden and
swampy. "Troth and small blame to the wild
crathurs to keep themselves out of it," used to
be a frequent observation of old Syl Walsh, the
naturalist, "Unless they'd a mind to be stiffened
up wid a wire of rheumatics run through every
bone of their mislucky bodies." So there is seldom anything to be seen moving upon its monotonous face save the scanty trickle of traffic passing between Fintragh and Lettercosh, the Inish's
two hamlets, scattered about the feet of its two
mountain-sentinels, Slievelone and Ben Teague.

Under these circumstances people sometimes
wonder that it should have been thought worth
while to establish telegraphic communications
with such an unpopulous and insignificant sort of
outpost. And, in fact, Anashee might have
waited for them long enough, had not a Person
of Importance chosen to build himself a summer
house there, and require none the less to be in
reach of the latest intelligence. Whereupon en-

sued the procession of lanky black-coated poles,
stalking in single file from a long step beyond the straits which make an Inish of Anashee;
and the birds of the air found an additional perch,
several miles in length, stretched for them to
light upon; and the little Fintragh post-office had
a new clerk, who understood the management of
"rael quare" clicking machine, which was like,
somebody said, a sort of a clock and a compass
bewitched, and which formed the central marvel
and mystery in this extraordinary method of receiving and sending messages, "all in a suddint
minyit." Speculation was rife as to the precise
means employed, and only a few ultra-conserva-
tive minds were content to explain it simply by
pishtrogues, that is to say, charms.

The Anasheans are stay-at-home folk. Seldom
do they journey as far even as to the adjacent
mainland, which they call going on shore; and
they had hitherto had no experience of the telegraph. Indeed a considerable number of them
had not any word for it in their language. For
on Anashee the old people are almost all Irish-
speaking, with little knowledge or none of Eng-
lish. Their children generally possess both lan-
guages, and converse in one or the other according to convenience. But their grandchildren,
being set to unlearn Gaelic at the whitewashed
National School, often accomplish that task with

a thoroughness which precludes verbal intercourse between the first and third generations. Few of the gossoons and colleens nowadays can speak Irish themselves with fluency, though some still understand it; and curious lopsided dialogues may not uncommonly be heard proceeding in the Sassenach on their own, and the Gaelic on their elders' part. This comes rather hard on the old folk, sometimes afflicting them with, as it were, a kind of twofold deafness, which makes the world seem all the stranger and dimmer to them, as they sit "bothered and moidhered" in their corners, amid a Babel of meaningless chatter, like exiles in a foreign land. They *collogue* much, however, with their contemporary neighbours; and now animated discussions were carried on among them, respecting the choice of an appropriate term for the latest wonder of these "quare times altogether." The old Gaelic tongue may be dying, yet it still retains at least one characteristic of a living and vigorous language in the capacity for evolving new words, which are genuine, legitimate products of its own, and not illogical misapplications, or incongruous loans, such as "wire" or "telegram." Anthony O'Keefe suggested that they should give it a name signifying: *a fishing-line for news*, and spoke often at length, with much earnest eloquence in favour of his proposal. But the fancy was too fine-spun for the taste of the majority. That thin tight thread, almost imperceptibly appearing and vanishing on the empty air, could so hardly be imagined the really efficacious element in the matter. Most people put more faith in the tall black posts, which at all events "had the look of being made for something." Therefore the name finally adopted was: *sgeul ar bata,* "a story on sticks," and it remains in use to this day.

It seems suitable enough, for by every message that comes to the office, and goes forth in an ominous tawny envelope, some kind of a tale is pretty sure to hang, and the same may be said of those despatched from thence. Anashee cannot spend sixpences on mere trivialities. Very few of them do come and go, except when the Person of Importance is in residence, and that seldom occurs, as he has grown tired of the place. Perhaps some one might like to learn the contents of the very first telegram that came clicking into Fintragh post-office? I am able, as it happens, to report them word for word—they were only a carefully counted sixpence-worth—but they need some preliminary explanation to make their purport generally intelligible.

The telegraph-poles might have seemed less certainly essential to the production of those astonishing phenomena, had it not been for the droning hum which runs through them inces-

santly, audible to even the unheeding passer-by,
and swelling into a sonorous wail, if he stop and
press his ear against the wood. This experiment
at first used to be tried by everybody with deep
interest, and sometimes with awe. They compared the sound to all sorts of things, such as
"the say-waves and a cross cow roarin' agin one
another in a storm of win'"—a duet which may
now and then be heard on the surf-bordered pastures of Anashee—"wid a quare kind of lilt
through it," some one would add, "that you
might take for keenin' or singin'." Many people
were vaguely of the ópinion that the sound had
"some manner of manin';" but only one person
claimed that he could actually make sense of it.
This was the above-mentioned Anthony O'Keefe,
younger brother of Cornelius O'Keefe, who farms
a rather large bit of land near Fintragh, and is
better off than most of the islanders.

His neighbours have always held that Anthony
is not quite "all there," and this belief, although
it has the effect of diminishing their regard for
his opinion about ordinary matters, does somehow
make them attach more than usual weight to it
when anything abnormal or occult is concerned.
Accordingly they are not inclined to reject him
as an interpreter. There is a touch of uncanni-
ness, too, about Anthony's appearance, which
helps to heighten the probability of his conver-

sance with secrets and mysteries. So likewise
does his propensity for swift and solitary wander-
ings, that cause his lean, black-frock-coated form
to appear promiscuously at and in unexpected
times and places. "That fellow does be skytin'
over the counthry," Syl Walsh has remarked,
"for all the world liked a one of them long-leggy
wather-spiders on the smooth of a pond. You
niver can tell for a second where the fantigue 'ill
take it to be shootin' itself to next—or him aither."

On a certain warm, hazy July afternoon, these
roving habits brought Anthony to the eastern
corner of Anashee, where the broad Meenmore
bog merges into a belt of fine short grass, which
is all too soon lost again among the sapless grey-
green bent and half-buried furze-bushes on the
white sand-hills of the shore. For: "You might
think there was a somethin' about in this counthry wid a grudge in it," I have heard Pather
Maguire dolefully declare, "that would be doin'
its best to skimp every mortal baste of gettin' a
bite or sup." Just here meet two roads, one
skirting the beach, the other striking out across
the width of the bog towards Fintragh, with the
telegraph posts keeping it company. Under the
first of these, on a swarded bank, Anthony found
three people reclining in a scanty shadow; a
couple of small boys, and a tall young man.
Larry and Pat Lenihan lived close by, and were

minding their goat, as little gossoons may, when
lucky enough to find such a good excuse for
not attending school; but Christy Rourke had
come from Anthony's district away beyond the
bog near Fintragh, and the blue-handkerchiefed
bundle which lay beside him showed that he was
leaving home, as young fellows must sometimes,
"like it or lump it." Christy was lumping it, to
judge by his looks, which were downcast and
moody.

"Musha and is it yourself, Christy?" Anthony
said upon recognising him. "I'd ha' thought
you'd be across the ferry agin now, for I seen
you startin' off out of our place this mornin' at
all hours of earliness, ould ages, anyway, before
I quit."

"Sure where's the hurry?" Christy replied
gloomily. "I'm sleepin' at me uncle's, over beyant Goulanephin, and if I get there by dark,
'twill be plinty time enough. It's an outrageous
hot day; I'm kilt thrampin' under the sun's blazes."

"That's because you haven't the wit to be
thinkin' of somethin' diff'rint all the while goin'
along," said Anthony. "I'm tired tellin' people
they had a right always to be doin' one thing and
thinkin' of another, and then they wouldn't git
torminted."

"Bedad now that's accordin' to what the other
thing was," said Christy. "I should suppose there

might be many a one 'ud only tormint you twice
as much."

Anthony presumably was not prepared to de-
fend his favourite theory from this particular
point, for sitting down, and leaning against the
post, he observed with an abrupt change of subject: "To your sowls, but there's a great
whillaloo goin' through it this minyit. What
are they at wid it at all at all?"

Larry and Pat at once sought to listen with
such precipitation that their heads collided from
opposing sides of the pole; after which Larry,
having kicked his junior, said: "'Deed is it
howlin' mad. But that's all I hear—like the
win' in a hole—ne'er a word whatsome'er—or
the river under the bridge when it gits among
the stones."

"And what else would the likes of you be settin' yourself up to be hearin'?" said Anthony.
"If the river was swimmin' thick wid troutses,
divil a one you'd catch wid just lookin' at the
runnin' wather. It's a line you'd want to fetch
them out. And it's the very same way wid the
runnin' sound. Sorra the word there's in it unless for them that has the sinse to be fishin' out
the manin'. Up there over our heads—it's a
line, so to spake, dropped into the noises of the
world, same as a line dropped into the say.
That's what I do be tellin' the folk up at our

place, but they're as stubborn as pigs wid their *Story on Sticks*, begol are they ——"

"And what are you hearin' in it now?" Christy enquired hurriedly, less from curiosity than eagerness to avert a recapitulation of those arguments.

Anthony replied with mysterious mien: "Och, that would be tellin'," but almost immediately began to tell, with one ear applied to the resonant pole, and one eye, shining from beneath a furtive, grizzled black fringe, fixed steadily upon Christy.

"Let me see now," he said, "it's about lads it is mostly—two lads and a letter—it must ha' got that comin' through some post-office. And Mack's the name of them: Jack Mack and Mick Mack—young chaps, much of an age."

"Jack Mack and Mick Mack—Micky Macky, Jacky Macky," Pat began to say with delighted chuckles, and seemed disposed to continue the repetition, but was peremptorily bidden by everybody to "hould his gab."

"Livin' at home wid their mother, they are," Anthony proceeded. "That's a widdy, and as dacint a poor woman as ever I—or anybody—seen, and farms the little bit of land she has, away at our—about the distance of from here to our own place—she and the two sons. And an ould uncle she has livin' on shore, as far, maybe, goin' in the opposite direction. I disremimber

the name of it—I mane I can't exactually hear
it. He's a warm man, anyhow, they say; Faylix Rooney his name is, and the grand-daughter
—Rose they might be callin' her—is an oncommon pretty-lookin' slip of a girl, bedad, is she,
red hair or no." Anthony emphasised the last
words strongly, while intensifying his watch on
Christy. "Well, now, the ould man, havin' ne'er
a child of his own left, always thought a dale of
his niece, the widdy's sons, these two fellows, Jack
Mack and Mick Mack. You be aisy there, tee-
heein', Pat Lenihan; what else would I be callin'
them by, barrin' their own names? But the one
of the two he thought the most of ever was
Mick the youngest. If you axed me me own
opinion, I wouldn't say but that Jack was the
makings of a better man. Not that there's any
great harm in Mick, mind you, but Jack most
whiles seems to be more raisonable in his notions, and plisanter in his timper."

"And he might be that same, begorrah, and
none too raisonable or plisant all the while,"
commented Christy.

"Ah, sure now, Mick's apt to be gittin' more
wit prisintly; he's no very ould age on him yit.
And there's a dale of good nature in him, I'm
thinkin'. Leastways, so they're talkin' inside
here," Anthony continued, ostentatiously listening again. "Only of an odd while when he gits

annoyed. And the trouble this time was all about an old skewbald pony. You see the way of it was, the mother of Jack and Mick does sometimes be hard set to get along, for the conthrariness of things is onaisy enough for anybody to contind wid, says she, let alone a widdy woman on a little bit of wet lan'. And the winther and spring we're just after comin' through bates all for as unchancy a saison as I have in me remimbrance. And that was the raison why Mick took off wid himself about Easter to thry could he save a thrifle at a job of work he'd heard of over in Glasgow. So the widdy after that had some bad luck and losses, that kep' her behindhand a bit wid her rint, and when the uncle, ould Faylix Rooney, heard tell of it, what does he do but offers to buy the ould skewbald off her for a five-pound note? Faix now, tellin' you the truth, the baste isn't worth it, and 'twas only be way of a compliment and convanience to her he done such a thing; for the crathur's as ould as a blind crow, and that broken-winded you'll hear it along the road ten minyits before you see it; and has a bog-spavin on the off hind leg of it the size of a jackdaw's nest."

"And, more betoken as cross as a weasel, you might say," put in Christy. "Would as lief take a bite out of your arm as look at you, if it got the chance."

"Well, at all events," Anthony went on, "the ould man said 'twould do them finely just to drive under the car wid Rose as far as the short step to mass of a wet mornin', and other times 'twould be welcome to the run of its teeth in the field, and a wisp of hay in the shed. So the widdy and Jack were both of them ready and willin' to let him have the crathur, and small blame to them. Howane'er, you must know the youngest son, Mick, had always the greatest opinion of it at all. He consaited the aquil of it didn't exist on Anashee; and when he got word in Glasgow of the ould pony bein' sold out of the place, leppin' he was and ragin' mad. And he up and he writes home the most outrageous letter to his brother Jack, that they got last night."

"Outrageous you may call it," said Christy.

"Givin' them all dog's abuse," said Anthony. "For the buyin' and sellin', and sayin' ivery sort of thing agin his ould uncle and the granddaughter, Nellie——"

"I thought you said it was Rose they called her," Larry objected.

"Who's talkin' now?" said Pat.

"Rose she is, to be sure—I heard wrong that time," Anthony said, listening once more. "And he took and passed a remark about her hair bein' red. 'I give you me word he did,' says his poor mother. 'And, in coorse, no girl in the world 'ud look the way he was after that,' says she. Done for himself entirely he has, if ever it comes to their knowledge over at Kilmacrone."

"I thought you said you disremimbered," a shrill voice began, but it was silenced in some sudden way.

"They'll have no more to say to him, that's certain," said Anthony, "and he that was always so great wid them, troth was he. But you see Jack was downright infuriated wid the letter, and maybe no wonder; and as ill-luck would have it, he'd settled to be steppin' over this very next day, and bring along the ould pony, and sleep the night at his uncle's, on his way to a job of work in the county Roscommon. And what's he done but took Mick's outrageous letter wid him to show to the uncle and Rose? And it full of *ould robbers* and *red-nobs*, and the mischief knows all. Their poor mother thried her best to dispersuade him of bringin' it, but sorra a word would he mind her."

"And why wouldn't he take it?" said Christy. "Didn't the young rapscallion say as plain as he could write he didn't care who seen it, and anybody might repate ivery word of it and welcome over at Kilmacrone?"

"Och, maybe he did," said Anthony. "She didn't tell me—I mane I don't hear it that way. But supposin' so itself? Sure there's plinty of

foolish talk people has out of them when they're
annoyed about anythin' that's gone agin thim,
and no manin' does be in it, good or bad. Look
at the say over there whitewashin' the black
rocks," Anthony said, pointing across a silvery
foreground of sand, and a creek of blue water,
to the dark wall of cliffs with a tossing snow-line
at their base. "You'd think it had a notion of
knockin' thim flat wid its rowlin' agin thim.
But sure not at all. Just a sign it is there's
been some rough weather out beyant the bay.
And that's so to spake the way the young chap
was flingin' himself about like, when he wrote
his fool's letter. Sorry enough he may be by
now—and it this moment of time walkin' over
to his frinds in his brother's pocket. Through
fire and wather Mick 'ud go for any one of thim,
his mother says, if he wasn't deminted wid his
fantigue about the ould pony."

"Is it anyways like *his* ould baste?" Larry
enquired, pointing to Christy with his thumb.
"For it's as ugly as ever I seen."

Larry was finding this part of the story intolerably dull, but Anthony would not be interrupted: "And if Mick himself doesn't mind,"
he went on, "his poor mother at any rate's in
the greatest distraction over it, by raison of all
the ugly mischief it's apt to make. Says she:
'Sure, Jack wouldn't go for to do it at all, if he

considhered a bit, for he's a rael good-natured fellow. But off he's took wid himself hot-fut, and he'll ha' done it before he knows rightly where he is,' says she. And says she: 'It's a sort of thing you can do while the clock's strikin' one; but that git undone agin you can't, if you had while it would be strikin' ivery mislucky hour from now till the world's indin'.' So says I to her: 'Mayhappen he might have time to change his mind while he would be trampin' over to his uncle's place, that's a good long step,' says I——"

"I didn't know you knew the mother of Jack Mack and Mick Mack," Pat said, and stared interrogatively.

"There's a dale of things there's no call for little spalpeens to know," Anthony replied with loftiness, and resumed: "Truth to say, I misdoubt if there's much chance he will. For I've an idea in me mind that Jack does be gittin' more than a trifle jealous now and agin of his mother and the ould uncle thinkin' that much of his brother; because the both of them had always a great wish altogether for Mick—let alone if be any chance Jack had e'er a thought of the granddaughter—Rose. Mind you," Anthony said, fixing his furtive gaze still more steadily upon Christy, "I'm not *hearin'* any such thing: it's just a notion I have of me own. But in coorse if that was the way of it, he'd be all the readier to take advantage of any bit of foolery Mick might have went and done, that 'ud give himself an ugly appearance, and make the girl and iverybody think bad of him. 'Twould be only natural, maybe, in his brother Jack, and you couldn't expect anythin' differint."

"Well now, yourself's the comical man," Christy said, closely examining the texture of the worn turf-carpet. "It's the quare romancin' you have about blathers and nonsense and nothin' at all."

"Nothin' to you it may be," said Anthony, "but it's a dale to your—to the mother of the lads I was tellin' you about. Frettin' herself woeful over it she was this mornin'. Wonderin' I was what misfortin ailed her, when I seen her cryin' away fit to fill her bucket, and she fetchin' wather at the little ould well, the time I went by. So then she tould me all about it. 'Deed, now, I'm sorry in me heart for the crathur worryin' herself there her lone."

"It's just a pack of lies you're puttin' on me," Christy said, clutching his bundle suddenly and bouncing up. "I well know she's more wit than to be frettin' about any such thing—a dale more. She was apt to get a bit discouraged bein' left all by herself—divil aught else ailed her. And I'll not be stoppin' away from her very long."

His general smouldering ill-humour seemed to

have flared into a special resentment, and he stood swinging his baggage defiantly, as if waiting for some further affront or contradiction.

"Sure then plase yourself," Anthony said, twirling himself round away from the oracular pole, and beginning to fumble for his pipe, "very belike you can hear and see ten mile off —— It's no need you have to be throublin' yourself wid gettin' a story off the sticks for other people."

"There now, you've gone and stopped him," Larry said, reproachfully glowering up at Christy, "and I was just about axin' him the ould pony's name. Git on, Anthony O'Keefe, there's a good man, and niver mind him. *I* believe ivery word you're after sayin', lies or no."

But at this moment a barking sound rose hard by, and over the crest of the nearest sand-hillock a small pony plunged at a clumsy canter, with a yapping, reddish-brown, short-legged terrier wriggling along in pursuit. And: "Land's sakes, if Thady's took to his capers, it's time for the pair of us to be steppin' on," Christy said. "For ne'er a minyit's pace he'll lave me. So good-day to you all."

Whereupon he captured the dangling rope-bridle, and departed leading Thady, a rough, parti-coloured animal, with quaintly cropped ears and shaggy feet. Christy's countenance wore a rigidly resolute expression.

About an hour later, somebody thrust a head in at the door of the miscellaneous store, which contains also the little post-office of Skaine, the first village you come to after going on shore from Anashee. "I'm wishful," it said, "to be sendin' one of them telingrams."

"Then why don't you step indoors and write it down on the form?" said the presiding official rather tartly.

"How can I, unless I'd bring the baste I've got here in wid me?" was the answer. "When it's leggin' home on me he'd be, if I let go me holt of him half an instiant." So the message was dictated from outside, and paid for with a sixpence, which had been destined for the purchase of more substantial goods.

Now this same telegram, which towards sunset reached the office at Fintragh, was the very first one to be received there. Its arrival seemed such an important event that the tawny envelope was conveyed to its destination by Mr. Crowe of the shop himself, with an escort of several neighbours, all curious in their minds. These people were, I dare say, somewhat disappointed when they heard its contents read aloud, and may have felt disposed to form a poor opinion of such communications, as being meagre and obscure. But to the person most concerned, who had been sitting forlornly by her faded hearth, and forecasting black troubles ahead, it was quite intelligible, and so consolatory that she made herself a cup of tea, and went to bed with a much lightened heart.

This was the telegram verbatim: "*From* Christy Rourke, Skaine, *To* Mrs. Rourke, Fintragh. *It's tore up. Don't be fretting.*"

And meanwhile along the wide, grassy-bordered road to Kilmacrone, the wind was having a paper-chase with a handful of white fragments which looked as if they had once formed a letter.

Lightning Source UK Ltd.
Milton Keynes UK
UKHW02n0941221018
330967UK00008B/654/P